Fleur McDonald has lived and worked on farms for much of her life. After growing up in the small town of Orroroo in South Australia, she went jillarooing, eventually co-owning an 8000-acre property in regional Western Australia.

Fleur likes to write about strong women overcoming adversity, drawing inspiration from her own experiences in rural Australia. She has two children and an energetic kelpie.

Website: www.fleurmcdonald.com
Facebook: FleurMcDonaldAuthor
Instagram: fleurmcdonald
TikTok: Fleur McDonald (Author)

FLEUR
McDONALD
SHOCK WAVES

ALLEN&UNWIN

SYDNEY·MELBOURNE·AUCKLAND·LONDON

First published in 2024

Copyright © Fleur McDonald 2024

Allen & Unwin
Cammeraygal Country
83 Alexander Street
Crows Nest NSW 2065
Australia
Phone: (61 2) 8425 0100
Email: info@allenandunwin.com
Web: www.allenandunwin.com

Allen & Unwin acknowledges the Traditional Owners of the Country on which we live and work. We pay our respects to all Aboriginal and Torres Strait Islander Elders, past and present.

A catalogue record for this book is available from the National Library of Australia

ISBN 978 1 76147 009 7

Set in 12.4/18.2 pt Sabon LT Pro by Bookhouse, Sydney
Printed and bound in Australia by the Opus Group

10 9 8 7 6 5 4 3 2 1

For my true north

AUTHOR'S NOTE

Detective Dave Burrows appeared in my first novel, *Red Dust*. Since then Dave has appeared as a secondary character in sixteen contemporary novels, including the latest, *Voices in the Dark*, and seven novels set in the early 2000s in which he stars in the lead role. These seven novels are *Fool's Gold*, *Without a Doubt*, *Red Dirt Country*, *Something to Hide*, *Rising Dust*, *Into the Night* and *Shock Waves*.

In these earlier novels, Dave is at the beginning of his career. His first marriage to Melinda has ended due to issues balancing their careers and family life. No spoilers here because if you've read my contemporary rural novels you'll know that Dave is currently very happily married to his second wife, Kim.

I had no idea Dave was going to become such a much-loved character and it's reader enthusiasm that keeps me writing about him. Dave is one of my favourite characters and I hope he will become one of yours, too.

CHAPTER 1

He kept his head down, running, as the misty rain drifted downwards in sheets. A gust of wind shifted the rain sideways, and an extra heavy shower pelted him from above. His hands, although cased in gloves, felt like they were frozen around the jerry can that pulled heavily on his arms.

Larger raindrops hurled down, seeping through his black clothing. Everything he wore was as dark as the night. He was grateful the dense clouds blocked out the moon and the stars—anything that could have lit his face. A couple of well-aimed stones had taken out the closest streetlights, and one of the other members of the team had taken care of the security and building lights illuminating the front of the Kallygarn Shire Council building.

Now all three of them were under the verandah, packing jerry cans around a sixty-litre oil drum.

Six filthy oil-stained hands worked quickly. None of them spoke. They had practised this many times, leaving nothing to chance.

'Shit,' he muttered as he jammed his fingers between two of the cans. He tried to shake out the pain, but the cold had already crept through his joints, making his fingers throb harder.

Neither of the other two said a word until minutes later.

'Done?' Their leader glanced at a watch. The hands on his own watch, glowing green, told him they'd been there for six and a half minutes.

It was time to go.

'Thirty seconds,' the third voice answered.

With fingers still aching, he turned and ran back towards the black car that was idling at the end of the pathway, ready for a quick getaway.

As the driver he was responsible for getting them out of here safely. His heart had started thumping when he'd slipped into the driver's seat about an hour and a half before, but now it threatened to break free of his rib cage and hurl itself out into the open.

Deep breath. Check the surrounds.

Ten more steps and he'd be in the car.

The hardest part would be done.

Hopefully once they drove away his heart would stop hammering so hard that it made him want to gasp.

A mixture of rain and sweat on his brow tickled as it ran downwards and he swiped at it before taking a breath and glancing along the road. The street was still empty;

no cars, not even a stray cat, which was a stupid observation, because he couldn't remember the last time he'd even seen a cat.

Thank fuck. If a cat appeared at his side now, he'd probably leap to the moon.

A distance away, a streetlight glistened on the wet bitumen and murky shadows stretched out.

Adjusting his night-vision goggles, he checked left again—empty.

Right—car lights.

He froze.

Three steps left to the car.

Thin beams approached from the far end of the street, reflecting on the wet road. Hissing tyres drove towards him.

'Shit!' They hadn't practised being caught. In hindsight, that's the first thing they should have made plans for.

He looked back at the other two, waiting for them to notice. To tell him what to do. But they were running towards him as fast as their crouched gait would let them. They were thirty metres from the ute.

He flicked his eyes back to the lights, thinking how stupid he must look, dressed in black with a balaclava and night-vision goggles, standing out here in the drizzle. A fox caught in the spotlights.

Twenty metres.

He caught a flash of blue inside the car as its lights flicked to high beam.

'Jesus, is that the cops?' he managed to whisper.

Ten metres.

But then white blinked orange and the car turned down another street. Everything fell into darkness again.

'Let's go.' The words were said calmly, without panic, as one of the others passed him on the way to the ute. 'Now.'

He knew not to argue.

The last few steps to the car were the quickest he had taken that night, and he yanked open the door, tumbling inside. Warmth from the heater stung his freezing nose and made his fingers burn with cold as he brushed the rivulets away from his eyes.

'Good job,' the leader told him. 'Now let's get out of here. Fast. We've got ten minutes.'

'Did you see that car?' he asked. Surely, they could hear his heart pounding. Weren't theirs?

The gears grated as he shoved the stick into first with shaking hands. There was no getting around the panic that was rising now. They couldn't go back, even if one of them wanted to. Everything they'd worked for had been set into motion.

'Wouldn't have seen us.' The answer was from the back seat. 'Too far away.'

He pulled at his face mask and tried to rub his wet cheeks dry.

'Put that back on.' The instruction was gruff from the back.

'It's wet.'

'Wait until we're on the open road. There might be cameras on the edge of town.'

He struggled to put the face mask back on, screwing his nose up at the cold moist material. 'Fuck's sake,' he said. 'This is Kallygarn, not bloody Sydney.'

'Fine, leave it off if you want to spend some time in the clink,' the front passenger said.

Angrily, he turned the steering wheel, and before long the car exited the town boundary. He kept his foot as flat as he dared. Even though he was wet and cold, he was grateful the crappy weather meant most people were tucked up in their houses, next to a fire, staring blankly at their TVs.

The front tyre clipped a rumble strip, making them all jump.

'Steady there.' That voice from the rear seat was in his ear. Soft and unruffled.

He refocused, clenching the steering wheel tightly as he directed the car back into the middle of his lane. The passenger in the front turned up the heating to full. Warm air blasted out, causing the windscreen to fog up.

His wet sleeve smeared across the glass and he swore softly.

'Eight minutes.'

He squinted, peering at the road in front of them, frightened he might miss the turn-off.

A different type of adrenalin was running through him now.

Euphoria.

They had done it!

They had really done it! They'd finished the job and now they had to make it to the lookout in time. He had to see it happen.

5

Their message would finally be out there.

Around the next corner and through the large salmon gums that lined the road, the spotlights picking up their glittering trunks, wet from the rain.

The speedometer told him it had been one point three kilometres since the turn-off. He pushed his foot down now, checking each mirror and seeing nothing but black.

The sign: *Knobbly's Observation*.

Blinker on. *Tick, tick, tick*. The only noise in the ute.

They each sat upright, holding themselves tightly, fists clenched on their knees. Shallow breaths. Waiting. Hoping.

The car exited the T-junction at speed, gravel flying from beneath its wheels.

'Four minutes.'

He fought to hold the steering wheel in line as the gravel bit at the tyres, trying to throw it from the road, but his driving expertise kicked in and he held the ute steady until it came out of the fishtail and straightened.

Up and up they drove, around the sharp corners that led to the summit of the hill just outside of Kallygarn.

Inside the car was quiet. Two more corners.

Another minute ticked by.

Then they were at the top and the soft glow of the lights of the town below were in the distance.

A smattering of illumination amid the darkness.

He angled the car so they could all see, turned the engine off and cracked the windows just enough that the cold air would keep the windscreen free of condensation.

'Ten, nine, eight . . .'

He tapped on the steering wheel, in time to the countdown.

'Seven, six, five . . .'

Now his leg took over, jiggling up and down.

'Four, three, two . . .'

Bright yellows and oranges shot into the darkness before they heard the explosion.

Slivers of fire flew skyward with trails of sparks and debris, outlined by the light from the fire burning in the building below.

Shrapnel began slamming onto roofs, creating extra devastation. Noises of windows shattering and walls crumbling reached them.

A second explosion. Smaller but still destructive. This one silhouetted the billow of thick black smoke that was hurtling into the atmosphere.

Moments later, lights came on in every house in town; high-pitched, fearful screams floated to them on the wind. The loud screech of the fire brigade shed doors opening echoed across the night, and then the shrill sound of the police siren, the red and blue lights reversing out of the station and racing down the main street in the direction of the blast.

With binoculars, they could see every last detail; the fire lit up the fire-fighters, dressed in yellow, pulling the hose from the truck.

The heavy-set policeman was standing back, his arms crossed over his chest, face awash with horror.

People were beginning to crowd onto the streets, dressing gowns wrapped tightly around them; others had shrugged into jackets and jeans. Most had their hands over their mouths, wordless at the destruction before them.

The passenger in the rear of the vehicle leaned back, arms crossed. The rear-view mirror showed a satisfied smirk. The face mask now lying on the seat.

'Good job, everyone.'

'Yeah, that's gonna stir up some shit.'

'Fuck 'em.' The driver felt a rush of satisfaction. They were unlikely partners, him and these two others, but their goals were aligned.

They would make a difference.

'Come on,' said the voice from the back seat. 'We'd better get out of here.'

CHAPTER 2

'What are you doing here?' Detective Dave Burrows stood at the office doorway of the Rural Crime Squad, hands on his hips. 'You're supposed to be home, resting, not sitting at my desk.'

'Says who?' Bob Holden was in the office chair, his feet on the desk. This had been his desk until he had taken medical leave recently. Now it was Dave's. 'Just checking to see if the outline of my arse is still in the chair.'

Making his way around the edge, Dave put down the pile of files he was holding and sank into the chair usually reserved for visitors. He didn't bite. 'How are you feeling?'

'Fine and dandy.' Bob's voice was upbeat but lacking its usual humour and warmth. 'What's going on here, son? Got any good investigations on the go? Tell me all!'

Dave assessed his friend and colleague. His face had that puffy look, as if he was on a steroid treatment, and his hair seemed to have thinned even more since they'd caught up three days ago.

Still, as Bob had told him, 'Chemo does that, son.'

'Coffee?' Dave asked now.

'Nah, I'm fine.'

'You don't look fine,' Dave said as kindly as he could. 'And I'm pretty sure you haven't and won't be gone long enough for the indent in your chair to be any different.'

Bob glanced around the office, as if searching for something new. Trying to pick up what they might have changed in his absence. But Dave had refused to alter anything. There wasn't any point because he was sure Bob would soon be back heading up the Rural Crime Squad again.

When they'd been paired together four years ago, Dave hadn't seen that Detective Sergeant Bob Holden was the mentor he'd needed. He'd only registered an old soak who spent as much time as he could at the pub, even during work hours.

After a few false starts and harsh words, they had become not only partners but best mates, and now it was Dave checking in on Bob.

'Where's Betty today?' Dave asked.

'Ah, the light of my life,' Bob said with the ghost of a smile. 'She's working a late shift at the hospital. She sends her thanks.'

'What for?'

'Taking me to the treatment the other week when she couldn't. She said she hasn't seen you since then.'

When Dave had picked Bob up from the hospital that day, Bob had vomited before they'd even reached the car. By the time Dave had managed to get him home, all the older man had wanted to do was crawl into bed and sleep.

Dave had sat next to the bed for an hour, holding a vomit bag out for Bob three times, before Betty had arrived and was able to give him antinausea medication. His normally strong and energetic partner hadn't had the power to move. Not to go to the toilet, or the bathroom, or even to roll over.

Still, despite the cruelty of the treatment, Dave kept hoping that every drop of chemo in Bob's veins was on a seek and destroy mission to get all the cancer cells in his body. Every single damn bit of it. Because Dave couldn't imagine a world without Bob.

He waved away the thanks.

Bob took his feet from the desk and put them on the floor, leaning forward to move the bucking bronco figurine to its normal spot next to the phone. Dave had shoved it out of the way when he'd spread out some paperwork the day before.

'There's a place for everything and everything in its place,' Bob said, before giving a grin that ended up looking like a grimace. His teeth had turned yellow and chalky and his skin stretched across his face, somehow tight but saggy. 'Now, what's going on here that you need help with? I came over especially, so no more comments about my looks—or I might think you're trying to crack on to me.'

Dave thought Bob looked a little wistful as he glanced across to the pile of files that had been plonked down moments before.

He snorted. 'You're the last fella I'd be giving the eye to.'

'Glad to hear it.' Bob cracked another gnarly smile. 'Well, come on, cough up. Anything good come across your desk? Or mine, as the case may be.'

'You're supposed to be on medical leave.'

'Ridiculous.' Bob shook his head as if he were disgusted. 'I'm as fit as a fiddle—' he paused '—on drugs.'

Dave laughed at the unexpectedness of the comment. 'Well, if you're so on song, you'd better have a read through this file.' He passed over a thin folder. 'Some bastard has shot a couple of horses from the highway. They were on private land, in the front paddock. Owner was away for the weekend and came back to find them both dead.'

'What possesses some people?' Bob took the folder and placed it on the desk, not opening it. 'Were they stallions or stud breeders?'

'Just two ordinary horses. The owner's kids used to ride them in a pony club.'

'Don't suppose there're any cameras close by?'

'I don't know. Lorri was running out the door to respond to a report of some fuel that had been stolen from a piggery down south. We've been so run off our feet with you and Parksy off crook. Two men down means we're a one man and one woman squad at the moment.'

Bob nodded and tried to swallow a few times.

Dave went to the kitchen and brought back a glass of water, placing it in front of him.

'Ulcers,' Bob said.

'In your mouth?'

'Yeah. Can be a side effect of the treatment.'

'Have you heard how Parksy is?' Dave poured himself a coffee and sat back down, flicking through the folder that was on the top of his pile. Then he stopped and looked over at Bob. 'If Betty's at work and you're here, should I ask how you got to the station?'

'I drove. I might not be looking the best, but I'm still operational—' he wagged his finger at Dave '—to a point.'

'So, you're lonely and decided to come in here and give me the shits, did you?' He looked over the rim of his mug and saw the twitch around Bob's mouth. Good. They all needed a laugh right now.

Parksy was only three months post a major heart attack and surgery, while Bob was having treatment for melanoma. A few of the constables had commented recently that joining the stock squad wasn't good for your health.

'I knew you'd be missing me,' Bob said, flipping open the folder to look at the information on the two horses that had been shot.

'Don't be so sure.' Dave's tone held humour. He repeated his earlier question. 'Any news on Parksy?'

'Last I heard they were ready to book tickets to go to France, Germany and Italy as soon as the doctor's okay came through.' Bob paused to line up the pens and paper on what had been his desk. 'Pretty big disappointment, really. He's a great team member and we could do with him back here.' He looked around and spread his hands out. 'I thought this job meant everything to Parksy; the way it does to me.'

'Maybe the missus pulled rank. I'm still waiting for Betty to do that to you.' Dave was serious. Bob and Betty had only been together for a couple of years, and he knew Betty had many plans and dreams for them both.

'Like to see her try.' Bob's tone was gruff. 'You're pretty short-staffed, son, just to state the obvious.' He brought a shoulder up in a half shrug.

'Well, it's a good thing we're not too busy then.' There was no way Dave was going to let Bob worry about what was going on at the office. His partner had bigger things to think about.

Dave picked up three thick files and placed them out of Bob's reach.

'I think we've all had a pretty good reminder that we don't know when our health is going to give us a swift kick up the arse because we're not invincible,' Dave said.

'True enough, son, true enough.' Bob flicked through the sparse information on the horses then pushed the file away. 'What are we going to do to get you some more help?'

Dave gave a soft snort and shook his head. 'You really think the brass are going to throw a few more detectives my way? Every other squad is screaming for more manpower, too. The other day a fella asked me what was more important, kids or cows.'

14

'Hard to argue with that.' Bob's strength seemed to disappear. His head dropped into his palm and he looked at Dave with weary eyes.

Dave pretended not to notice. 'We make do. Always have. This isn't something you need to concern yourself with. Karly Hepworth, the constable I met up in Meekatharra when we were looking into Leo Perry—remember that guy who disappeared when the fire went through his farm—she had her name down to do the detective course. She was keen to join us.'

'That's a start. What about Shannon?'

'I don't think she's got any desire to join the stock squad,' Dave said with a grin as he thought about the forensic pathologist he'd been seeing recently.

'Idiot,' Bob muttered, rolling his eyes. 'Like that was what I meant.'

Dave studied Bob. 'Want me to take you home?'

'Now why would I be wanting you to do that?' He flipped open the folder again.

''Cause you look dead on your feet.' Dave was quiet for a moment, then added, 'I bet you a slab of Carlton Draught you haven't read a word that's written on the first line of that report.'

Bob ignored Dave. 'Let's talk about how we're going to get you some more detectives.'

Dave folded his arms and leaned back in his chair. 'What are you doing this for, mate?'

'Doing what?'

15

'Seriously, Bob, why are you in here? Betty would murder you if she knew you were at the station. Not sure I've got the ability to keep her out of gaol if she does that either. I bet she thinks you're tucked up in front of the fire at home.'

'Where else am I supposed to be?' Bob asked simply. 'This is my life. It has been for over thirty years.' He stood up and walked to the wall, stopping in front of a framed certificate. 'My first award,' he said. 'Back when I was a young whippersnapper. Reckon I would have been about your age when I got this, son. The bravery award. You've heard me talk about the story. The car accident; the family that died. The people I pulled out. I've got the burns to show from it.

'I remember them every day, just as I remember every other person I've helped, every other victim of crime.' Bob took a deep breath, trying to keep his voice strong. Then he put his fist to his chest and thumped it lightly. 'They're all in here. They won't leave me and I won't leave them.

'So, you tell me, son. Where else am I supposed to be? Sitting at home waiting to die? Ha! Nah, that's not for me. This—' He spun around and faced Dave, his arms outstretched towards the office again. 'This is my life. Betty is going to have to understand that. And if she doesn't, well . . .' His voice trailed off.

Dave nodded. He understood. When the hardest, most awful things had been going on in his life, he had always buried himself in work, too. It was that responsibility towards the public when they were lost and vulnerable

16

that had kept him going. That duty had always fired Dave on, along with every other copper he knew.

'Anyway, son, I'm not dead yet. Stage four melanoma doesn't necessarily mean a death sentence, so I'm told. Plus, I've still got a few things I want to do here.'

'But the chemo knocks you around?'

'Yeah, gives me a bit of a tickle from time to time.' He threw Dave a glance. 'You saw that first-hand. But that's not gonna stop me, is it? Wouldn't stop you either.'

Dave nodded again, and waited, his mind ticking over.

'Right, enough of this talk,' Bob said after the silence had stretched out for an almost uncomfortable length of time. 'What about these horses?'

Without answering, Dave got up and tipped what was left of his cold coffee down the sink and poured another one as he thought about Bob's statement.

Wouldn't stop you either.

Bob was right. His responsibility was to help.

Dave hoped he wouldn't live to regret the words he was about to say. 'Well, if you're feeling up to it, I've probably got something a little more meaty.'

Bob raised his eyebrows. 'Don't tell me you've been holding out on me, son.' He took his handkerchief from his pocket and mopped his brow, before taking a long drink of the water Dave had placed in front of him.

'I don't know that holding out is quite the right term,' Dave said with a grin. 'How about we get back on the road? Just you and me, like we've always done. You've got a two-week break on your chemo, haven't you? So let's go and hit up some abattoirs, check the paperwork and stock and remind everyone we're still around. The abattoir in Stockdale has started up again recently and the new company has employed a few of the blokes that were there before, but there're some new ones, too. Wouldn't hurt to show our faces.' Dave looked at his friend expectantly.

Bob stared at him deadpan, then shook his head as if disgusted with Dave. 'The something "more meaty" you have for me is a trip to abattoirs. Don't give up your day job or start a career in comedy.'

CHAPTER 3

'I've written all the instructions out clearly so you shouldn't have any issues,' Betty said. 'He's got to take tablets at breakfast, lunch and before bed. Some he has to take with food. Please make sure he doesn't miss any of them, Dave . . .' Betty's voice trailed off, but she came back strongly. 'I know he's got his watch alarm set in case he gets busy during the day, so he shouldn't miss the timing.'

'No worries, Betty.' Dave checked inside the bag, glimpsing the handwritten instructions.

'And if he gets a temperature or starts to feel even the slightest bit unwell, you'll have to bring him back to Perth, Dave. Immediately. Not tomorrow or the day after. Like yesterday.'

His stomach sank a little. 'What does it mean if he gets a temperature?'

'He'll have an infection somewhere. The chemo decreases his immune system and makes it harder for him to fight anything off. If the doctors don't get on top of it right away, then there could be . . . consequences.' Betty looked down.

'Right.' Dave wished he'd taken a bit more notice when Bec and Alice had been sick. He could remember something about Panadol, and Melinda saying it helped bring the spikes down, but it wasn't a medicine he'd ever administered.

Betty was watching him closely, her face showing her misgivings. He couldn't let her change her mind now. Straightening quickly, he placed the bag of medicine carefully on the back seat and smiled over at her. 'Not a problem. I'll look after him, Betty.' He made his voice convincing.

Betty shifted from one foot to the other, and Dave suspected she was trying to work out if he was up to the task.

'I'm sure there won't be any problems,' Dave continued, 'but how about I send you a text every night we're away? Then you'll know how Bob is, and if I've got any questions you can answer them. Does that sound okay?' Dave smiled now, putting his hand on her shoulder.

With a sharp glance, Betty covered his hand with hers. 'Please, you've got to be careful with him. He's not as well as he's pretending, and the chemo . . . it really knocks him about.'

'But he comes good a few days after each treatment, doesn't he?'

As if unwilling to admit this, Betty gave a half nod. 'But he hasn't been having the chemo for too long. Once it builds up in his system, there'll be more bad days than good in between each session. We won't really have any idea how it will affect him until it happens.'

Dave's heart squeezed tightly. God, his mate was having a tough time as it was. He didn't need things to get worse.

Moving away quickly before turning back to her, Dave held her eyes. 'If I could, Betty, I'd take the treatment for him. Bob's my best mate and I hate seeing him like this, but this trip is really important. It might perk him up a bit. Give him something to hold on to.'

Tears filled Betty's eyes. She blinked them away before they could spill over. 'I agree, but please be careful.'

'I've been wondering—' Dave cleared his throat as he tried to find the words he needed. 'No one has said anything about Bob's prognosis . . .' He let his voice trail off.

He watched her swallow a couple of times, then it was her turn to clear her throat.

As she was about to speak, the front door was flung open with a great shove and Bob stood on the doorstep, overnight bag in hand. He looked torn between excitement, relief and concern.

It seemed everyone was a bit nervous about this trip.

Betty started to fuss again, probably pretending that she and Dave hadn't been talking about Bob. 'Dave's got all the medication on the back seat and I've given him clear instructions on when and how you must take them all.'

Dave shot a glance at Bob, who was looking longingly at the troopy's open passenger door.

Betty touched Bob's arm. 'You're going to be a long way from the doctor, sweetheart.'

21

'Reckon they've got docs and hospitals in the places we're going to. No need to fret,' Bob said, patting her shoulder.

She paused, then stared Bob straight in the face. 'I hope you really enjoy yourself, my love.'

Bob turned to her and smiled. 'Dave here is reasonably responsible, you know.'

'It's not him I'm concerned about,' Betty said, throwing Dave a wan but amused smile. 'I know how persuasive you can be when you want something. Don't listen if he's wanting to do anything stupid, Dave. Promise me.'

'But what's stupid? How do I tell?' Dave asked with an innocent look.

Betty couldn't help but laugh this time, while Bob smirked and put his overnighter on the ground.

'You know exactly what I mean.' Betty pretended to look indignant.

'Nope, not getting involved,' Dave said, holding up his hands and backing away. 'Only going to say I'd like him alive as much as you would, Betty.'

'For god's sake! Stop it, the two of you,' Bob said. 'We're only going away for a few days.' He put his arm around Betty's shoulders and turned her towards him. 'Now, give us a kiss and head inside. There's a good—'

Betty swatted his hand. 'Don't you dare pull that good girl stuff on me, Bob Holden.' She landed her lips hard on his and then disappeared inside the house.

Bob gave Dave a knowing wink. 'Well, there you go, son. For some reason that good girl stuff gets her all hot and bothered under the collar. Not sure why.'

'Couldn't imagine,' Dave said and slammed the back door shut while Bob got into the passenger's seat.

'Ah, this will make a nice change,' Bob said as Dave turned the key. 'I'm sick of bloody hospitals and doctors and needles and being stuck inside. Let's get out bush where we can both breathe better.'

'Sure thing, boss.' Dave started the car and headed towards the highway.

'What's the plan?'

'I made some calls to the new Stockdale abs and they're expecting us tomorrow. Thought we could stay at Hydmere tonight, then head down to Stockdale tomorrow.'

'Son, we could make it to Stockdale today.' Bob's face creased into a frown.

Dave nodded. 'We could, but if we take it slowly you'll probably find the rest of the trip a bit easier.'

'Oh yeah? Did Betty tell you that? I reckon she'd prefer me to be wrapped up in cotton wool and locked away from the rest of the world, but I don't see any point in that, do you? I'd rather drop dead chasing some bastard who's just nicked a couple of hundred cattle than cark it in some hospital bed.'

'If it's all right with you, I'd rather you did neither.'

Bob shot Dave a look and didn't answer.

The ticking of the blinker filled the silence and Bob moved in his seat, pulling the belt away from his neck.

Dave had to grip the steering wheel tighter to stop himself from looking over. Was Bob uncomfortable? In pain? Tired? Could he breathe?

They were questions Dave knew Bob wouldn't answer, unless he was asked them straight and he chose to give the information. Which would only happen if he was close to dying. Inwardly, Dave cursed the tough Australian male exterior. Life was much bloody simpler if everyone just said what they were thinking and feeling. What they needed help with. It was easy if you knew you were going to make someone laugh or smile, Dave thought, but those hard conversations—they weren't simple or easy.

Shannon's words from their last dinner popped into his mind.

'Do we have something here, Dave, or is it still a fly-by-nighter for you?'

He'd watched her twist her long dark hair around her pointer finger as she spoke, looking at him intently. Dave loved it when she did the finger and hair thing.

What did he want? One moment he was sure that he wanted Shannon to be around all the time, and then he got frightened.

'You haven't answered my question,' Shannon had said, this time more quietly. She'd picked up her wine glass and sipped so she could hide her shaking hands.

But Dave had noticed. He'd smiled and reached for her, entwining his fingers with her free ones. 'It's not a fly-by-nighter,' he'd meant to say. Instead words he hadn't practised came out. 'It's pretty hard to have a proper relationship when you're a pathologist and I'm a detective, isn't it? I mean, you can be called away at any time, and so can I. I wonder how that will work for us later down the

24

track. You know, if it got really serious and we decided to have kids or something.'

As he'd said the words, his stomach had clenched into fists and he'd wanted to double over with the pain. At that moment he knew with certainty that there would be no more children for him.

Shannon had taken another sip of wine and was then quiet for so long Dave had been frightened she'd never speak to him again.

'Son?'

Starting at Bob's voice, he realised the car in front of him had moved forward at the green light and he was holding up the traffic.

'What's bothering you?' Bob asked.

'Nothing. Everything is fine. Are you okay?'

Dave felt Bob's eyes on him.

This time Dave looked over. 'Okay?' he asked again.

A moment passed before Bob answered. 'Now, son, I think we should get something clear. If whenever I move, cough or blink, you think I'm dying we're going to have trouble. How's about we just get on with the trip as we normally would. None of this cotton wool shit. Last time I looked you're not Betty.'

Dave gave an appropriate reluctant smile, glad that Bob hadn't pressed him further about his own thoughts. 'I think Betty would like it if I monitored your every movement.'

'And then reported back,' Bob agreed. 'Probably every hour.' He fixed Dave with a steely stare. 'And that isn't going to happen, is it?'

'Not on my watch. You've got to be a little understanding, though. Betty loves you and wants to know you're all right. I'm stuck in the middle here. But, look, I do understand what you're saying about watching you like a hawk. I'll try not to let the nurse in me come out too much.'

'Don't worry, son, you shouldn't find it hard. Not in your nature.' This time Bob gave a wicked smirk. 'Now, update me on everything I've missed out on with your life.'

'Nothing to report.' Dave changed lanes as they headed towards the hills and out through the state forest. 'Mark is still holding control over Melinda, and she seems pretty happy with that.' Dave's ex-wife had always let her father take charge. 'They're keeping the girls under tight rein, too.' It had been a while since Dave had had any contact with his daughters, Bec and Alice. To be fair, both the girls were still too young to call or write to him.

'I can't imagine Mark sitting down at night and helping them write something to me unless it read, *I have won and you are still married to the job.*'

A familiar anger bubbled inside him. He took a breath and kept talking. 'No letters from Melinda or the lawyers about letting me have some custody of the girls. Sweet FA.' He tightened his fists around the steering wheel as he thought about the last parcel he'd posted to the girls. A few weekends had been spent in bookshops, searching high and low for a story with a kelpie as the main character. He'd given both girls stuffed toy kelpies earlier, telling them the dogs would never leave their sides, especially if they were frightened. If Dad couldn't be there for his daughters, the kelpies would be.

When finally Dave had found what he'd been looking for, he packaged it up and dropped the parcel to his lawyer's office. Mark had forbidden him to know even their postal address. His lawyer, Grace, would post the book out and then charge his account triple.

There had been no reply.

'Maybe that's a good thing,' Bob said. 'I know you want to hear from the girls, but whenever you hear from the lawyers or Mark, without stating the obvious, you get a bit uptight, so let's run with the no news is good news.'

Dave didn't answer. That wasn't exactly true.

'Bec's birthday last week, wasn't it?' Bob ran his open palms up and down his pants as the sun danced across his lap.

'Yep.' Dave glanced out the window, racking his brain for another subject that didn't involve hospitals, cancer, death or his family. Something without emotion.

'Couple of good footy matches on the weekend.'

What the hell? Bob and he didn't talk about footy. They only kept track of what was happening in the AFL because footy was a great conversation-starter in the bush.

Bob just ignored his attempt to change the subject.

The trees on either side of the road were thick as they wound their way through the hills. Rubber marks covered the road where young hoons had given their cars a workout. There were plenty of plastic chairs tied to the trunks of the tall gum trees.

An empty chair meant someone had died there in a car accident. An empty space at the table.

His mother-in-law, Ellen, had been shot by a criminal who had been seeking revenge on Dave. Memories overcame Dave as he heard Bulldust say, 'I've lost my patience,' then a gunshot. Then a second shot, mixed with screaming and shouting and Ellen falling backwards, while his young daughter, beautiful little Bec, had blood streaming from her mouth and arm.

Sometimes Dave felt like his daughters had died alongside their grandmother because he rarely saw them now. When he did, the visits were short and sharp, never more than an hour long and usually in some out of the way place.

All thanks to Mark. That bastard had managed to convince Mel that Dave's choice of career had put them in danger that day and would continue to do so for as long as he worked as a copper.

'Three?' Bob asked.

Dave blinked, then frowned. What had they been talking about?

Bec. Her birthday.

'Ah, four.'

'I'd like to say that time has gone quick, but it hasn't really, has it? Not when you think about all the shit that's gone down since Bec was born. Did you get to see her?'

'Just put a birthday present in the mail via Grace.' Again, he felt Bob's eyes on him. 'What else am I supposed to do?' His tone was louder than before, feeling judgement, even though he knew there wasn't any. 'I couldn't just turn up at the house, could I? I don't know where they live, and if I did find out, Mark would probably have me arrested. Now that's a good look. A detective with a rap sheet.'

The rage sat heavily in his chest. These days he didn't want to belt someone or find a hitman for Mark—oh yeah, in the early days he'd flirted with that idea. He would've been able to find one easily, too.

In the end he'd decided he couldn't put his girls through any more death or grief. No one that young should lose access to their own mum, because she was too lost in the deep depths of her own sadness as Melinda had been.

Dave's rage had become helplessness, and then anguish. And he knew that, in time, the loss would decline and one day he might start to feel normal again. *Might* being the operative word.

Or perhaps it would become that new lot of buzz words he'd read in a magazine a while back: *A new normal.*

It sure as hell couldn't be the old normal.

'I didn't say a word, son.' Bob's words were heavy. 'I'm sorry you didn't get to see her. No word from your lawyer then?'

'Radio silence. Nothing since I signed the divorce papers.'

'Divor— What?' Bob turned in his seat now and looked at Dave fully. 'You never said anything about any divorce.'

'You knew we were always going to get there. Mel wanted it. Mark wanted it. Actually, I reckon that fucker needed it. Just waiting for the final court date before it's official.' Dave shrugged as if he didn't care, trying to ignore the stone that had found its way through his veins and into his heart and sat there constantly now.

Bob clapped a heavy hand onto Dave's shoulder. 'Shit, mate, I've been caught up in my own stuff. I had no idea.'

'You've had more important things on.' Dave glanced at the speedo, making sure it was a steady one hundred and ten. He knew the patrol cars loved hiding on the side roads, or driving slowly along the highway, catching people who thought the laws weren't for them. Even as an officer, he mostly liked to obey the rules that were for everyone. Not necessarily the ones inside the force, though.

'When did all this happen, son?'

Dave hated the rough-gentle tone of Bob's voice. He swallowed. 'Last week. Bec's birthday.'

'Bitch,' Bob breathed. 'Bet they did that on purpose.'

Dave shrugged and changed the subject. 'I had a letter from Mum.'

If what was left of Bob's eyebrows could have shot off his forehead, they would have. 'Your mother? Geez, son, what else have you been keeping from me? When was the last time you heard from her?'

'Who knows. My brother has disappeared, and she wants to know if I can help look for him.'

'What did you say?'

'I haven't answered her.'

Bob snorted. 'Why am I not surprised? Has anyone told you that you are the epitome of an ostrich?'

'Not since the last time you did.'

Bob shook his head as the forest line made way for open paddocks covered in a rich, deep green of wheat crops with grey granite outcrops and the occasional large salmon gum tree.

'Well, you've just strengthened my resolve not to die,' Bob said, a laugh in his voice. 'I was pretty keen on that anyway, but you've just proved you still need me around.'

Dave let out a bark of laughter. 'If that's what it takes, mate, I'm happy to have a screwed-up personal life for you to fix.'

CHAPTER 4

Hoisting the shopping bags out of the ute, Darryl Wilson pushed open the wire swinging gate with his foot and walked up the cement path. The edges were overgrown with weeds and the dandelion puffs gathered in the corner of the verandah, waiting for someone to come and sweep them away.

There was no one going to do that.

Darryl took a deep breath and readied himself before pushing the handle down with his elbow and heading inside the s'house, the shopping bags hitting his thighs as he walked. 'Hi, love, I'm home,' he called into the dimness.

There was a shuffling sound from the lounge room, and he put his head through the doorway, smiling. 'I'm back, love.'

Jasmine was facing away from him, but he knew the expression that would be on her face. Boredom and frustration. He expected her to at least turn, but she didn't move.

'Love?' Darryl set down the shopping bags in the hall and moved into the lounge room, pulling the curtains open. Dust particles danced in the mid-morning sunlight as he turned and looked at his wife. 'Jasmine?'

His smile fell away. She was holding a thick, creamy piece of paper in her hand. A piece of paper that was expensive and out of place in their dark, rundown s'house, where the carpet was threadbare, and the walls were covered with a lining of black soot from the open fire.

He walked to the couch and sat down next her, taking the paper gently from her without looking at it. 'All right, love?' He tugged at her hand, which was now in his, encouraging her to look at him.

Finally, Jasmine turned her eyes, which had turned a deep green with sadness and despair. 'They're going to do it . . . Take you to court,' she whispered, tightening her weak hands around his. 'The lawyers. They say they need—' she took a short, sharp breath and swallowed, then spoke again '—a meeting with you . . . As soon as you—' another breath, another swallow '—can get to Perth.'

He mashed his lips together, feeling how frail she was, how paper thin her skin was. The longing for Jasmine to be fit and well again slammed into his stomach so hard he wanted to bend over and hug his knees to his chest.

But Darryl would never let anyone see how distressed he was at the gradual decline in her health. He was stoic and unemotional. Or at least that's how he wanted everyone to see him.

'Wellll,' Darryl drew the word out in his well-known laconic style, 'guess we always knew that was on the cards, love.' He put the paper down, still not looking at it. 'I'm not worried about those bastards, and you shouldn't be either. We'll fight it. Now, I'll put the kettle on and make us a cuppa. Tea or coffee?'

'How can we? . . . We don't . . . have the money.' Jasmine pumped her hands up and down weakly, her eyes boring into his.

Her eyes were the strongest part of Jasmine now. They'd always been expressive. When she smiled, her eyes grinned. When she laughed, they danced. Serious? They were calm and genuine. Loving? Well, that was when, even thirty years on, Darryl's breath caught in his throat and he wanted to fold her into his chest, breathe in her shampoo and hold her until time ended. Another feeling he would never let anyone else know he experienced.

'Don't you worry about it, love—okay? I don't want you stressing about something that might take years to get to that point. Anyhow, I've got a plan.' He got up and kissed her head. 'Tea or coffee?'

'Hot chocolate . . . please.' She pushed herself from the couch. 'You always have . . . a plan.' She stood carefully, holding on to the frayed arm to get her balance. Her hand shook wildly, and he reached out to steady her.

Jasmine moved her head ever so slightly. Upwards, defiant of the disease that was robbing her of her life, still wanting *needing*—her independence.

His Jasmine was still there underneath every laboured breath, every tremor in her limbs. The strong, determined woman he loved, and who he'd do anything for.

Still, Darryl took the hint and moved away, picking up the shopping bags again. 'Did Cheryl drop the mail in? That how you got the letter?'

'No. George . . . after you left to go to town . . . Got it last week . . . by mistake . . . Wanted to bring it sooner . . . He's been busy.' Jasmine's breath was as fast as her steps were slow and careful. Her hand outstretched, not quite brushing the walls, in case she needed more support.

They were thin walls that divided the house's living areas: a kitchen, lounge and bedroom. All tucked inside a large shed: a s'house.

Darryl had promised Jasmine he'd build her a house on the eastern side of the farm, overlooking the granite hill, parts of which turned into a small waterfall after rain. Bottlebrushes grew in abundance through the cracks of the granite and formed a mass of red flowers during spring, while orchids and wildflowers played peek-a-boo at the bottom of the rocks.

He'd told her the colours of the bottlebrushes would match her hair and she'd smiled and kissed him.

Never in his wildest dreams would he have thought that trying to provide a comfortable life for his wife would send him to gaol.

But the letter was proof that it could. He knew without looking at the words, what it would say: *Darryl John Wilson charged with Illegal Clearing of Vegetation.*

Five years ago, a wildflower enthusiast had been looking for some kind of orchid, and seen him in action, pushing the bush over with the dozer. Turned out Big Brother had been watching also. Later in the year, as the trees and bushes had dried out, and he had burned the piles, the satellite had captured images of smoke billowing from the back of his farm.

Five bloody years ago!

Then that Arsehole from the Department of Conservation and Land Management had turned up and asked to see the area. Darryl had tried to tell him that this was his land and he could get nicked, until the prick had sprouted off about some part of an Environmental Act that Darryl knew nothing of.

He wasn't allowed to say no.

Arsehole had taken photos, asked questions and frowned deeply as Darryl and Jasmine had given him a cup of tea and waited for his decision.

They would receive notification, Arsehole had told them, of the process to come, but they were in violation of the Act and would more than likely be prosecuted.

Radio silence for five years. Both Darryl and Jasmine had begun to breathe easier after the first three months of not hearing anything, then six months after the initial visit all their time and energy had been absorbed with Jasmine's diagnosis. The possible land clearing charge, forgotten.

The government hadn't forgotten though.

Out of the blue, a letter, followed by an email. It was

time. Darryl had been the one operating the machinery, so the charges would be laid against him only.

The government. A mob of cocksuckers who had no idea what it was like to live in the real world.

Still, as far as Darryl was concerned, he and Jasmine had won. So, if the government thought putting him in gaol for something that couldn't be reversed was worthwhile, well, go right ahead.

Except that would leave Jasmine here by herself, getting weaker and sicker as each day passed.

The fact Darryl never had enough money to build the bloody house anyway had always stuck in his throat. But, by clearing the land, he'd opened up another twenty hectares for his livestock to graze on, with a lovely little spot in the middle for their dream homestead. And he was keeping a hold of that dream, while the sheep happily used and made them money on those twenty hectares the government wanted to gaol him for.

In the thirty years they'd been married, not once had Jasmine asked how his plans for the house were going. Nor had she resented the few rooms inside the shed he'd built just before they married.

After a couple of years living in the shed, she'd quietly planted lawn under the temporary clothesline he'd erected outside. There was a paved path and a fence surrounding the shed, to keep the chooks in and the dogs out. Even a few pots with roses that Jasmine picked when they flowered and then brought inside to the table.

The shower and toilet were inside the shed, but outside the walls of their rooms, with a twin-tub washing machine near the tractor and sheep-dipping race. Jasmine had never complained about any of it.

'Being here with you is enough,' she'd always whispered into his ear on the nights he'd apologised to her.

'Sorry, love, the crop didn't do as well as I thought it would.'

'Sorry, love, the sheep market has gone belly up. Can't get what the lambs are worth.'

'Sorry, love, the wool market crashed last week, just as we put our clip up to sell.'

'Being here with you is enough.'

Darryl hated those words and the guilt they brought as much as he hated that twin-tub washing machine. Still there wasn't money for a frontloading machine, so every day, he lit the donkey hot water system, filled the drum with water and Jasmine's sweaty clothes and bedsheets, then washed them and hung the wet washing out to dry. It wasn't hard work, just time-consuming when he knew things could be easier.

Every time he did it, he silently apologised to Jasmine that she'd had to do the washing like this for so many years and he hadn't realised how annoying it was.

If it was hot outside, he could hang the sheets on the line. If it was cold and rainy, there was a makeshift clothesline in the shed, between the wool press and wool bins. Didn't matter that the sheets smelled faintly of sheep and wool and oil when he went to get them in—the whole area did.

Sometimes the chemical drums emitted acidic or metallic smells and that ended up on their sheets, too.

On those nights, as Darryl was tossing and turning, unable to sleep, he had a secret thought. Was it him who had caused Jasmine to get sick by asking her to live so close to chemicals and farm equipment? Then he'd shake his head. Not likely. It's not as if they showered in the chemicals.

Darryl just wished he could build Jasmine something comfortable and cosy. Homely. The house she had always wanted.

It was too late now.

He refocused on Jasmine's words.

'George didn't have much . . . news.' Jasmine took a breath and continued, while Darryl pretended that her intake of breath didn't hurt him.

Her breathing had started to become a problem in the last few months and Jasmine's specialist had indicated the downward slide had begun. After four and a half years of holding the muscular dystrophy at bay, this was the beginning of the end.

Of course, the bloody disease had been present for a long time, they just hadn't realised. The fall that had broken her leg had been what finally got the doctor asking more and more questions, and then suddenly they were told why Jasmine had been falling so often, and why her face had drooped slightly, and now they were here.

After that recent specialist appointment, Darryl had taken Jasmine home and set her up with her panic button, then he had taken his gun on the pretence of shooting the foxes who were killing the new lambs.

Instead, he'd taken rum from his secret stash and driven to the spot where the house was supposed to be built and drank until the bottle was empty. Then he had stared at the gun and stroked it, wondering what it would feel like to place the cold barrel against his forehead and pull the trigger.

Life really hadn't worked out how he'd planned. Was he really useless at farming? That's what the angry stock agent had said that day he'd accused him of purposefully miscounting the lambs he'd sent on the truck.

'There should have been at least another eight thousand dollars in that payment,' Darryl had said. 'Where's it gone?'

'Mate, if you're accusing me of stealing stock, let me tell you, I wouldn't steal yours. Lightweight, underfed shit—that's what your lambs are. You're lucky you got what you did, because if I'd been the buyer, I would have slapped you with an NCV on that load.'

NCV. No Commercial Value.

Was that him as well as his stock?

When the tip of the barrel had found its way into his mouth and touched his tongue, the metal had been cold and hard. Darryl didn't want the hand he'd been dealt. He wanted to rage against everything. Jasmine should be well. They should be doing things together as they'd always done.

There had to be a way to make things return to normal, didn't there? He was powerless in every aspect. Powerless against the government, powerless against Jasmine's disease, powerless against all the resentment he was feeling.

Death seemed like a good—no, the best—option.

But then who would look after Jasmine?

The same question echoed in his mind now as he thought about the impending court case and possible gaol time. Maybe Jasmine would be in a home by then. Or worse.

'He did say . . . Steph had the baby . . . Little boy. Mitch.'

'That's great.' Darryl lit the gas and put the kettle on the burner, getting out two mugs from the cupboard. One was a travel mug. Jasmine could use the lid if she was worried about her hands not being able to hold the mug. 'Another farmer for the district.'

'I wish I was . . . able to help . . . Them being our . . . neighbour.' There was a heavy sadness in her voice that Darryl ignored.

'I got your medications,' he said, indicating the paper bag with the chemist's logo. 'And a treat.' He rustled around in another bag and found the packet of Tim Tams. 'Your favourite!'

Jasmine seemed to put her grief of being childless aside and grinned. 'Treat me . . . like a queen.' She pulled out a chair and tried to sit down, knocking it over in the process. 'Damn it!'

Darryl knew better than to try to pick the chair up for her. He poured the hot water into the mugs and stirred in half a teaspoon of sugar for Jasmine. He put their drinks on the table.

A few minutes passed before Jasmine had managed to right the chair and sit down. Her face was flushed and she was breathing hard, but still Darryl pretended not to notice and pushed her cup towards her. He left the lid within reach, letting Jasmine choose whether to use it or not.

Jasmine took a Tim Tam and bit into it, smiling again. 'Yum,' she said, her eyes sparkling. Then she became serious and reached out her hand. 'Thanks, love.'

'For what?' he answered, rubbing his thumb along her hand. He didn't give her the chance to answer. 'I've got to go out and check the ewes in a while. Want to make sure they're all upright and happy with no lambs stuck.'

Jasmine pulled her hand away and nodded. 'How long . . . until they finish . . . lambing?'

'They should be done. I'll see what we've got and then organise Smoky to come and do the lamb marking in a couple of weeks. Probably should have rung him before now, but somehow time has got away on me again.' He looked at his watch, then stood up, taking his cup with him. 'Better go or the day will get away, too. See you at lunchtime.'

Darryl wanted to fuss and make sure that Jasmine had her panic button close to her, but past experience told him that would only annoy her. He wasn't good at that type of thing anyway.

Perhaps he could suggest they take a drive to their neighbour's and see the new baby when Steph came home from the hospital. Still, that offer could make her happy or sad. Safer not to suggest anything. Instead, Darryl tucked his notebook and the letter into his pocket and left Jasmine sitting at the kitchen table, smiling vaguely after him.

CHAPTER 5

Darryl unhooked the piece of wire that looped over a wooden post and held the cocky gate upright, then dragged it to the side so he could drive into the paddock.

He splashed through a small puddle on the way back to his ute, feeling the cold water soak through his jeans.

What the hell was he going to do?

Now he'd read the letter, it sounded like the government was really going to come at him. Just for trying to have a go and make a success of his business. To make his farm a smidge more profitable than it would have been with the bush still standing. He chose not to think about the house that should have been built there; and it would have only taken a hectare or two, not the whole twenty hectares.

He and Jasmine had always paid their taxes and stayed out of trouble. And now, for twenty hectares, he was likely going to gaol? Why?

The ABC radio news came on and he glanced at the clock on the dash.

Eleven o'clock.

How on earth had it got to late morning and he was only just getting out into the paddock? Every other farmer worth their salt would have been out the door by seven thirty at the latest.

You had to go to town and do the shopping and pick up Jasmine's medication, the logical part of his brain told him. *That's no excuse. How about you're useless?*

'Investigations into the Kallygarn Shire Council offices' bombing are ongoing,' the news reporter on the radio said.

Turning up the volume, he put the ute in first gear and slowly started to navigate the edge of the paddock, looking for any ewes that were down and not able to get up. That could indicate a lambing problem or that she was too weak, or too fat, to stand.

Take your pick.

Except Darryl knew his ewes weren't too fat.

'Major Crime, the Bomb Squad and Forensics are being called in to examine the crime scene. It is still too soon to determine if this was a deliberate act.'

Noticing a hole in the fence, Darryl stopped the ute and got out, grabbing his pliers and a roll of wire from the back. Cutting the right length from the roll, he weaved it through the fence and proceeded to twitch the wires together.

His stomach was fizzing as he listened to the report. The bombing had happened only hours ago.

'We're securing the scene and waiting until the required squads have arrived before we can investigate the origin and cause of the explosion,' the officer in charge, Senior Sergeant John Campbell, was saying.

'Tamara Goyder, a resident of Kallygarn explained what she experienced,' the reporter continued.

'We were all sound asleep but something woke us. Probably the loud bang, I guess. The windows were shaking and we were confused for a bit. Thought the world was ending actually.' The laugh that came over the radio was self-deprecating. 'My hubby, Darren, got out of bed and went to the window and then called me to have a look. All we could see was an orange glow on the clouds, so we knew it was a fire, but not what was burning. Debris was falling down all around us and we were too scared to go outside. Bricks were landing on our roof . . .'

'Did you have any damage to your home?'

'A few dents in the tin that's all. Nothing like the council offices. There didn't seem to be much left when we were able to get outside and have a look. The fire brigade put the fire out quickly, thank goodness. The offices are very close to the supermarket and post office, so if they'd gone up in flames, the town would be without some services that we rely on.'

'How do you feel about the explosion? Do you think it was deliberate?'

'Deliberate?'

Darryl straightened. She sounded awfully surprised at

the question. He wondered why, when that would have been his first thought.

'Who would do that? God, I hope not. Pretty scary to have something like that happen here in little Kallygarn. Nothing much ever happens here.'

'In other news . . .'

Darryl tuned out for the next news item as he put his pliers back in the toolbox. He hung his hands over the edge of the tray and looked out across the paddock, reflecting on the season.

It was a hard one. Early in the season, not much rain had fallen before the cold had set in, resulting in little feed growth. The crops were stunted and patchy. Some parts of the paddocks hadn't germinated at all, although on the heavier country, which held on to moisture, it looked like the crop had got away well.

That last rain had been helpful to build the soil profile moisture bank, and a few warm days would certainly help the crops, but for now it was too cold, this deep in winter, for it to kick the feed along. He wished the bitter cold hadn't affected the soil temperature so soon. When it began to drop, the grass didn't grow as quickly and it didn't take long for the hungry, milking ewes to get on top of what was in the paddock.

The lambs weren't plump and happy like lambs should be, they were 'woody'. An incredibly untechnical term, but a word that every stock farmer understood—they weren't getting enough milk from their mums and therefore not enough nutrition.

And that started a cycle of problems. The lambs were hungry and had started to pick at the grass before their tummies were ready for solid food. Grass would cause their tummies to get upset, they'd get the shits, which stuck around their arse and tail, and then the flies turned up.

There were a few lambs that already had large dags hanging from their arse end. Perhaps he should have brought some oats or lupins out here to supplementary feed them. How much did he have left in the silo? Probably only a few tonnes and that wouldn't be enough to get them through winter.

This season was bringing a never-ending circle of things that weren't right and a merry-go-round he couldn't get off.

What would it be like, he wondered, to blow up his house? His shed? His possessions? Himself?

Darryl could imagine the noise of the blast, then the thudding of debris hitting the ground. The sheep would take off in fright across the paddock, stopping only when they came to a fence and maybe not even then. Afterwards a silence would reign across the land as everything he had owned would cease to exist.

He would cease to exist.

What did he feel for his farm and stock? His life?

Switching his thoughts to Jasmine, and the dreams he'd had before they'd married. Along with the ones they'd had together in the years that followed. The lost goals—no children, very little money and a mountain of regrets.

There were no emotions inside his body when he thought about what they had planned for. Yet mention the government and his anger and frustration flared so quickly and violently, he could easily hurt someone.

Back in the ute, Darryl continued to circumnavigate the paddock, looking for problems, but he wasn't concentrating on the livestock or the feed. He was back to fuming at the government, at the Department of Conservation and Land Management and anyone else who had a hand in throwing the judge and jury at him.

Maybe he could appeal to their human side. He could show them photos of Jasmine and tell them why gaol wasn't an option. No one with an ounce of compassion would want Jasmine to be without her husband while she was declining.

Would they?

'Who's going to look after her if I'm not there?' he would ask them. 'You?' Then he'd scoff at them, because he knew that not one person in those glass high-rise offices would give a toss whether Jasmine had anyone to care for her. They were only interested in the crime he'd committed. No mitigating circumstances would stop what had been put in motion.

The slow flush of red-hot anger started at the base of his throat and worked its way downwards until it reached his chest. Now, the fury turned into a bubble that spread across his body. Darryl wanted to punch something. Or someone. The bloke called Arsehole would be a good start. He was the one who had caused this problem. He'd been one of those from the high-rise buildings in the city. Six hours drive to the west on the highway.

Chapman Hill, the closest town to Darryl's farm was five hundred kilometres to a town called Stockdale, on the coast, where a few locals took their summer holidays. And four hundred kilometres from the town in the news, Kallygarn. Darryl and Jasmine lived in the middle of nowhere. On the long edge of a strange-shaped square, if someone drew a line between all these towns and Perth.

'It was only twenty hectares,' Darryl muttered. 'Twenty bloody hectares. Not enough to make any difference to anything! It's my land. I bought it, paid the interest on the loan from the bank. How the hell can the government tell me what to do with my place?'

It was only twenty hectares. The words he repeated almost daily. Sometimes incredulously and sometimes in anger.

Maybe he could offer to plant some trees around the boundary or something. If they were worried about wildlife, there was still plenty of bush near the granite hill that would protect any animals.

A quiet chirp from his glovebox interrupted his thoughts.

He took his eyes away from the paddock and looked at the scratched and worn latch that would open the door.

The ute was shaking slightly from the idle of the engine and the vibration seemed to run through his body like electricity. The world came into sharp focus. Had he imagined the noise?

There it was again. A soft chirp.

He didn't move a muscle, nor his eyes.

The ewes turned to look at the ute that was motionless in their paddock. It only took seconds for them to let out a loud baa and start to run across the paddock in hope Darryl had the feeder on behind him and that there would be a trail of supplementary grain on the ground when they arrived.

The lambs bleated and tried to follow their mums; some kept up, some tangled their newborn legs together and fell over, then scrambled to their feet, calling out in panic. They ran blindly, thinking each ewe was their mother, trying their udders only to get kicked away or rolled over on the ground as the ewes kept running in anticipation of a feed.

But Darryl was towing nothing. Soon he found himself surrounded by the mob, sniffing and looking up at him. Their barley-coloured eyes assessing each move he made.

They fossicked and sniffed around, pawing at the ground. To no avail. The ground was empty of any grain and when they realised that, most started to move away, calling to their lambs. A few stragglers, still hanging around hopefully, looked up at Darryl as if he'd failed them.

'Take a number,' he called out. 'The rest of the world is disappointed in me, too.'

Another chirp. From a phone he never took into the house.

Forgetting about the sheep, he smiled as he reached towards the handle and pulled it open. Inside, along with dirt and nuts and bolts and blue raddle, was a little black phone. He pulled it out and looked at the screen. Pressing a few buttons, he then held the phone to his chest as if it was a letter from a lover.

CHAPTER 6

Bob stretched out on the bed and closed his eyes. It frustrated him how easily he tired these days. Normally on a night like this, he'd be in the bar, laughing and joking with the locals, but all he wanted to do tonight was sleep. It was a bone-weary tiredness, yet when he lay down and closed his eyes, his body refused to succumb to the welcome blackness.

Dave had been right—breaking the trip up into two halves was the best way to go. Bob could never admit this.

His mobile phone dinged but he ignored it. Betty had already called twice today and she would be in bed by now as she had an early shift tomorrow. If Dave needed him, he could knock on the door. There was no one else Bob wanted to talk to.

Finding the remote control by feel, he hit the on button and made sure the channel was on the ABC, then shut his eyes again, waiting for the late-night news. They'd missed the seven o'clock news and they'd been talking about Bob and Johnny's work together when the radio news would have been on, so they hadn't seen any up-to-date headlines.

He massaged the scar on the back of his arm where the doc had taken out the melanoma. The doc had had to go in hard, not wanting to risk leaving any cancerous cells behind. Fifteen centimetres by eight. Sometimes, the damaged skin prickled as if there were pins and needles inside, and part of it was still numb. He assumed the feeling would come back in time and he hadn't mentioned it to anyone because a little numbness was better than the alternative. Plus, Betty had told him that scar tissue was an ever-moving beast and it would be about eighteen months before the area settled properly.

The anchor of the current affairs program droned on about something to do with politics and a federal sitting member for somewhere in Queensland who was embroiled in another scandal. Bob sighed. He was tone deaf to this shit.

His watch's alarm would go off dead on ten pm as a reminder to take his nightly tablets, so he would watch the real news then. Not this dramatised crap every tellie station seemed to want to put out.

There was already a glass of water on the bedside table, and he hoped there would be no reason for him to get up again tonight. His legs were aching with tiredness and, yet, all he had done was sit in the passenger's seat. Even though this trip was what Bob needed right now, he wouldn't be much use to Dave over the next few days. Still, he'd take feeling crap if it meant the open spaces and paddocks.

During the drive out of Perth, he'd noticed lambs running along a fence parallel to the road. Their pure joy in life had lifted some of the weight from his shoulders.

The calves in the paddock near Corrigin had ripped away from their mothers' udders at the sound of the troopy and watched it go by with suspicion, while milk had dripped from the corner of their mouths. They had put a smile on Bob's face which hadn't left.

As they'd driven into Hydmere tonight, the railway crossing lights had started to flash and the boom gates lower. The driver had stuck his hand out the window and waved at them as he'd passed with carriages full of grain, headed for the city.

Life in the bush was simpler and slower. Nicer. Bob was glad to be back.

Dave had suggested a late start tomorrow, but a lie-in wouldn't be enough to make up for the sleepless nights he had these days.

Three nights ago he had got up about eleven pm and sat in the lounge room waiting for sleep to come. Betty had bought him a rocking chair and a pair of slippers when the treatment had first started. He'd scoffed when the chair had been delivered, telling her he wasn't that old yet, but there was something comforting about the gentle movement back and forth. And the slippers? He'd asked whether he needed a cigar and a glass of port as well.

Betty had lightly batted his arm and dropped a kiss on his cheek. 'You'll get used to them,' she'd told him.

Bob hadn't been so sure.

For years, he'd wandered around in bare feet, not worrying about the cold. And a kitchen chair had been the choice, to watch the tellie, because he never knew when he would have to go running out the door to an investigation.

To his surprise, Betty had been right. With all her years working as a nurse, she understood how simple things comforted.

That sleepless night, the soothing motion of the rocking chair hadn't stopped the thoughts the way he'd hoped. Instead, there had been no other option other than to sit with them, no matter how uncomfortable or sad they made him.

Were there any regrets? Oh, too many to mention.

Did he wish things worked with his first wife and they'd had children? The jury was still out.

Would he have worked as hard if he'd had kids? Stayed out bush as much? Drank as much? And had the drinking heightened the likelihood of getting melanoma?

The answers to the working and the bush were still a loud yes. That was his life and he loved it. There was nothing he would change about his career, which probably answered the question about his first wife, if he was truthful.

The booze? Well, if it had contributed to the cancer, it didn't matter now. What was done was done. He'd given a philosophical shrug at that one.

Later, he'd got up to make a cup of tea and had sat at the kitchen table trying to scratch out some letters.

Dear Betty, glad you turned up when you did. I'm really happy that you're in my life. Meeting you up north was timing at its best, and the last couple of years have been the happiest . . .

He'd screwed it up and tried again.

Dear Dave, mate, glad to have known you, son.

Son. There was no denying Dave was the closest he'd ever had to a son.

Somewhere from deep within, the lump that had been sitting at the base of his throat since the diagnosis burst. He had let the tears fall—knew he'd tell no one about them—and when they'd stopped of their own accord, Bob had picked up both pieces of paper and taken them into the lounge room. With a deep breath, he'd thrown the letters on the fire and stared deep into the flames as the orange glow leapt and danced in front of him.

In the car this morning, the urge to tell Dave had been strong. Turning words over, trying to find the right way to tell Dave how important he was, but each time Bob came up short. In the end, it was easier to say nothing and not embarrass either of them.

Anyhow he wasn't going to die any time soon. Dave was clearly stuffing his life up and still in need of some help, and Bob would make sure he was there to do just that: guide.

You won't beat me, he thought grimly as the strain of the late-night ABC news came on. *There's too much to do yet.*

With a groan he sat up and reached for the glass of water and tablets, swallowing them in one gulp. A reporter was out the front of Parliament House, talking about something the prime minister had said. Bob was sick and tired of people talking and nothing changing. What would it take for everyone to stop bitching and take responsibility for their own actions. Fed up with politicians and society in general, he started to head for the bathroom.

A banging sounded on his door.

'Shit!' Bob took a breath as his heart jumped, hitting his rib cage hard, then he glared at the door as if it had reached out to slap him. 'Fucking hell.' He did up the drawstring on his pants and grabbed the handle, yanking it open, determined not to show he'd been rattled. 'Ah, it's you. See the light on and get lonely, did you?' He opened the door wider to let Dave inside. 'Sorry, I don't think you'll find me as comforting as Shannon.'

Dave brushed past and turned to face Bob as soon as he was inside. 'Don't you answer your phone anymore? I sent you a text.'

'That was you? I heard one come through.'

'How am I supposed to know if you're okay when you don't answer?' Dave's voice was tight.

Bob gave Dave a quizzical look. 'Well, I guess you knock just the way you just have. What's your problem?'

'There's been a bombing. During the early hours of the morning. At Kallygarn.'

Bob raised his eyebrows. 'That sounds all rather dramatic for our quiet state.' Even though he spoke calmly, the familiar rush of adrenalin flooded through him. Still, his bladder wouldn't hold for anyone or any news these days, so he went into the bathroom and started to relieve himself, waiting for Dave to speak.

'Just got a call from Lorri. She's been trying to get us since the news filtered through about lunchtime, but the mobile range out through the hills is average at best.' He paused. 'Kallygarn is only two hours from here.'

Bob could tell from Dave's voice that he was pumped, as if he wanted to get in the car and go straight there. At ten pm.

'I know exactly where Kallygarn is,' Bob said, flushing the toilet and coming back out again. 'What's the drum?'

'Not a whole lot yet. They've sent Major Crime, Bomb Squad and Forensics down there. No injuries. They'll have to wait for the scene to be assessed before they know more. It would have taken the teams six hours to get there from Perth and it happened late at night, so by the time they've gone over it good and proper, I guess it won't be until tomorrow or later that we get any information.'

'What was targeted?'

'The shire building.'

Bob flopped down on the bed. 'Someone upset they had to pay more rates?'

'Don't know. Lorri didn't think anyone had claimed responsibility.'

'Claimed responsibility? This isn't Iran or Iraq, son. If you haven't noticed, we're living in Australia.'

'I know, I know . . .' Dave's voice trailed off. His fingers tapped out a rhythm on his thighs, a sure sign he was agitated. 'Strange, though, don't you think?'

Bob snorted. 'Yeah, I reckon that goes without saying. When was the last time we investigated an explosion?' Bob scratched at his chin. Then his eyes dropped to the floor and he groaned. 'Old Donny Hancock and Lou Lewis.'

A feud which had started way out in the bush between retired detective Don Hancock and a bikie gang had spilled over in a Perth street, late one night. The gang had placed a bomb under Don's car, which exploded, killing Don and his civilian mate. A retaliation for a bikie death in which it had been alleged Don Hancock was the murderer.

'Shit,' Dave muttered. 'Could there be—'

'I've told you never to jump to conclusions,' Bob said. 'We don't know about this blast. A bloody gas bottle might have exploded.'

Dave gave him a disbelieving look. 'How often does WA have bombings? The relations between the coppers and bikies are pretty tense at the moment, and the bikies' MO is to shoot people or blow them up.' Dave shoved his hands in his pockets and rocked on his heels.

Bob held up his hands. 'Just calm the hell down, son.' Frowning, Bob threw Dave a look. 'I thought I'd got all the fire and brimstone shit out of you. What did Lorri say exactly?'

'Just that there had been an explosion.'

'Right, so my comment about a gas bottle coming to an unfortunate end might not be so wrong.' Bob gave Dave a hard stare. 'Anyone would think you wanted it to be the bikies.'

'I was just putting it out there . . .'

Bob gave him a steely look. 'Careful what you wish for, son. They're not to be played with.'

Dave walked over to the window and pulled the curtains back a few inches, staring outside, then closed them again.

'Do you think the bikies know we're here?' Bob asked with a snort. He couldn't help but take the piss out of his partner. When Dave didn't answer, he plumped the pillows and pulled back the covers.

With a last yank of the curtains, Dave turned and flipped him the bird.

'That's the way, son. Keep that up and we'll be back to buying you McHappy meals, because you've reverted to age five again.' Bob hopped into bed. 'Don't be an idiot. Go to bed and we'll see what news there is in the morning. Also, you're forgetting, there are three detectives stationed out of Stockdale, which is only a couple of hours away from Kallygarn. Just because we're in the area doesn't mean we'll get a look-in.'

'We'd have more experience than the locals.' Dave sounded as if he was daring Bob to disagree.

'For fuck's sake, son. What is it with you? Get back in your box. Just go to sleep and we'll see what the morning brings,' Bob repeated. By god he was tired. Surely Dave could head off now and let him sleep.

'Fine, fine.' Dave twisted his fingers together. 'Okay, I'll let you get to bed.'

But Bob saw his mate's agitation and he softened. 'What's going on?' he asked gruffly.

'Nothing.'

'Somehow I find that hard to believe.'

Jiggling on the spot, Dave just shook his head.

Bob stayed quiet, knowing Dave would talk to him in his own good time.

It didn't take long.

'I dunno. Just need something to do.' Dave pulled out a seat from the table and sank into it. 'Tonight, being here, and you not in the bar with me—it just doesn't seem right. Like I'm missing something. An arm or a leg.'

The words were like a blow to Bob's chest. He wanted to apologise but what did he have to say sorry for? Other than nothing.

If he had a choice, he wouldn't have cancer and he would be in the bar, talking to every Tom, Dick and Harry, swigging on beer and soaking up information and conversation as normal. A burst of anger, rose to the surface, catching him by surprise.

'Dave,' he said, 'I'm not going to be here forever. I understand that you're not enjoying this. Neither am I. But start growing a pair, because forever isn't on my dance card. It's not on anyone's.'

CHAPTER 7

The Stockdale cemetery was cold and empty, and Connie pulled her jacket tightly around her thin frame. She glanced around and, seeing no one else around, whispered to Dude to 'Come on out', then slammed the door of her second-hand Corolla shut.

Clipping the leash onto Dude's collar, she patted him, unwilling to walk through the gate yet, because that would make Brandan's twelve-month anniversary real.

But she'd brought the flowers and Brandan's dog, Dude, so of course she'd push open the gate that screeched louder than a cockatoo and weave her way through the rows until she stood in front of his grave.

Slivers of sun danced through the heavy canopy of gum leaves, and she tried to walk through each of them, hoping for one that was extra warm. Instead, she felt the heavy drops of dew as they dislodged themselves from the branches in the gentle morning breeze and landed on her jacket and in her hair.

A layer of ice covered the lawn, even though it was nine am and the sun was shining. Brandan had loved the frosts when he was little. She remembered him slipping outside while the rest of the household stole the last few minutes in their warm beds. His favourite joke had been making tracks across the lawn, pretending they were from an intruder during the night. The wicked giggle accompanied the cold wind in through the door, as he snuck back inside had given him away.

Dude's exhalations were in time with hers, both turning the air white as they breathed warm air out.

Her feet took her automatically towards the plot she'd visited every Sunday. She'd never missed one, since the funeral—even when she'd been struck down with the flu, she'd dragged herself here and told him about the week. About their mum, their family, and every bit of news there was. Right down to when Leopard, their newly acquired kitten, had upended the sugar bowl on the table and licked at the granules until Connie had turfed her into the laundry and cleaned everything up.

She didn't mind the cemetery now, but she had been uncomfortable when she'd first begun visiting. Not scared, but certainly uneasy. Many times, as she was leaving, she'd had to stop and look over her shoulder, thinking Brandan was watching her. Telling her not to leave him. Asking her to make people aware of how he'd come to his death.

She could *feel* him so strongly, he *had* to be behind her. But when she turned, the paths and grassy areas were always empty. And silent, so silent because the dead don't always speak for the living to hear.

For a while afterwards, Connie had gone to different mediums, hoping to hear Brandan's last words to her, but she'd been met with either sentences that were clearly made up by the medium or nothing. She couldn't believe that Brandan wouldn't have something to say. That would be unlike him.

Everyone must die. But not the young, surely. Yet, here in the cemetery was proof that people did die young.

The old, dirty, moss-covered headstones, telling her that children, mums, dads, daughters, sons, uncles, aunts were all buried here, loved by someone. Hated by others. Some headstones read of tragedy, others of a normal death. 'Death must come to us all no matter our age,' the minister told her once. 'Brandan's was an unfortunate accident.'

Connie understood, of course, that this was the circle of life. But, no matter how hard she tried, she couldn't agree with the minister about her brother's death—dying in a car crash at twenty-three. A car crash that he hadn't caused.

Tucking her blonde hair behind her ear, she adjusted the bouquet of banksias, gum leaves and bottlebrush flowers, heavy in her arms, and tugged at Dude's lead, which had wound around her wrist.

'Dude,' she told the border collie, as he stopped to sniff another grave, 'you can't piss on anything. Even if you find someone you don't like. You're not even supposed to be here, so behave.'

Dude turned towards Connie, and cocked his head, as if he understood, then led her through the perfectly manicured lawns and trees planted with precision across the grounds. The dog knew the way. He, too, was a constant visitor despite the signs reminding people dogs were not allowed in the cemetery.

'I thought you'd be here,' a voice called out, from a long way behind.

Connie turned and Dude, tongue lolling, lunged towards the end of the lead, letting out an excited bark. His tail wagged so hard Connie almost dropped the lead as the flowers jerked in her arms.

Tom jogged towards them as Connie gave a relieved sigh. She could always rely on Tom.

Now alongside Connie, Tom put his arm around her shoulders and gave a squeeze. 'How are you holding up? Hello, Dude. Yes, mate, I know you're there.' With his free hand he tried to pat the dog but didn't make contact as Dude jumped excitedly around.

Connie swallowed and let her head fall against his shoulder momentarily, then she straightened and handed him the flowers. 'Can you take these? They're as heavy as anything.'

'Hang on a sec, I've got to say a decent hello to Dude.' Tom held up his hand in a high-five gesture and Dude immediately sat, holding up his paw.

The sting of tears was hot. Brandan had taught Dude to high-five. Connie refocused on the flowers. 'I think the florist got a bit excited when she was putting all the flowers together. It's a bit over the top, don't you think?'

'I don't think any bouquet is over the top,' Tom said as they fell into step. Dude walked alongside them, his tail wagging. 'Kristy has done a nice job.'

Touching each headstone along the path Connie read the words silently. She knew all of them.

Sarah Convey, 65, beloved wife and mother of John, Anne, Graham and Kate. May she rest in the arms of our Lord.

Michael Hovey, 22, taken tragically on 16 December 1896. Much loved son of William and Deirdre Walker, brother to Holly and Sarah. Forever loved.

Brian Dearlove, 95, husband of Margaret (dec.). The Lord our God will be pleased to see his faithful servant.

They all showed the same thing: that time is precious and even the most valued of family or community could suffer the same fate, it only depended on when, where and how.

Her Aunt Mary used to say, 'Dying doesn't bother me. It's just how I get there that does.'

She didn't say that anymore.

'How are you feeling today?' Tom asked.

Her friend was looking at her, but she didn't turn her head to him. She was focused on the tall, black headstone three rows away, that had her brother's name engraved on it. She could pick it out from the entry gate.

'There isn't a day when I don't wish he wasn't walking in the door,' she said. 'Guess I won't ever feel any different.' Connie took a shuddering breath and looked towards the sky.

They came to a standstill in front of the grave.

Tom touched her hand. 'I care. Brandan was important to you.'

Connie gave a wobbly smile. 'It's tough without him. Mum's sadness is so heavy sometimes I expect the walls will fall in under the weight of her grief. And what pisses me off is I don't know how to help her. Did you know Mum hasn't been outside the house in four months?' As she traced the letters on the marble, her voice rose in frustration.

Brandan James Phillips. Much loved son of Josh and Georgia, older brother to Connie. Forever 23, forever loved and forever remembered.

The forever-remembered part was something her mum had insisted on, but the statement couldn't always be true. If Connie had kids, she'd tell them about the uncle they would never know, but once they were all gone, who would be left to tell of Brandan's practical jokes or loud laughter? He wouldn't be remembered when everyone who knew him was dead.

'You know that cow Jackie at the service station told me that everyone turns into a saint when they die and that Brandan wasn't any different . . . even though he drove too fast and recklessly, and it was his fault that he slammed into a tree.'

Tom grunted in disgust. 'Of course. It was nothing to do with the fact that the cops were chasing him.'

'None,' Connie answered bitterly, taking the flowers from Tom and laying them at the foot of the headstone. She reached into her handbag and took out a small banister brush and ran it over the grave, clearing away dust and cobwebs before getting out a small photo frame. This was the last photo she had taken of Brandan.

He was staring moodily at her, his black eyes unreadable, the heavy silver chain around his neck glinting in the afternoon sun. His haircut was new, a crew cut, much to their mother's disgust, and a dark green tattoo snaked out from under the collar of his T-shirt.

'Why would you defile your body like that?' their mother had cried out when he'd first come home with the inked serpent.

'Just to see your face, Mum.' Brandan had grinned, then he'd taken her into a hug. 'It's okay, everyone has them.'

'Brandan, you're not everyone. Don't follow the masses. Be yourself.'

Their mother had loved using Brandan's name.

Dude whined and pawed at the ground, then lay down heavily, next to Connie's and Tom's feet.

'Oh, Dude, I miss him, too.' Connie sat down on the grass, next to the dog and stroked his head, her eyes not leaving Brandan's photo. 'I know he wasn't perfect, but who is? Just because he was a bit of a rev-head and liked a drink, that didn't make him bad. It's not like he was bashing little old ladies for their pension.'

'He was a good bloke.' Tom put his hand on her shoulder. 'And there're lots of people who miss him. Don't worry about Jackie.'

'She's a sour-faced bitch,' Connie said.

Tom gave a soft laugh. 'Down, Tiger.'

'Brandan was kind. Don't you remember how he went out and bought me a hot chocolate every time I got sick? And he used to check on Mr Ganter after his wife died. He took him out in the wheelchair to the pub and helped him have a couple of beers and a bet on the horses. I didn't see anyone else doing that for the poor old bugger. Everyone kept saying he shouldn't do it. Wasn't good for the old bloke to be drinking and all that shit. Well, he was always laughing when I saw Brandan pushing him home.'

'He had a heart of gold, for sure,' Tom agreed.

The dew was seeping through Connie's jeans, making her legs and bum cold. She should move, but sitting here made her feel close to Brandan again. Anything for that.

With teeth chattering, she pulled Dude to her, wrapping her arms around his neck and leaning into him.

'And he used to weed the community garden at night so no one knew it was him.' The ball of emotion that Connie had been pressing down since she had woken up that morning was threatening to burst out of her. There were too many firsts in that first bloody year. Sounded like a stupid saying but it was true.

'He, uh, he . . .' She stopped talking and hid her face in Dude's shaggy mane. The dog turned his head around to see what was happening.

Tom reached out and rubbed a hand over her back.

'God, as if losing Dad a few years ago wasn't bad enough for Mum, and now Brandan has tipped her over the edge. She won't let any of her friends through the door. Says they wouldn't understand what it's like to lose a child. Aunty Mary's worried, too. Did I tell you she's coming over today from Kallygarn, just to be here with Mum? I'm so bloody grateful because I don't know how to make her see the sun is still shining. Maybe not as bright, but it still is.'

'I reckon it's great Mary wants to be with you both today. Rough times call for family and she's always been a huge support.'

Connie sniffed, then wiped her nose. 'Sometimes I think we'd be lost without Aunty Mary. I told her yesterday that Mum's made a shrine to Brandan in her bedroom. Photos from when he was a baby through until last year. T-shirts that he used to wear hanging from the window. Brandan's photo sits on her bedside table so he's the first thing she looks at when she wakes up and the last thing she sees when she goes to sleep. Aunty Mary says none of this is healthy and I totally agree, yet I don't know how to help her.' Her voice echoed across the empty cemetery.

'Georgia doesn't want to come here?' Tom asked.

'Nope. She's only ever seen the headstone in photos. Makes it too real, she says.' Connie scoffed as if she couldn't believe the stupidity in the statement. 'It's not like he comes home every night anymore, so I'm not sure how much more real you can get.'

They sat in silence until an unseen shed door screeched open and a lawn mower started.

'I used to feel him you know,' Connie said. 'I've never told anyone that before. When he first died and I came here.'

'Did you?' There was no judgement in Tom's tone. Only curiosity.

'Yeah, I kept looking over my shoulder, just to check that he wasn't there. He felt so damn real.'

'Dunno how true this is, but someone told me once that if a person is taken out of the blue, like Brandan was, then their soul sort of hangs around for a while. Just until both the people left behind and the person who's died get used to what's happened.' Tom picked at some grass and let it fall from his fingers, like confetti, as he spoke. 'Maybe that's what you were feeling.'

'Get used to it?' Connie whispered. 'Get used to it . . . How do we do that?' she asked, despair ripping through her stomach.

Tom shrugged. 'No idea, Con.' He looked around and then up to the sky. 'All this stuff is much bigger than you and me. Guess we'll never really know, will we? Not until we actually—'

Connie's hand shot out and grabbed his arm. 'Don't say it. I can't bear any more death.'

Rubbing his thumb over her hand, Tom looked at Connie. 'I'll do my best to somehow fix this.' He leaned forward and stared into her eyes. 'I promise.'

'How can you promise that, Tom? There's nothing—' her voice caught '—anyone can do.'

As she spoke a cold breeze swept through, tousling her hair and playing with Dude's ears.

The dog looked around as if he was confused, then shot to his paws, with a sharp bark.

'Dude?' Tom took the lead and tugged at it gently, but the dog ignored him.

Another few steps away and Dude whined, then let his mouth drop open in a smile, wagging his tail at nothing.

As quickly as it happened, Dude was back next to Connie, puffing in her face. She shivered and looked behind her.

71

CHAPTER 8

'Hello, Kate. How are you?' Clare Davidson put her handbag on the Chapman Hill post office counter, pulled out three envelopes and waved them around. 'Can I get some stamps, please?' Plucking at her hair, self-consciously, Clare once again wondered at the wisdom behind embracing the grey.

Kate just waved to her from the sorting room and made a wait motion. 'Just a mo',' she called.

Clare nodded her head to say there was no hurry.

A few moments later, and Kate was smiling over the counter. 'How are you, Clare? I haven't seen you in ages. Have you been away?'

'Wouldn't I love to have been on a holiday? No luck there I'm afraid, just busy helping family.'

'Don't get me started on family! My daughter, the one who lives in Sydney, has been asked to run the company she works for while the boss is away on maternity leave. I'll probably get the call up to do her washing and till

72

the freezer with meals!' Kate reached into the drawer and brought out a booklet of stamps. 'Three?'

'Yes, please.' Clare ran her fingers through her hair.

The door swung open and a cold wind blew through the shop as Hec Burton came in, leaning heavily on his walking stick. Pushing his glasses back on the bridge of his nose, he squinted at the two ladies as the door banged behind him.

'Good morning, ladies. It's a bit blustery outside. Have you—' He was overwhelmed by a sudden hacking cough.

'Good morning, Hec,' Kate answered over the noise. 'Have you come for your mail?' She moved towards the sorting room but stopped as Hec stamped his stick. 'You all right, Hec?'

The old man got out his handkerchief and wiped his mouth. 'No, not the mail!' He lowered his voice a fraction. 'Did you hear the news, ladies?'

'Nothing this morning,' Kate said, 'but I did hear the ambulance sirens last night. I think they were heading out the highway towards Perth on the Great Eastern Highway. Was there an accident? Oh hell, not someone local?'

Clare clutched her hands to her chin. The Great Eastern Highway was a death trap with all the truckers and idiot drivers. 'Oh, I hate hearing those sirens. Do you know what happened?'

'Stop twittering,' Hec said, waving his free hand around. 'You ladies talk far too much.'

Kate fixed Hec with a glare. 'It's a good thing you're ninety-two, Hec, because that was very rude of you.'

Hec flapped his hand impatiently. 'There's been a bombing! Someone has blown up the Kallygarn Shire Council offices!' He looked triumphant at their silence.

Kate and Clare looked at each other, then back at Hec, as their mouths dropped open.

'Ah-ha,' Hec said, gleefully. 'That's got you quiet, hasn't it? How about that then? A bombing.' He nodded, his grey, straggly eyebrows raised.

Kate recovered herself first. 'Kallygarn? That's a long way from here. Five hours? Nearly on the coast.'

'I know. But a *bombing*?'

'Are you sure it's true?' Clare asked.

'I heard it on the wireless news, on my drive here.'

Kate seemed to forget about Hec's startling revelation and tsked loudly. 'Hec, you're not supposed to be driving anymore. I thought Maisie had taken your keys away from you.'

Hec looked petulant. 'No daughter-in-law of mine is going to tell me what to do. I'm ninety-two and fought for this country. I—'

Kate came around from behind the counter. 'Come on, I'll make you a cuppa, and we can get your mail. I think the *Farm Weekly* is out today. That'll give you something to read until Maisie comes to collect you.'

'Mrs Cutterby, I am not a child,' the elderly man told her, his eyes ablaze.

Hastily, Clare interrupted. 'Tell me about the bombing, Hec. Sounds intriguing.' She caught his gaze, giving Kate time to get into the back office and call Maisie. 'I can't believe I haven't heard about it. Was anyone hurt?'

'Someone must be upset to do something so extreme. You'd need to have access to dynamite and detonators. I used to be an expert in explosives. They've changed a bit, of course, but setting a bomb isn't easy.' Hec was eager to share his knowledge.

'How do you know it was a bomb?'

He gave Clare a scornful look. 'It blew the building up. There's not much left, so they said on the news.'

'Can't always believe everything you hear,' Kate called from the back office.

Another customer came in and tipped his hat to Clare. 'Morning,' he said.

Clare gave him the once-over. Another older gentleman, not as old as Hec, and a farmer by all accounts. Flannelette shirt and a jacket with a machinery dealership's name embroidered on the pocket. She'd seen his face around town, but she didn't know his name.

The man turned his attention to Hec. 'Hec, how are you this cold day?'

'G'day there, George. Had any rain? Although it's almost too cold for a downpour, don't you think?'

'Certainly chilly enough, and there was a clear morning sky today. Get too many of them over the next month or two and we'll be getting a frost. No good for the crops.'

Not interested in George's summary of the latest farming news, Hec only just managed to wait politely for the last word, before rushing to pass on his own news. 'Just telling

Clare and Kate about the shire building in Kallygarn. Did you hear?'

'Sure did. It's a bugger of a thing to happen.' He turned to Clare. 'Excuse my language.'

'I can promise you I've heard worse,' Clare told him. 'I'm Clare. I know your face, but I don't think we've ever met.'

'George Tucker.' He took his hat off again, keeping it in his hands this time.

'Hi, George.' Kate appeared holding a pile of forms in her hands. She left them on the counter in a neat pile. Her eyes went to Hec. 'I've just called Maisie.'

'Well, thank *you* kindly,' Hec said, without meaning it and looked around for an escape. 'Have you come to pick up your weekly supplies?' Hec asked George.

'Mmm, and my neighbour's mail. I got Kate's message saying Cheryl was sick and not coming out today.'

'Don't worry about Darryl's. He was in early this morning and got his then,' Kate told him. 'Said he had to pick up Jasmine's medication. He didn't tell you?'

'No, but's that's fine,' George said. He turned to Hec who kept looking out the window, trying to move out of the line of sight from the street. 'That your car out the front, Hec?'

'It is.' The old man drew himself up as if ready for battle.

'Could you give me a lift to the cafe? It's smoko time. I'm ready for my cup of tea.'

'To the cafe? That's just across the road.'

'Let's walk then. I'm parched. And I need warming up.

That wind outside is like the grey ghost, it goes straight through you.'

'Right you are,' said Hec. He lifted his hat and turned to leave.

Kate disappeared again, then moments later was back with two envelopes and a farming magazine. 'Here you go, George.'

'Thank you kindly. Well, I hope you both have a nice day.'

The two men left, and Kate shook her head fondly. 'That Hec, it'll be a sad day when he's not around anymore. He would have been a right trick when he was young.'

Clare smiled. 'I don't know George, where's he from?'

Kate leaned against the counter and watched the two old men walk across the road. George had his arm out behind Hec in case he needed some support.

'He's got the last property up the Hubler Track just before it goes into Crown land. Never married and no family that I know of. Must be a lonely existence up there. At least an hour's drive from town.'

'How old would he be? Surely he's not safe up there by himself?'

'He'd be seventy plus, I guess, and fit as a fiddle. Look at him with Hec,' Kate said. 'George just seems to understand those few really old fellas who are left. How quickly did he work out that Hec didn't want Maisie to come and get him? Hec'll be AWOL for a while, happy as a pig in mud, enjoying a cup of tea and a chat. George looking out for him. They'll be yabbering about old times and stock prices and, best of all, Maisie won't find him for a little while!'

'I hope someone is as kind to me in a few years.'

'He's a lovely old bloke. And he's very good to poor Darryl and Jasmine. I hear he often looks after their place when they've got to go to Perth for Jasmine's medical appointments.'

'How's she going?'

Kate shook her head. 'Not really sure. They keep to themselves.'

The two men disappeared into the cafe, just as the low rumbling began rolling around the sky.

Clare looked up. Clear blue.

Kate grabbed the counter. 'Earthquake!' she cried.

The words didn't compute in Clare's head. Nothing was moving or shaking.

The low growl had become a roar from . . . where?

A flash of black and silver, then another.

One motorbike went past, then two, side by side. Another, and another. Revving their engines, filling the air with a deep roar. Black leathers, black helmets, black sunglasses, long beards streaming to the side in the wind.

'Shit! Bikies!' Kate's voice was shrill. 'Here?'

Kate and Clare pressed closer to the window as the riders parked in the main street, near the pub.

On the fuel tank of the closest bike, Clare could see a black triangle with a claw hand imposed over the top.

They didn't look like the friendly bikies that she'd met over the years. The ones who did toy runs for disadvantaged kids. These ones looked like bad news.

The men gathered in a group; each one took off his helmet and put it on the handlebars of his bike. Jackets came off, showing tattoos running over arms, necks. One had the claw hand tattooed on his forearm.

'I've seen that logo before,' Kate whispered.

'Why are you whispering?' Clare wanted to know. 'They're just out for a ride.'

But Kate was shaking her head. 'No, no, no. I've seen that logo on the seven o'clock news. I reckon that's the gang that blew that copper and his mate up in Perth a while back. Or maybe they murdered someone, I can't remember, but I know I've seen that claw on the news.'

Clare took a closer look. Beards, earrings, hard faces. 'Well,' she said briskly, 'who knows? Stay out of their way and I'm sure they'll stay out of ours. Anyhow, I'm late for my catch-up. Lovely to see you, Kate.' Picking up her handbag from the counter, she smiled and headed out. What a lot of things she had to tell her knitting group this morning.

CHAPTER 9

As Bob cracked open the car door, the whomping sound hit their ears. 'They're here already,' he said, looking skyward.

'Chopper?' Dave asked, coming around the side of the car and staring into the sky, trying to see where the aircraft was.

'One of the commercial TV stations for sure. Vultures.'

'They're pretty late, unless they've been here since yesterday and just keep putting the bird in the air in hopes of seeing something different,' Dave said. 'It's over twenty-four hours since it happened.'

Grey clouds hemmed out any blue sky, causing the choppers to fly low over the town.

Both men turned their attention to the levelled building. Blackened bricks and mortar, shattered glass and the stench of burnt carpet, curtains and furniture met them. In among the rubble, men wearing protective coveralls, holding cameras, evidence bags and notebooks combed what was left, looking for evidence.

They reminded Dave of busy ants crawling over a lolly.

To their left was a police van set up as a control station. Inside would be computers, whiteboards, all sorts of radios and equipment, and possibly the officer in charge. They needed to find whoever that was and introduce themselves.

Still, not a high priority for Dave; he was too busy absorbing the scene. What he wouldn't do to get down and dirty on this case.

He felt Bob knock against him, pushed by the force of the wind, which brought his attention back. 'So what's the plan?' Dave asked Bob. His hands were in his pockets to keep them away from the biting gusts, whistling through the trees and freezing everything in its path. The south coast of Western Australia was often at the mercy of the gale-force blasts and sometimes experienced four seasons in one day.

Many years previous, after his father had kicked Dave off the family farm, he'd worked on the coast, down towards Stockdale. So many days had started with clear skies, a gentle puff, but by lunchtime a howling sea breeze had thrown up heavy, scudding clouds, sometimes even a shower or two. During harvest there had been days where the mercury had hit forty-five degrees before the cool change had come through. Then the temperature had plummeted six or seven degrees in five minutes and kept going south. Dave had learned never to leave home without a jumper, no matter the season.

'I don't have a plan, son. I guess we should find whoever's in charge and see what information they can tell us.' Bob nodded towards the scene. 'Good thing Kallygarn is on the way to Stockdale. This should sate your appetite to see what's going on if nothing else.'

Dave chewed the inside of his lip, recalling their conversation with Lorri that morning. No one injured. Building demolished. Major Crime called in. Lorri seemed short on facts, but he wasn't surprised. If a gang of bikies had done this, then the squads involved would be keeping quiet. The bosses wouldn't want any slip of the tongue getting back to informants.

The silence gave weight to his theory.

Yet, it niggled him that this was a small country town with few people. Why would the bikies be interested in Kallygarn? Unless the target had been inside the council building. He made a note to ask what departments had been housed there.

'Detective? Excuse me, could we get a statement?'

Bob and Dave turned to see a young man dressed in a suit walking quickly towards them. He was hauling a microphone with a long lead trailing behind him. A cameraman was running towards them, too, a heavy camera on his shoulder, trying to get in front of them before the reporter got too close.

Behind, a woman in high heels ran awkwardly, microphone outstretched, desperate not to miss out on information.

Two others, having seen the approach, threw open car doors and raced towards Bob and Dave, notebooks in hand, pens behind their ears.

Bob held up his hand. 'Sorry, everyone, we know nothing. We're not part of the investigation.'

'Then why are you here? You're stock squad, right? I recognise your uniform. Do they think a farmer has done this? Has the shire issued an infringement to a farmer? Or has there been stock stolen in the area?'

Dave licked his lips to stop himself from smiling. He could see the headline now: *Farmer's Beef with Shire.*

Bob smiled benignly and shook his head. 'You're wasting your time with us, mate. Like I said, we're not involved. You're probably wasting your time full stop. No one is going to give you anything, so you may as well go back to where you've come from and wait for the official word.'

'Where's the fun in that?' The journo smiled back, turning on the charm. 'Come on, mate, you can give me something, surely? I've got a job to do here.'

'As do the people working here,' Dave said. 'You'll just have to wait.'

'I've been told—' the woman started as a print reporter spoke over the top of her.

'Can you confirm that this was a premeditated act?'

Dave could see Bob was getting annoyed, so he shouldered his way in front of him and faced the reporters. 'Not sure how many times we've got to tell you, no comment. If you don't move on, I'll begin issuing infringement notices.'

The first journalist on the scene took a step forward, daring Dave to do just that. 'The public have a right to know—'

'The public have a right to know the correct information at the most suitable time. Anything else would be irresponsible. Now, leave.'

One of the print reporters turned away. 'Might as well stand down, boys and girls. Not going to get anything here.'

Dave began to open the door for Bob when he heard a voice calling out.

'Bob? Bob Holden? That you?' A giant-sized figure was standing at the door of the control centre, looking towards them. 'Geez, what are you doing here? I heard you were just about cactus, mate.' A senior sergeant, wispy white strands across his forehead and red cheeks from the cold wind, approached the two detectives. He threw a look at the reporters.

'You lot can get lost. There's nothing coming from us today.' He made a shooing motion with his hand and ignored the pushiest reporter, who again tried to speak. 'Scram. I'm not joking.' Motioning for Dave and Bob to follow him, he moved towards the crime-scene tape. 'Come on, fellas.'

Dave waited until Bob moved in the direction the senior sergeant was going. He had yet to introduce himself and Bob had yet to acknowledge his words, but Dave had seen the recognition flash across his face.

Behind the safety of the crime-scene tape, and away from the prying eyes of the reporters, the man finally stopped and turned to Bob. 'It's good to see you upright, mate. Heard you were gunning for the grave.'

'Johnny. I'd lost track of you. Didn't know where you were stationed.' Bob opened his arms and gave the man a brief, heavy hug, which was returned, then they slapped each other on the back for good measure. 'It's great to see you, old friend. You're looking good. And don't worry, it'll take more than a few mongrel cancer cells to keep me down.'

Standing back, Dave was struck by the deep emotion in both men's voices. These two had clearly been partners once and been through some shit together. Shit that Dave knew nothing about, despite his closeness to Bob.

'Dave, son, this is Johnny Campbell. Johnny, this is Dave Burrows, he's heading up the stock squad while I'm on sick leave. He's top shelf.'

'Good to meet you, Dave.' Johnny held out his hand. 'Any friend of Bob's is a friend of mine.'

'Likewise,' Dave said, grasping the giant policeman's hand.

Johnny's gaze went back to Bob. 'How're you getting on, mate? You're looking—' he gave Bob the once-over '—okay.'

All three of them knew that wasn't the case. Bob hadn't shaved that morning and the shadow of stubble across his face was so unusual that Dave had to hold his tongue when he'd thrown their bags in the back of the troopy.

The message he'd texted to Betty the night before had said Bob was holding up pretty well, though he was tired. Now he wondered if he'd told a fib. Bob's face was a funny shade of dark and red mixed together.

Dave hoped the red tinge wasn't a sign that Bob had a temperature.

'The alternative isn't very good, Johnny, so I'll take where I am at the moment.' Bob tilted his head towards the crumbling building. 'Looks like there's been a bit of bang. That must've been a busy night.'

'Tell me about it. Mate, you should have been here,' Johnny said. 'Me and the missus, we were sound asleep then the windows were shaking, glass rattling. Thought it must've been an earthquake, 'cause we get a few of them around here these days. Then I saw the glow off the clouds and worked out it was something else. Jeanette's mother's crystal even fell off the shelf, everything rattled that hard.' He gave Bob some kind of private-joke look. 'Not that they're any great loss.'

Bob laughed, shoving his hands in his pockets and rocking on his heels. 'You in charge here at Kallygarn?'

Johnny gave a brief nod then went on with his story. 'Rained cats and dogs, except it was bricks and mortar and glass. Should have heard that shit hitting the roof. Would've thought we were in a war zone with all the bangs and crashes.' He bent down to inspect some rubble. 'Still, we were lucky no one was killed. And on the upside, the local glaziers are going to make some money out of it. Along with the motel and pub. Probably the caravan park, too. Can't get a bed in town because the coppers have got them all booked. Major Crime, Arson, Bomb Squad. You name it, they're here.' Johnny straightened and looked up as an officer held out something and motioned for another policeman to come over with the logbook, so he could document whatever evidence he'd found.

'Yeah, we had trouble booking a room at Stockdale,' Bob told Johnny. 'They must be using that as a base, too. What's that, two hours from here?'

'Just under.' Johnny stretched. 'Bloody hell, what I wouldn't give for a coffee. The force is too tight to send a kitchen bus this far out of Perth, and the cafe got some damage from falling tin and bricks, so they're not opening. Tell you what, gives a whole different meaning to the line from *Henny Penny*, "the sky is falling".' He shook his head in disgust. 'What a bloody mess,' he said, nodding towards the street. 'I had to hold the council depot off from getting the street sweeper out until we'd given the area a once-over.'

'Any leads?' Dave asked.

Bob stumbled over a rock that lined some garden beds and Dave's words fell away as he reached out to grab Bob's arm so he didn't fall.

Bob yanked his arm away and spoke loudly to cover his embarrassment. 'Who was the target?'

Johnny seemed to ignore the exchange and answered Bob's question. 'No one really knows. So many offices in that building. The Kallygarn Shire Council, Departments of Transport, Agriculture, Conservation and Land Management—or CALM in the much-loved government world of acronyms—the post office, Centrelink.

'We're even in there.'

'Coppers sharing with govie workers?' Bob raised his eyebrows.

'The old cop shop was put out to pasture when they found asbestos in the roof a couple of years ago, so we managed to get us a dusty old office out the back. That's gone, too, along with all the computers and records. Reckon there'll be a few locals who probably hope their drink-driving charge might be forgotten because they only got it in the last couple of days. I have bad news for them.' Johnny laughed and Bob joined in.

Dave didn't say anything, still smarting from Bob's reaction to his attempt at help.

They walked together in silence, taking in the destruction.

'Do you know what the explosive was?' Dave asked.

'Still working on that.'

'Was anyone pissed off with the shire? Or any other department? You perhaps?'

Johnny laughed. 'Only every drunk and speeding driver I've booked since I moved here.'

'Well, reckon all of this should keep you occupied for a while.' Bob shoved his hands in his pockets, while the rest of the officers worked the scene.

'It will at that. Anyhow, you never said why you've suddenly showed up in town.' He turned to face the two men, and Dave glanced at Bob. Johnny was his mate, and he wasn't sure how much Bob would be happy to share, so he could answer. It was clear from Johnny's earlier comments that a lot of the force knew Bob was on medical leave.

'Checking out the abs down in Stockdale,' Bob told him. 'Just reopened and there're some new faces. Heard anything about it?'

Johnny tapped his foot for a second. 'Nah. Should I have?'

'Not at all. Thought I'd ask the question, that's all. No news is good news.' Bob continued to gaze out across the wreckage and Dave thought he was building up to say something, but he just turned and held out his hand. 'We'd better let you get on, Johnny. We've still got a fair drive to go and you've got your work cut out for you and the rest of the crew, here. We don't want to hold you up.'

Johnny took Bob's outstretched hand and held it tightly. 'Call in on your way back. Jeanette would love to see you.'

'I'm sure that's not the case,' Bob said, and the two men shared another look that Dave couldn't distinguish.

'Tell you what,' Johnny said, 'why don't you come and have a steak sandwich over at the pub before you head off? We can have a decent yarn without being interrupted. You fellas got time? The pub is only three streets away.'

Johnny looked so hopeful Dave felt the word 'no' die on his lips.

Bob still wasn't looking that flash and the time to take his next lot of medication wasn't far away. Surely Johnny could see that his old mate needed a rest.

'That's sounds like a bloody good idea,' Bob said.

CHAPTER 10

The smell of stale beer and wood smoke hit Dave as he entered the pub, and he just knew that the bar was going to be sticky the minute he leaned his elbows on it to order. Not that any of them would be having a beer, but he'd be buying lunch.

'This way.' Johnny indicated a doorway that led through to the dining room, shutting them off from the rest of the bar.

Considering it was only lunchtime the front bar was rowdy; men in farming work boots, jeans and Hard Yakka shirts were holding beers and laughing.

'Looks like that's the end of a field walk or something,' Johnny said as pulled out a chair at a table in the furthest corner away from the throng.

'Johnny! Hey, mate!'

They all turned at the voice and Johnny raised his hand in a wave. 'Jacko! How's it going? What's happening out there in the front bar?'

A man walked up to the table and nodded at Bob and Dave. 'We've been checking out everyone's barley crops. We've done some trials of short-growing varieties that seem to do better in our climate than on the coast.' He grinned. 'How have you managed to get in here for a feed, when you've got all that going on out there?'

'Copper has to eat, too, you know,' Johnny said. 'You boys all on the beers?'

'You know what it's like, when all that's finished there are beers to be had.'

'Make sure you don't let anyone drive if they've had too much, Jacko.'

'All over it, mate,' Jacko said with a good-natured grin. 'We've got a bus.'

'Good to hear.'

'You got your own farm, Jacko?' Dave weighed into the conversation.

The young man with sandy hair turned to look at Dave and gave another smile. 'Sure do. Best place in WA, I reckon. God's own country.'

Bob laughed. 'Every farmer says that about their piece of dirt, mate.'

'It's true though,' Jacko said earnestly. 'Although it's good to get off your own place and see how other farmers do things. There's always a lot to learn from each other, but I still like my patch best!'

Johnny leaned forward and spoke quietly. 'Don't suppose you saw anything unusual in all those places you went today, mate?'

'Like what?' A confused expression crossed the young man's face.

Hoisting one shoulder, Johnny said, 'Oh, I don't know. People in places they shouldn't be; anything that raised an eyebrow.'

Jacko's smile fell away and was replaced with a deep frown. 'You reckon we might've seen something to do with what's happened out there?' He jerked his head towards where the shire council building had once stood.

'Even the smallest detail might help us later on. Want to mention it to the boys so they can get their thinking caps on?'

'Sure. I can do that.'

'Good job, Jacko. Have a great afternoon, but don't let anyone drink and drive. Got it?'

'Yep. No worries.' Jacko gave a small salute before he left and Johnny turned back to Dave and Bob.

'He's a good fella.'

'It's great these young blokes get to go around and learn different things from a range of people,' Bob said. 'For so long it's been that they just follow what their dads did and the grandfathers before that. Agriculture isn't quite like that anymore.'

Johnny rolled his eyes as he handed out menus. 'There're plenty of other states that haven't changed the way they work,' he said. 'I was talking to a mate over east the other day.' He shook his head in disbelief. 'They're still using harrows because Dad thinks it's a good idea, if you can believe that.' Moving his gaze to Dave, he explained, 'In case you don't know, mate, that's where they work the country up and back to get rid of all the weeds or to break up big clumps of dirt. Makes the topsoil so fine that any time they get a wind, it disappears towards the next town.'

Dave opened his mouth, but Johnny kept talking so he opened the menu instead.

'I said to him, "Mate, haven't you heard about nil-till?"'

'When did you learn anything about farming?' Bob's tone held humour and disbelief in the same measure. 'That was never your thing. In fact I can't believe you're in a one-horse town without a cappuccino strip!'

'Maaaate,' Johnny drew out the word, 'I've been in Kallygarn for nearly ten years now. I learn through osmosis. Listening, watching. You know how it is.'

'You at your best,' Bob said.

There was a sharp beep and all eyes turned to Bob, whose watch was emitting a high-pitched alarm. He quickly pushed his fingers to the button on the side of the watch and distracted everyone with a loud: 'So, who's having what to eat?'

Johnny didn't say anything, while Dave discreetly got a pill tube out of his pocket and handed it to Bob. His partner leaned back in his chair after tapping his finger at a chicken schnitzel for Dave to order for him.

'I'll have a steak. Medium, with mushroom sauce,' Johnny told Dave. 'And a lemonade.'

Dave went across to the bar and waited until someone came to take his order.

'You're a bit early, fella,' the barman said, coming through the doorway. 'Don't usually open the kitchen until eleven thirty.'

Dave looked at his watch. It was just after eleven. 'Any chance you can fire up the grill early?'

The man looked over to where they were seated and nodded towards Johnny who gave him a cheery thumbs up.

'You all coppers?' he asked as he turned on the till and hit a few buttons.

'Yeah.' Dave leaned on the counter and felt the stickiness he had expected.

'Here to help out with the bomb?'

'Nah, mate. Bob and I are stock squad. Rural Crime Squad. Passing through.'

'I see,' he answered, although it was clear he didn't. 'Right, whaddaya want?'

Dave was glad the barman didn't show any curiosity as to why they were there and gave him the order. 'Can I please get a receipt?'

'Sure thing, fella.' The man's sausage-like fingers took the chit from the till and handed it over. 'Reckon we can do with all the help we can get at the moment. Don't know what would have possessed someone to blow up the council offices.'

'It's not been established as to whether it was an accident or deliberate,' Dave cautioned.

Putting the lemonade on the countertop the barman leaned forward, interest in his eyes. 'Do you know much about what happened?'

'We're not involved in the investigation,' Dave told him firmly. 'But I want to reiterate that nothing has been established as to whether it was accidental or not.' From the front bar, a loud voice boomed through the walls and the barman's face changed from being interested in what Dave had to say to annoyance as he listened to the words from the loudmouth.

'Fantastic. Just who I don't need,' the barman said and went through the small doorway between the bars, not giving Dave an opportunity to thank him.

Dave collected the drinks and went back to the table. It sounded like whoever was in the next room was greeting everyone with gusto.

'Ah, Crabby, what's new, mate? Good to see you. And Kenny boy, how's things? I heard your wife had a bub the other day. Congratulations on being a new father.'

'Who's that?' Bob leaned back on his chair to try to peer through the gap. 'Sounds like the town crier!'

Dave finally got eyes on the loud-mouthed man, who was wearing moleskins and a checked shirt, and working the room like he was a celebrity. His pasty face didn't look like a farmer's, but he was wearing the farmer's uniform so . . . Dave assessed him for a moment then turned back to the conversation at the table.

'That, my friend, is Dan Hinderkin. Shire councillor. Failed farmer. Local business owner. All round tosser.'

'Certainly knows how to hold court,' Bob observed.

'Yup, and trust me, he does it regularly. Somehow, he manages to get most of the locals listening to what he has to say and even, at times, agreeing with him. Sometimes I think they listen to humour him, but other times . . .' Johnny gave a heavy sigh. 'Other times I think some people believe his bullshit. Well, they must, because they voted him back in again last year. Christ, I wish they hadn't. You know how often he's on my doorstep telling me how to do my job?'

'It sounds like once would be more than enough,' Dave said.

'Not a truer word spoken,' Johnny agreed. 'Smart fella, this one,' he said with a smile at Bob. Then he changed the subject. 'How many weeks of treatment do you have to have?'

Bob gave a one-shouldered shrug. 'Who knows? I'm just taking each day as it comes. That's the best way to manage any expectations. If I haven't got any, I can't get disappointed, can I?'

Johnny laughed. 'You're still the same, Holden. Pragmatic as always.' He turned his attention to Dave. 'So you're heading up the Rural Crime Squad now?'

'Only until Bob comes back,' Dave said quickly. He turned to Bob. 'Won't be long and you'll be back in the driver's seat.'

'Mmm, we'll see.' Bob took a sip of the water that Dave had collected then turned his attention back to Johnny. 'Dave here is a good copper. Lot of experience as a detective and he's from a farm to boot, so he's got all the skills needed—' He broke off as the voice from the front bar broke through their conversation.

'I tell you, mate, our town gets blown up and no one seems to care why. See now, that's the question. Why? Why did someone feel that they had to cause so much destruction? To get attention of course. But there's a deeper question. Why did they want that attention? Now that's where the answer will be, you mark my words. Once the coppers work out the why, the who will follow. See? I can only hope the police are up to the job.' He didn't sound as if they were.

'Maybe this fella could join the force,' Bob said.

Johnny rolled up the sleeves of his jacket and checked his watch. 'I've offered him that position before.'

Dave laughed, then Bob and Johnny followed.

'Tell me, Johnny—' Bob leaned forward, speaking quietly as his laughter died away '—what've you got? Was someone targeting the shire council building?'

Heaving his heavy shoulders skywards, Johnny took the slice of lemon out of his glass and sucked on it before answering. 'We don't know anything yet. However, I'm running with the theory that, yeah, someone had the building as a target, but the official line is "Evidence is still being collected and collated". But I've started a very quiet little investigation, checking to see who is pissed off and if there've been any threats made towards anyone who works in that building. Which is a bloody lot of people.

'Threats are taken very seriously, even in a little town like this. I've been a copper all over Western Australia and I can tell you that sometimes the tiniest towns are more dangerous than cities. So every time a drunken idiot turns up and gives the shire president a mouthful, or an upset woman tells the local sitting member that she's going to make his or her life hell, I always follow it up.'

'I agree,' Bob said. 'Small country towns are great places for people who don't want to be found to hide out in.'

Dan's voice came through from the front bar again. 'Take your pick, mate: conservation, local rangers, ag depart-ment. They're all in that office. Any one of them could have been the target because the departments want to make hard working blokes' lives a misery. I mean remember when—'

'Are you sure this bloke is a councillor?' Dave looked over his shoulder, incredulous.

Johnny held up his hand and waited.

'You're right, Dan,' another voice came. 'The amount of red tape those government departments create just to give themselves jobs—you can understand why someone would want to blow them up. Might have been waiting years for a permit to do something and they got sick of all the follow-up phone calls and requests. Who knows? Govie workers are all just out for themselves.'

'Agreed, Mick.' This time the voice was lower and softer. Another commentator. 'I find the local government's ethics questionable, even contradictory. I had to fill out two different forms to have a fence put up, on my land. Why should I have to do that when I fairly and squarely bought it, built a house and paid the debt off? Surely the council has no right to tell me what I can do within the boundary because it belongs to me?'

'Ah, but they can, Howard. And they do.' Dan sounded as if he was sharing a secret with a lover.

The bar was quiet for a few moments until Dan was back again.

'Come on, you guys, you know as well as I do that the new estates in towns all across this great state of ours have rules the owners have to comply with. My friend in Stockdale is building a house and they were told by the shire council that they had to choose a lighter colour roof. Something to do with energy efficiency.

'They're trying to control us—dictating what colour the roofs are going to be on our houses on our land that we have bought with our hard-earned money. If they're doing that, what else will they claim is under their jurisdiction?

'See, that's why I wanted to become a councillor. To keep every other councillor honest, to make them look at each decision they make. To stop the dictatorship.'

'Jesus,' Johnny said, 'he's really getting on his soapbox today. Wait here.' He pushed his chair back and strode into the front bar.

'Sounds like that fella's a loose cannon,' Bob said quietly as he slipped another plastic vial out from his pocket and shook a couple of tablets into his hand. He swallowed them without water, while Dave busied himself lining up the salt and pepper shakers and sachets of sugar and sweetener.

'It actually sounds like he's trying to hoodwink everyone,' Dave said.

'He's crazy, son. I don't know, these people just seem to think that the world would run without any rules. What would happen if we didn't catch the murderers and put them away? Or thieves, paedophiles, you name it. The world would be lawless.' Bob now took a sip of water just as his mobile phone beeped. He groaned. 'Two guesses and the first one doesn't count.'

'Stop it,' Dave said. 'She cares.'

'I'm a grown man. I know when to take my medication.'

'And she's a nurse and also knows when you have to take your medication.'

Grumbling, Bob took his phone out of his pocket and looked at the message. He harrumphed, pressed a few buttons then replaced it.

Johnny came back into the dining room, behind Dan. It was clear Johnny had asked to speak to him privately.

Dave and Bob kept their eyes away from them, leaning in towards each other, pretending to talk, but both were listening.

'You can't talk like that with the authority you have, Dan.' Johnny's voice was low and urgent. 'You just upset all the other people in town and make them angry towards the shire council. Then my job gets harder. What do you think would happen if some people decided to drive on the right-hand side of the road, rather than the left? These rules, mate, they're there for a reason, whether you like them or not.'

'Get away with you,' Dan said, a laugh sneaking out. 'I'm only telling it as it is. I'm not having a crack at you, Johnny. I do understand the need for rules and laws. But why should the shire have a say on what colour everyone's roof is? Or whether someone can put a fence up or clear some bush on the land they own?

'People buy lifestyle blocks because they want to do what they want on them, not to be told they have to leave fifty per cent of their block as virgin bush, or that the house has to be x number of metres from their boundary. Ridiculous!'

'Do what they want? Geez, Dan, if there weren't rules everyone would be growing pot on these lifestyle blocks!'

Dan fixed him with a 'you know what I mean' and 'don't be ridiculous' look. 'I've got a lady who spoke to me the other day about a bird aviary that is causing some consternation between her neighbour and herself because it disrupts the neighbour's view of the valley. Yet the bird aviary is on the lady's land, so why the hell should she have to shift it?'

Johnny held up his hands. 'Look, mate, could you just keep your opinions to yourself until we get a handle on what the hell is going on? All right?' Red flamed across Johnny's beefy cheeks and he pushed the strands of hair back to cover his bald patch. Then he adjusted his belt and pants, just to remind Dan he was a copper, and looked hard at the man standing in front of him.

Dan stared back, and when Dave flicked his eyes up and back down quickly, to assess the situation, he thought Dan might take a swing at Johnny. There was a lot of anger in the rigidity of his body.

Instead, he took a deep breath and mirrored Johnny's actions, before pasting a large smile on his face. 'Sure thing, Johnny. Whatever you ask.'

Dave knew he didn't mean those words.

CHAPTER 11

Spook didn't mind the Chapman Hill pub. The fire was roaring in the corner and the beer was cold. So far, everyone had left him and his gang alone, and that was another thing he liked about it here, everyone minded their own damn business. Either that or they were shit-scared of the Sinners, and that was a good thing to like, too.

The two massive silver rings he wore on his ring and pointer finger glinted in the light as he waved to the publican again. 'Another,' he said, his raspy voice still loud over the music.

The publican, Spook knew, was doing a very good job of hiding the fact he was petrified of the twelve men who were in his pub. He was a thin man with a pointy nose and bulging eyes.

Spook named him Bug in his mind. His spindly arms made him look as if he'd blow away in a heavy breeze.

'Sure, and your friends?' Bug answered his wave.

The twelve other bikies were lined up at the bar, each drinking different brews, bowls of chips in between them. Just one more drink each and they'd have to leave. They had places to be tonight.

'Line them up when they've finished,' he said.

When they'd first arrived, there had been five other locals in the bar. One had been near the TAB bench, another two sitting at the bar talking to Bug, who had been wiping glasses behind the counter. The last two were at a table, menus in front of them.

Three had left, speedily enough for Spook to know his gang's entrance was the reason they were departing. The other two older men in the corner ignored the group, ordered lunch and kept on talking.

The TV was on at the end of the bar, the volume switched all the way down, and after Bug put down a middy glass and sorted through the coins on the bar for the change, he nodded towards the news bulletin.

'Bad business, that bombing in Kallygarn.' He swiped at non-existent dust or liquid on the bench and straightened the towel. His forced friendliness only irritated Spook. What was the point in pretending to be welcoming when all the barman really wanted was to get them out of his pub?

Spook wanted to snarl at him just so he could see the man shrink back into himself.

Be a man, serve the beer. They'd move on soon enough.

Instead, Spook ignored him and waited until he'd nervously moved down the bar to pull another beer and put it in front of Wolf, who'd just finished his first and turned to watch the TV.

The anchor was a blonde woman with a large nose. Her mouth moved and he tried to work out what she was saying, but the picture changed mid-sentence. Men dressed in blue coveralls searching the burnt-out shell of a building. One of them put what looked like a small piece of brick into a plastic bag. Spook snorted to himself. There was a shitload of stuff to go through there. The coppers wouldn't be finding anything any time soon. There wouldn't be much to find anyhow. Looked like the place had been totalled.

He breathed deeply in through his nose and out again, before tugging at the end of his beard, which was touching his neckline and tickling him.

Good job, he thought. *That was a very good job.*

Calypso pressed up next to Spook, and he turned to his friend. Together they had carefully chosen men who had the same ideals. It had taken time, but now the Sinners were held in awe and fear by police, by other bikie gangs and by the general public. They ran a tight club. If they had to question any member's loyalty, and didn't like the answers, that member disappeared. So no one put a toe out of line; the consequences weren't worth it. Spook and Calypso had proved their ruthlessness time and time again. Once in, always in, with complete allegiance.

'A good job,' Spook said, nodding at the news anchor who was on another story now.

'Pity they didn't take out any of the pigs at the same time,' Calypso said.

The door pushed open and a couple walked in, took a look around and then walked out again.

Bug looked despairingly after them, then back at the men sitting at the bar. He poured another beer and punched at the buttons on the till with more force than necessary.

'Reckon he might want us to leave,' Calypso said.

'Too bad,' Spook answered. 'Free country and we're paying for the beer.' He picked up his glass and walked over to a table underneath a window, near the two elderly gentlemen. They were just about finished their meal, still deep in discussion.

'—I tell you, Hec,' one of them said, 'it's much easier getting the fertiliser in bags.'

Spook pricked his ears up, listening to the old fellas talk.

'I know most people think I'm old and silly, but I don't care. I fill the bags to a weight that I can still lift on the back of the combine. There's no need to waste money on a new front-end loader or auger just to help with my seeding program. I make do, and as you would know, Hec, when you're our age you've got to find ways to manage your jobs.'

'I'm a bit older than you George, but you're right. That's what our generations have always done. Make do. Ah damnation, looks like I've been found.'

Spook turned after feeling the wind hit his back and saw a woman dressed in pants and a black jumper, with her grey-streaked hair pulled tightly off her face in a bun. Her gaze swept across the bikies and her step seemed to falter until she drew herself up and clutched her handbag tightly.

'Hec, it's time to go,' she called from the door.

The man called George rose and indicated for the woman to come further into the pub. 'Come and have a cup of tea, Maisie,' he offered.

'No, thank you. I'm just here to take Hec home.'

The older man sighed, took a chip from his plate and swiped it through the gravy, then finished off the last of his drink, sucking loudly through the straw.

'Guess I'll see you next time I escape,' he said to his friend. He gathered his walking stick and leaned on it heavily, shuffling across to the woman. 'That's if she doesn't hide my car keys again.'

George picked up the plates and took them back to the counter, thanking Bug. 'You always do a great steak and mushroom sauce, Jeff. Thanks again.'

Spook kept his eyes on George, assessing the sprightly but older man. He looked like he could lift a few bags of fertiliser if he had to.

'Terrible thing to happen at Kallygarn, George,' Jeff repeated his earlier words.

'It really is. How can anyone think it's all right to go around bombing things? Especially in Australia. We're not that kind of country.'

Wolf turned and spoke directly to Bug and George. 'Bullshit,' he said. 'That bombing is the best thing that's happened to this state in years.'

'Why would you say that?' George asked, a confused expression crossing his face.

''Cause the pigs need to diiieee,' Bear, another bikie, snarled.

Jeff moved closer. 'Now let's stop—' He jiggled up and down on the spot.

But George interrupted him. 'I don't see how you could think that,' he said to Bear. 'I understand you might not like the police.' He paused and Spook watched his alert eyes cast across Bear's jacket. 'I guess that, ah, goes with your line of work, but that blast brought a building down in the dead of night. No lives were lost. What were you hoping to achieve?'

'George, might be time you headed over to pick up your supplies,' Jeff said. His fingers tapped up and down on the bar as Bear stood, towering over the old man.

'Anything that brings the coppers undone is a good thing,' Bear said.

'See, I don't understand your thinking,' George said, not backing away.

Spook had to give it to George, he didn't seem the slightest bit worried about Bear.

'Yes,' the old man continued, 'there was a blast, not sure if it was intentional or not. You might not like the police, but it was a shire building without anyone in it, so I really don't understand how you think it achieved anything.'

Bear took a step towards George. 'It's the act,' he whispered. 'And the fear that's left behind. The fear of what could happen.'

Spook stood up now and came across, backing George into the bar. He held up his hand. 'Stand down, Bear.'

Bear glared at George for a moment before sinking onto a bar stool.

If they had been in the clubrooms Spook would have backhanded Bear, but instead he turned to George. 'Sorry about that, friend,' he told George. 'My colleague is getting a bit out of hand. Before you get any ideas, we haven't done anything, as you implied.' He nodded towards the TV. 'We're just showing a bit of appreciation for someone else's handiwork.'

'This is such a shame,' George said slowly.

Spook had to admire the older man's courage. Not too many people would stand up to him. Spook was six foot seven, bulky and bearded.

'What's a shame?' sneered Bear from the bar stool that he'd been relegated to.

'You know,' George's tone was conversational, 'that old bloke who was in here with me before you lot turned up? He's a veteran. Fought for this country. Seems to me you just like to terrify our citizens. You make a mockery out of what good people have done to get this country where it is today. Let me give you all a piece of advice . . .'

Spook leaned forward and George mimicked his action. Calypso was now close by and the others were on high alert. Everyone was aware of Bear, coiled and ready to spring at Spook's command.

Jeff looked like he was about to have a heart attack. 'George!' he called out, edging closer to the phone.

Everyone ignored the troubled bartender.

'I'm gonna call the cops.'

It was an empty threat.

Bug wouldn't do that, Spook knew. The Sinners' reputation went before them. No matter how freaked out Jeff was, he'd be too worried about the repercussions. Spook didn't take his eyes from George. It wouldn't take much to fell him. A push to the shoulder. A swipe to his ankles. He really didn't want to hurt this man, but . . .

'Most people in this town have no respect for others who make threats against authority. If you lot don't want to fit in, then I'd suggest you get back on your bikes and head for the hills.'

The swish of the water in the dishwasher echoed loudly around the large room, then Spook brought his hands together, slow clapping. 'Thanks for your advice,' Spook said, with a shade of laughter. 'We'll take it as soon as we've finished our beers.'

The tension left the room like an audible sigh, and George nodded at Bug. 'See you another time, Jeff. Thanks for the feed.' He drew his jacket closer around his bony shoulders and walked to the door. As he was about to leave, he turned back around and locked eyes with Spook. 'Just remember. Respect.'

CHAPTER 12

'Okay, I'm ready.' Cheryl closed the rear doors to her van and checked she hadn't left anything on the bench just inside the door.

'You sure you're feeling well enough?' Kate handed her friend a water bottle she'd just filled from the tap.

'Fighting fit and full of energy. That cold was just a blip,' Cheryl told her and reached in through the window to start the van, then bent down to tie her shoelaces in her sturdy boots. 'These keep coming undone since I got them wet when I was at Darryl and Jasmine's the other day.'

'Any news on Jasmine?' Kate was leaning against the doorframe now and her Australia Post uniform had a smudge of dust on the shoulder.

'I can see she's declining. When I was there last, she was finding it hard to talk and breathe. It really sucks.' Cheryl climbed into the ute. 'I reckon Darryl is doing everything now. I noticed the clothes on the line were hung out like a man had done it.'

'At least he's doing it,' Kate said.

'Too right. You know Darryl is a good bloke. He's looking after Jasmine, and I heard he was still captaining the bowls team and cooking the barbecue for the club fundraiser the other day.' She paused. 'Can't understand how he's comfortable with leaving Jasmine at home by herself when he goes so far away.' Cheryl shrugged. 'Anyhow, you can't fault the community spirit in the guy, even when things seem to be pretty hard at home.'

'I noticed there was a flash-looking envelope in their mail the other day. Any word on what that was?'

Cheryl put her hands on her hips. 'That's a bad question to ask and you know it.'

Kate grinned. 'Ah yes, but you and I can talk, because we work for the same company.'

Not about to admit she didn't know what the contents of the letter was about, Cheryl took the moral high road and shook her head. 'Not about things like that. Anyhow I'd better get on.' Putting the van in gear and with a wave, she turned down the main street and headed north. She loved this drive. Ninety kilometres, one way, dirt roads, twelve deliveries to all different sorts of mailboxes. Some were forty-four-gallon drums, one was a microwave and the Connor family had made theirs from a fridge. Trouble with that one was the bees loved to get inside and create a hive in spring. Every. Damn. Spring! She'd been stung three times in one go last year.

Sometimes Cheryl sprayed the mailboxes with chemicals to discourage the bees from even trying to swarm there. Between them and snakes, plus the occasional roo or emu, her job was reasonably hazardous.

Her phone rang and the caller ID showed Darryl's name. With no cars in sight, she answered. 'Darryl, hi. I've already left.'

'Damn, have you? Jasmine needs another script filled.'

The gap in the conversation let Cheryl know that he was very much hoping she would turn around and head back to the chemist for him. A glance at the clock on the dash showed she was fifteen minutes behind schedule already. She sighed. 'Has the chemist got the script?'

Darryl sounded relieved. 'Yeah, the doctor has faxed it through to them.'

'Okay, I can turn around. I'll be late to you, though.'

'No trouble. I'm just going to check on the blokes who are camping out the back of the farm and then I'll be back at the house.'

Cheryl lifted her foot and pulled over to the side of the road, before flicking on her blinker and executing a perfect U-turn as she pointed the van back towards town.

'Visitors? That's nice for you.'

'Oh no, nothing like that. A few blokes who ride motorbikes are staying here. They've been here for a couple of days. I'm running wood out to them every day, so they can keep the campfire going.'

'Kate told me there was a group of bikies in town. I think they scared a few people.'

113

'They're friends of a friend of a friend,' Darryl said. 'I'm just helping them out.'

Cheryl felt a burning need to ask why he had a dangerous bikie gang staying on his farm but didn't. 'How's Jasmine?' she asked instead.

'Okay. Physically, I mean. Mentally? She's a bit stressed. We got a bit of bad news and tension tends to make her symptoms worse.'

'Sorry to hear that,' she said. Then, unable to help herself, she asked, 'Don't the bikies stress her out? They freaked out most of the people in town. Especially poor old Jeff over at the pub!'

'She doesn't know they're here. I got them to come in the back gate and they're camping near the granite outcrop. They're just a few old blokes who like to ride bikes. They seem nice.' There was a pause. 'Still,' he said in a low voice, 'what would I know?'

Cheryl didn't answer his question. Best he didn't have any idea of who he was dealing with. Jeff had told her he'd rung a copper mate of his and been told they *were* a gang and a bloody dangerous one; the cops had even interviewed some of them over the disappearance of some woman a few months back. They were known as the Sinners apparently.

'You okay, Darryl? You're sounding pretty flat.' Cheryl flicked on her blinker to turn into the main street and navigated the van into a parking bay at the back of the chemist. Putting the phone up to her ear, she got out and slammed the door, not bothering to lock it, and headed around the edge of the building and back onto the main street on foot.

'Yeah.' His voice was still low but there was optimism in his tone. 'Maybe these new drugs will do the trick. I really hope so.'

'I do, too.'

A silence and Cheryl heard an intake of breath before Darryl cleared his throat.

'Anyhow, thanks for getting the medication. I'll catch you later on.'

Cheryl went to say goodbye, but Darryl had gone.

Inside the chemist she asked for Jasmine's script and the pharmacist tutted. 'I've got it all made up here.' She handed over a small box in a paper bag. 'And the doc sent this one for Darryl.' A second paper bag.

'Cheers,' Cheryl said. 'I'll get them out to them now.'

'Just make sure you tell Darryl that he has to take those meds with food and the doc wants to see him in a couple of weeks. Can't start this type of medication and not go back to see the doc. He's going to have to make time. I've written all the instructions on the box and made a note inside the bag, but it needs to be reiterated. Since he's not coming in, you'll have to tell him. All right?'

'Sure thing.' Cheryl glanced curiously at the second bag in her hand. 'I'll let him know.' *If I see him*, she added under her breath. It hadn't sounded like Darryl intended to meet her at the mailbox.

'Good-oh. Drive safely on your rounds.' The pharmacist was drawn away by another script to fill.

Back in the van Cheryl headed back out to the dirt road, breathing in the frigid air through the crack in her window. Cereal and canola crops grew on farms along the road. Occasionally, she'd come across a paddock that had ewes with lambs at foot, grazing on clover and grasses. If she was lucky, some of those lambs would be galloping close to a fence line, or a dam embankment, pigrooting and kicking their hind legs off the ground, enjoying the feel of the sun on their bodies. They always made her smile. Just like little children off exploring.

The first mailbox was an easy drop-off. She pulled up next to it, wound down her window, throwing the bundle of mail into the large opening and watching with satisfaction as it landed in the middle of the drum, safe from any rain, prying eyes or wind that might spring up in the afternoon. She checked to see if there was any return mail, but the red hankie that would usually hang from the drum on a stick to indicate there was, wasn't there so she drove on.

Over the next half an hour, she delivered ten lots of mail and picked up five return deliveries. Mrs Cooper had met her at the mailbox in trackie pants and a short-sleeved T-shirt, puffing slightly. When Cheryl pulled up she'd still been fifty metres away from the road but she held her granddaughter's birthday card up and waved it.

Cheryl couldn't pull away knowing Mrs Cooper had something for her, so she waited, tapping her fingers in time as Keith Urban sang about somebody like you. Who 'you' was, she wasn't sure. Nicole Kidman maybe?

'Thanks for waiting,' Mrs Cooper said, puffing slightly as she came up to the window.

'No worries. Amber's birthday in a couple of weeks?'

Nodding, Mrs Cooper tried to smile, but it was a little wobbly. 'I'm sending it in hope her mother will show her the card. I need Amber to know I haven't forgotten her, no matter the silly disagreement between her father and us.'

Cheryl remembered Amber's last birthday. She'd turned six and Mrs Cooper had done the same thing as today.

Only to have the card returned to sender.

'Bloody families,' Kate had snarled as they sorted the mail and saw the envelope. 'Why would they hurt her like this?'

This had resulted in a conversation between Kate and Cheryl to see whether or not they should play the good Samaritan and just keep the card, so the Coopers didn't have to go through any more pain. But that went against the law and, if they were found out, they'd both lose their jobs.

Cheryl had delivered the card back to the mailbox and watched Mrs Cooper crumple when she saw her own handwriting on a white envelope.

'Mr Cooper well?' she asked now, trying to avoid the emotions that were crossing the older woman's face.

'Yes. And Mandy and Byron are coming to stay next week, all the way from the Gold Coast. It's been a while since they've been home, so we're looking forward to their visit.'

'Wonderful. Okay, I'd better get on.' She held her hand out for the card and Mrs Cooper wavered before giving the envelope a kiss.

'For luck,' she said and then looked back up the driveway with a determined look on her face. 'God knows why I'm trying to get myself fit and lose weight when there's not a huge amount to live for,' she said, but took a resolute step forward. 'Still, here I am! Thanks, Cheryl. See you next week.'

Cheryl waved and drove on. Now the US country music star, Martina McBride, was singing about how blessed she was, and Cheryl realised she felt the same. She knew more about these people on her mail run than she did about her neighbour in town. Well, sort of. Mail was personal and what people sent and received told you a lot about them.

The Matthews, two stops back, had a large share portfolio. They were always getting letters from a stockbroking firm, and three months back, they'd bought a brand-new Nissan Patrol wagon, even though their crops had failed last year.

And young Ally Mason, well, she was a bookworm and music lover and didn't like socialising much. The number of parcels she got from the Doubleday book and music club would have been enough to keep anyone at home for a very long time!

The next stop was Darryl and Jasmine. Cheryl had known there had been something wrong for about six months before word snuck out to the rest of the town that Jasmine was ill.

The letters from the hospitals had come thick and fast and, some weeks, the two deliveries Cheryl made weekly hadn't been collected from the mailbox, indicating no one was home. When her last four drop-offs were still there, she'd picked them up and driven up the driveway to the house, leaving all the mail on the kitchen table so it didn't get stolen or damaged if it rained. There were plenty of window envelopes from hospitals in the bundle. Cancer had been her first thought.

Then Jasmine's diagnosis had become public and Cheryl wished she hadn't been half right.

Through the car speakers, Kasey Chambers plaintive, nasal voice asked if her heart was too broken and did she cry too much. Cheryl had to take a breath to keep her own tears at bay.

Did Jasmine cry when no one was around? When she sat in the makeshift lounge with worn furniture and ugly surrounds?

Did Darryl cry when he was out in the paddock? Did he pull up somewhere, under a tree, next to a hill and look out across the land, the bush, the carpet of pink wildflowers that were beginning to poke through and let the tears fall?

She hoped they did, crying being cathartic and all.

The mailbox drum that Darryl had painted to look like the Very Hungry Caterpillar came into view and she lifted her foot to slow down. A peak inside the barrel showed it was empty, so nothing to take back to town, but she saw a twenty-five kilo bag of . . . something sitting on the ground.

She grabbed the two-way mic. 'Darryl or Jasmine, you on channel?'

No answer.

Checking up the road, there was no sign of a ute coming towards her. Slowly, she got out of the van, hoping to catch the glint of a ute window in the sun hurtling down the driveway. Nothing.

Putting the mail and two packages from the chemist into the drum, she repeated her call over the two-way.

'Gotcha, Cheryl.' This time Darryl's voice crackled with static as he answered.

'There's a bag here at the bottom of the mailbox, is that something I need to take back into town?' she asked.

'Nah, mate, all good. It's chook wheat for the Fullestons down the road. Bronny's coming to pick it up at lunchtime.'

That was the one thing about Darryl, Cheryl thought as she told him to have a good day. No matter how tough things were in his life, he always looked out for his neighbours.

The dirt road was still moist from the recent rain and Cheryl had spent most of the trip out avoiding the water-filled potholes. The wet gravel had clung onto the wheel-tracks of the motorbikes as they'd entered Darryl and Jasmine's driveway and she could see them clearly follow the road towards the house.

Surely, Jasmine would have heard them drive in, she thought, as she remembered Darryl saying this morning his wife didn't even know the bikies were on the farm. That they'd come in the back way.

The front gate didn't look like the back way to her.

Still, that wasn't any of her business.

Cheryl stretched her arms up, trying to relieve the tension in her shoulders. There was a light shower of rain headed her way. That wheat shouldn't be out in the rain. Getting wet would make it go mouldy and that would kill the chooks.

Grasping the bag by the top, she went to drag it under a tree, but it was too heavy. It felt like a tonne of bricks. Or a bag of cement! Cheryl tugged again and left it where it was, still wondering what was inside. Not wheat, that's for sure. The two edges had been handsewn together so she couldn't check. Ah well, whatever it was would have to get wet, because the drizzle had started.

That was none of her business either. Still, it seemed odd that Darryl would have forgotten where the bikies had entered his place and what was in the bag waiting for collection.

Back in the van, she looked at the motorbike tracks again, a feeling of unease rolling through her. Her gaze followed them into the farm. An isolated and quiet area. Now hosting a notorious bikie gang.

'I hope you know what you're doing, Darryl,' Cheryl muttered as she pulled away.

CHAPTER 13

Puddles lay in the lined grooves of the bitumen where heavily loaded trucks had gouged wheel tracks. The table drains were full of water and Dave had the windscreen wipers on.

The *swish-swish* was the only noise inside the vehicle; the couple of questions Dave had asked since they'd left Kallygarn forty-five minutes ago had gone unanswered and Bob seemed lost in memories as he stared out of the window. Occasionally, Bob would softly thump his fist to his knee, but not say a word.

Paddocks with deep green cereal crops went back as far as the eye could see, although there was the occasional one sporting tall canola plants covered in flowers. The contrast between the fluoro-yellow flowers and dark purple heavy clouds almost made Dave's eyes hurt.

He glanced across to Bob. The side of his head was leaning against the window. His eyes were closed, and he wasn't moving. Dave checked Bob's chest and saw the steady rise and fall of someone who was asleep.

This trip wasn't really going as Dave had planned. He'd hoped it would be the same as always. Talking, slinging shit and laughs, with the odd deep and meaningful conversation. Usually about Dave and Mel. The kids. Shannon.

Sometimes Bob would talk about Betty and the choices they'd made since they met a couple of years before. He always liked to pretend he was the tough, gruff copper, without any emotions, but it didn't take much to see that Bob was very much in love with Betty.

He smiled, remembering the first case Bob and he had investigated together. Bob hadn't stopped calling him 'son', and Dave had been ready to punch him.

Thankfully, his previous partner, Spencer, from Dave's first post as a detective at Barrabine, had read him the riot act and told him to pull his head in. Calling him 'son' was Bob's way of saying he saw Dave in a great light, that he was his protégé. It had taken Spencer's death, and Bob's support of him through that and his relationship troubles, for Dave to realise that Bob was a top-shelf bloke and a cracker detective to boot. And now here they were, best of mates.

Bob looked frail and small as he slept against the window, and a strange mixture of anger, hurt and love swamped Dave. He was angry with the disease. Hurt that perhaps the job and the amount of time Bob had spent outside in the elements had caused the cancer—detectives from the stock squad rode motorbikes and horses, spent hours in the stockyards in all sorts of weather, and even though Bob always wore a hat, he'd been too much of a tough bloke to wear sunscreen.

But being outside wasn't the only thing that caused melanoma.

Most of all he loved the annoying, clever, witty old bastard who slept alongside of him now. The fear he was going to lose him, the same way he had lost Spencer and Mel and his family—every other person he loved—drove a stake into Dave's heart. Perhaps he shouldn't get close to anyone again. Could it be him that was casting bad luck on his loved ones?

Had he pushed his family away? Was it because of him that Mel wanted to divorce him? Well, yes. That last reflection was true. Mel loathed his job, hated that he was away so much and despised that he had brought Bulldust into their lives.

Ah, Bulldust; the root of Dave's problems. Bulldust had many job descriptions—the cattle duffer, the murderer, and mostly, the Dave Burrows-hater. His need to destroy Dave had landed him a lifetime sentence in gaol.

Bob gave a quiet snore and Dave wished with his whole being he could change what his partner was going through. Not knowing what the diagnosis's end game was made it hard to ask for change. If Bob was to get better, well, that would be his wish come true. For Dave, Betty and everyone who loved Bob. For Bob, too.

If the worst was to happen, well . . . Dave's shoulders slumped. He would do anything to change that.

Exhaustion had been oozing out of Bob when they'd finished lunch. He hadn't eaten much, just pushed the food around the plate and pretended to take bites. Instead, he'd talked to Johnny, laughed, and slowly faded after an hour or so.

When they'd walked to the troopy after lunch, Johnny had clapped Bob on the shoulder and they'd gripped each other's hands for a moment longer than normal. Neither of them said a word aloud.

Something had passed between the two men that Dave wasn't privy to and he was curious as to their history. Still, Bob wouldn't tell him anything until he was good and ready, so instead of thinking about what it could be, Dave reached over and turned the CD player on, low enough to hear but not wake his sleeping passenger.

He focused on the road. Stockdale was less than a couple of hours drive from Kallygarn, and by his calculations, they should arrive about two pm. Loads of time to check into a motel, have a shower and then find the officer in charge at the cop shop and introduce themselves.

'We were partners about thirty years ago.' Bob's voice broke in over the music.

Although startled from his own thoughts, Dave didn't turn his head. His friend's voice sounded a bit like he had a cold and he didn't want to see Bob's tears. The road held better things to look at.

Shifting in his seat, Bob turned back to face the front and wiped his hand over his face and thinning hair.

Dave felt his partner's eyes on him, as if he was waiting for a reaction. Fighting down all the questions, Dave stayed quiet. Spencer and Bob had both taught him that leaving silence was sometimes the best way to get information.

'We started at the academy together,' Bob said finally as he fumbled with the lid of a water bottle. 'I didn't think he'd get through, you know. Even though he was built like a brick shithouse, Johnny was soft and considerate. Back then that didn't make for a good copper. We were supposed to be tough, in your face, men's men, you know? Don't show emotion, don't have feelings, don't let anyone's story affect you.

'The old fellas occasionally gave out a backhander to help encourage someone to talk, and a couple of punches wasn't out of the ordinary either. Guess that sounds shocking in this day and age, when we could all get the sack for doing something like that, but we all did it and, well . . .' His voice faded a bit as he wiped his hands on his jeans. 'You know how it was, son. You've been there, heard the stories.'

Dave kept his eyes focused to the front. Some of the people he'd gone through the academy with had dropped out for the same reason. Butter soft. Others had stayed at entry level, as a street copper, and were bloody good at what they did. A handful had ended up in higher management, and while Dave had celebrated with and congratulated those police officers, to him, that wasn't what being a copper was about.

No, he was glad he didn't have to argue the toss with the bureaucrats. Being a detective suited him. Being there for the public suited him.

'We were stationed in the hills, where it was pretty quiet,' Bob continued, oblivious to Dave's thoughts. 'It was almost like a country town, but only half an hour away from the city centre, so the night we came across a bloke who had been throwing stones at cars from a bridge, well, that was pretty unusual.' Bob took a few deep breaths.

'You don't have to tell me,' Dave said. As Bob spoke, he realised he didn't want to know Johnny and Bob's secret anymore. Some things were best left unsaid.

'Yeah, I do. Just so you know.' Bob stayed silent for a few more seconds and then continued on. 'He was high for sure. And once us boys in blue turned up . . .' Bob gave a huff. 'You've seen what can happen sometimes, son—he scarpered to the edge of the bridge and climbed up on the ledge, threatening to jump.

'Now, one thing Johnny was good at was talking people down. Gift of the gab. He could tell you that the sky had turned pink overnight, and he'd have you believing exactly what he was saying even if you were looking at blue. So Johnny spoke to this kid. Told him he should come away from the edge, didn't want to see him get hurt; the same sort of shit we say when anyone's life is in danger.

'Not to mention it's a bloody risky thing to do, throwing rocks at cars. There's a high chance someone could die. We wanted to get him back to the station and give him a talking-to, as well as getting him the help he needed. Once we'd done that, maybe we'd charge him.'

'Shit,' Dave said as he held the troopy steady on the road. A grain truck was in front of him and one behind. Cautiously, he pulled to the right to see if he could pass. Coming towards him was a set of headlights. Dave was glad the other vehicle had their lights on. It was such a grey, rainy day it was hard to see other cars from a long way back.

'Anyhow, we finally got him off the bridge and took him down towards the car.' Bob shook his head as Dave moved the troopy back in behind the truck. 'He was apologetic, and now that we'd spoken to him a bit we thought he was a good kid.' There was the huff again, as if he was disgusted with his own inexperience. 'What we didn't do was frisk him for weapons. We were just out of the academy—that's no excuse, I realise, but we were pretty green.'

Dave went to tell him it was okay, everyone makes mistakes, but Bob mistook what he was about to say.

'I know, we were dickheads.' Bob gave a tiny smile. 'So was he. Johnny had the passenger door open and was reaching in to pick up the radio when his leg started to feel wet. I was a few yards back and then I heard Johnny yelling, "You mongrel, you dirty, fucking prick."

'One right hook had the kid spinning and a couple of jabs had him on the ground, bleeding. There was a knife on the ground—Johnny had knocked it out of the kid's hand.

'Back in the day I used to be able to run, so by now I'm hightailing it across the footpath but Johnny's lost it.' Bob gave a giggle now. 'The kid had pissed on his leg and into the cop car . . . On the seat! There was a puddle right where Johnny had to sit.'

A grin spread across Dave's face, too.

'But then . . . I didn't think things were gonna get out of hand but they did. The kid made a couple of cracks, comments that would normally be water off a duck's back, but not that night. Johnny was bent right out of shape.'

Bob was looking less amused at the memory now.

'We took him to the hospital, did the right thing. He had a couple of loose teeth and a broken jaw. Johnny's a lot harder than he looks and he's got that six feet plus height behind him, which gives him a bit of extra strength. The doc was a bit suss towards us but we kept saying it happened when the kid hit the ground after he'd pulled the knife and we'd had to manhandle him down.'

'They believed you?'

'If they didn't, the hospital staff never said anything. And all the coppers did, or at least if they worked out what had happened, they kept their mouths shut as they'd all had an incident like that.

'Anyhow, after we got the all-clear from the hospital, we took him back to the station and charged him with carrying a concealed weapon, throwing rocks and other objects at vehicles, urinating in a public place, and a couple of other things. But then suddenly we had a problem 'cause it turned out the kid was the son of one of the state pollies.' Bob let that revelation hang in the air.

Pollies were well known for putting pressure on coppers to drop charges, or have the hierarchy investigate coppers who they thought were being unfair.

'Shit.'

'Oh yeah. Big time. Of course, his dad didn't want the kid charged because of the bad press it would bring. Let's not worry about the fact he could've killed someone by throwing those rocks. The little snot told his dad that Johnny had assaulted him. We denied it, of course, but the minister wanted us investigated. Our boss shut it down and Johnny's rep took a bit of a battering, although—' he gave another grin '—his street cred among the constables shot up sky high.'

Dave knew how handy street cred was, especially after he'd gained some himself when he'd been shot by Bulldust in Queensland.

'Even though the investigation was only a quiet one, it caused a fair bit of angst with Johnny's wife. She was embarrassed that there was an inquiry. Did you know,' Bob turned to look at Dave, 'being a copper's wife gives them standing in the community?' Bob gave an unkind laugh. 'Not really, but she couldn't be told. Then when that didn't work, she refused to believe Johnny had hurt anyone . . . could harm anyone.' There was a pause and then Bob said, 'To be fair, if I hadn't been there, I might've thought the same thing.'

'Hang on, so you told her that Johnny belted the kid?'

'Nah, only that he injured himself when he fell. Johnny was the arresting officer, so it rested on his shoulders. But his missus thought he was covering for me—that I'd been the one who'd assaulted the kid and now wasn't taking responsibility.'

Dave shook his head and held up his hand so Bob didn't say anymore because the two-way radio had suddenly come to life and was blaring with some truckies talking for a few moments. 'Sorry, go on.'

'Anyway, she got all snarky, told Johnny that he should be telling the truth. He said he was, but she refused to believe him. Got so serious for a while he thought their marriage was gonna fold.'

Bob took a long drink from the water bottle and rubbed his hands over his face again. 'There was no swaying her opinion of me. Johnny told me to keep out of her way but, in hindsight, maybe that was the wrong thing to do.' He stretched his arms towards the windscreen and his voice sounded tight when he spoke again. 'You know what it's like trying to reason with someone who's got an idea in their head that can't be changed. To this day, she thinks I was trying to throw Johnny under the bus.'

'Strange Johnny couldn't persuade her otherwise,' Dave said. 'She can't have had a lot of trust in him.'

'You're telling me nothing I haven't already thought. He gave up trying to convince her when she said if he didn't get a new partner, she'd leave. She wanted him out of the city and working in some tiny little country town where nothing bad ever happens. That way Johnny would be safely tucked up in bed next to her every night. Which, as you know, doesn't always work anyway.'

'She sounds like Mel.'

Bob stilled then nodded slowly. 'Yeah, well, there you go.'

CHAPTER 14

'Aunty Mary,' Connie said as she stirred a packet of sugar into her coffee, 'you can see what I'm talking about with Mum now, can't you? I'm really worried about her.'

'Yes, darling. There's some real trouble there.' Mary reached across to grab Connie's hand and squeezed it tightly.

'What do I do?' Connie leaned forward and rested her elbows on the table and then dropped her chin into her palm. 'Have you got any idea how I can help her?'

Mary's mouth twisted in thought. 'Connie, how old are you now? Twenty-two?'

'Nearly twenty-three. Same age as Brandan was.' She felt the back of her throat tighten at the mention of his name.

'Well, darling, you need to start living your life. You can't keep staying at home with your mother and feeling responsible for her. Georgia has to take some accountability for her life. I know that sounds harsh, but she's the only one who can drag herself out of the cycle of self-pity she's in.'

Letting the teaspoon fall to the table with a clatter, Connie stared in horror at her aunt. 'Self-pity?'

'I told you it would sound harsh. Georgia is not the only parent who has lost a child, you know. There are many other parents who are grieving as deeply as she is, and yet they can face every day. I'm sure it's not easy, and I would never go as far to say I understand what Georgia is going through. I loved Brandan, but I didn't give birth to him, so it would be very wrong of me to assume I could comprehend her grief.

'But from what I see, she's not only mucking up her own life, she's ruining yours as well. I can't stand by and let that happen . . .'

A tiny seed of hope bloomed in Connie's stomach. 'Did you have something in mind?' she asked quietly.

Pursing her lips, Mary didn't answer. Instead she asked another question. 'How do you feel about Brandan's death?'

'Angry,' Connie said without thinking. 'Really angry.'

'Why?'

Connie let her aunt's hand go and played with the serviette on the saucer. ''Cause it shouldn't have happened. Brandan was so young—' She broke off as the waitress, who had been at school with her, brought her toasted ham and cheese sandwich and Mary's chicken soup.

'Thanks, Lisa,' Connie said.

'Welcome. Hey, I saw in the paper today that there's a memorial to your brother. Can't believe it's twelve months already. That time's gone pretty fast.'

134

Connie was used to people's careless remarks by now, so she just nodded. 'Yep, it's been twelve months.'

'There was lots of talk after he died, about, you know, whether it was an accident or not. You know what I think?'

Mary cleared her throat and rearranged the cutlery in front of her. 'Lisa, was that your name?'

Lisa nodded and smiled. 'You're Connie's aunt from Kallygarn, aren't you? I remember when you used to come over for the school concert and presentation nights.' She flicked a glance at Connie, then back at Mary. 'Connie's lucky to have an aunt who cared enough to turn up to those things. Mine never did.'

Mary touched a napkin to her mouth, even though she hadn't eaten anything and nodded. 'Yes, I'm Connie's aunt and that's nice of you to say. But, Lisa, we don't care about your view on what happened with Brandan. Or anyone else's. I've found that people in small towns who have opinions on everyone else's business have very small minds.' She smiled not-so-kindly. 'I think the cook in the kitchen is looking for you.'

Lisa flushed red and looked at Connie as if waiting for her to say something supportive, but when she didn't Lisa turned and walked away without saying another word.

When she'd disappeared inside the kitchen, Mary grinned. 'There we are. It's much nicer in here without unwanted thoughts, wouldn't you say?'

Looking at her aunt in awe, Connie asked, 'How did you do that?'

'Do what?' Mary picked up her spoon and started to swirl it around in her soup, cooling it down.

'Speak to her like that. And have the confidence to do it? I mean, Lisa isn't as bad as some of the others but—'

'Connie, confidence comes from here.' She tapped her forehead. 'It's what we think of ourselves. Self-belief comes from how we learn and grow from our successes and failures, and the way we react to people's thoughts of us. You're only young, but you've already had far too many knockdowns, so you're bound to be feeling a bit wonky at times, and that's okay, darling. But this can't go on.'

Her throat was tight again, and Connie wished she hadn't started this conversation.

Mary kept talking. 'I've got another question for you. If you could change one thing in your life, what would it be?'

'For Brandan not to die,' Connie said immediately.

'Hmm. I wonder.'

'Of course that's what I'd change. If he was still here, Mum would be normal, you and I wouldn't be having this conversation. Life would have just gone on as we'd planned.'

'I'm not sure that's right, you know.' Putting down her spoon, Mary tucked her long grey hair behind her ears then brushed the crumbs from her bread roll off her puffer jacket.

Connie watched her aunt's manicured fingernails, painted purple, brush the crumbs away. She'd always idolised her aunt. Her mum was a wonderful woman, but it had been Aunty Mary she'd confided in when a boy kissed her behind the school library, and it had been Aunty Mary she'd told when she'd failed her maths test. Like Lisa said,

Aunty Mary had been the one who had turned up at every school concert and awards night, and she had driven the two hours from Kallygarn to Stockdale the day Brandan had been killed.

'Maybe I should have phrased the question a bit better,' her aunt said now. 'If you could change one thing after Brandan died, what would it be?'

'Mum,' Connie answered. 'I wish I could get her out and about again.'

'What about you? Would you like to get a full-time job?'

'Of course. You were the only person who knew I wanted to go to Perth and enrol in law. No one else.' Connie tapped at the table angrily. 'Far out! It had taken so long to work out what I wanted to do with my life, and then—boom!— Brandan died and now I can't leave Mum.'

Why was Mary trying to hurt her by bringing up her long-discarded dreams? The ones she'd never be able to do now. Or at least not until her mother started to improve . . . If that ever happened.

'You know I can't go,' she said to her aunt now, 'so why are you asking me these questions?' A little sob came from deep within her and, as it did, Connie realised how angry she was with Brandan, with her mother. The way her life was becoming about everyone else. Hiccupping, she picked up her sandwich and took a bite, hoping the food would stop the threatening tears. She couldn't, *wouldn't* cry. If she did, there might be no stopping.

'Yes,' her aunt said calmly. 'I know what your dreams are, but is there anything you want to add to them?'

Another bite of her sandwich to stall while Connie thought hard. Trying to imagine a life outside of her mother's sadness. 'Yeah, I want to live in Perth and earn enough money to buy my own house. I want to represent clients in the courtroom. Like they do on *Law & Order*. I want to wear beautiful shoes and clothes.'

'Good, you have a goal. Now let's look at some timelines. When can you enrol? And what do you have to do to be able to enrol?'

'What? I can't. Mum . . .'

Mary waved her hand as if nothing mattered. 'Humour me, darling.'

Connie stared at her, mind whirling. 'I don't know. Maybe towards the end of the year? I—' She shook her head. 'There's a bridging course I'd have to do and interviews, of course.' Connie could feel herself warming to the questions now. She had the answers because of the research and inquiries made only a few weeks before Brandan had died.

No. Not died. Been killed. By the police. Because they were chasing him.

Maybe . . . a thought flickered in her mind and she looked up at Mary, excited even to be thinking this way.

Mary was talking now. 'Because, Connie, you are not going to waste your life working in a job you don't like, living in a town you don't want to be in, and making sure your mother is okay. I want you to get angry. So angry you're prepared to take a risk! Change everything you know. Because if you don't start getting enraged and confident, then you're still going to be here in ten years' time. Do you want that?'

Until only minutes earlier, Connie hadn't been able to think ten days ahead, let alone ten years. But now she knew with clarity that she did not want to be in Stockdale in ten years' time. By then she was going to be wearing Jimmy Choo shoes and a gown in the courtroom.

And billing in ten-minute blocks to afford the Jimmy Choo shoes!

'Think about this, Connie,' Mary pushed her hardly touched soup to the side and leaned across the table. 'Five years' time, when you've finished university—'

'Seven,' Connie said, sitting up straight. 'It's going to take seven years and then some.'

A slow smile spread over Mary's face and she leaned her small, strong body against the back of the chair, her arms crossed over her breasts. 'In seven plus years,' Mary said, 'you might be able to send that copper who murdered Brandan to gaol.'

Connie didn't move, but she could see it in her mind: that prick copper up on the stand, stuttering and stumbling over her questions, not knowing how to answer because he knew he was wrong.

Connie flipping the pages on her desk looking for a trap and finding one.

The jury returning after deliberations.

The clerk of the court asking the accused to stand.

The judge. The judge with glasses perched on the

end of his or her nose reading the verdict. 'I find you guilty of murder.'

A cold breeze rushed past and knocked the menus on the counter over as the door opened and a couple of kids tumbled through, pushing their hair back from their eyes and laughing as one of them tripped over the school bag she was holding.

Connie turned back to Mary, anticipation on her face. 'Do you think I can do it?' she asked.

'I know you can.' Mary stared hard at her. 'When I was young, I had to fight like cat and dog in a man's world. We were clearing virgin bush, ripping up rocks, digging dams. I worked hard to make sure I was accepted. You will have to do the same, because industries where men rule are not easy places for women to be. You hear me? You'll need to hold on to your anger. Keep it, harness it and use it when you need to.'

'I will, Aunty Mary. I really will.'

'Good. In ten years' time that copper better watch his back.' Mary leaned forward again. 'I've got one more thing I want you to do.'

'What's that?'

'You find that copper and tell him you're coming for him. Not just you. We, as a family. We're coming for him.'

CHAPTER 15

Stockdale hadn't changed from ten-odd years ago when Dave had spent a harvest season there after his father had thrown him off the farm. He'd been lost and angry, and had driven hundreds of kilometres to get away from everyone in his family.

His two brothers had been allowed to stay on Wind Valley Farm, but not Dave. His mother hadn't known her youngest son was going to be kicked off. His father made the call and now Dave hated him.

He had needed to be far from all of them.

Way back then, he'd pulled up at the foreshore as a grey curtain of rain hid the islands, blue water and white sands. Frightened and angry, Dave had thought his life had ended.

How strange to sit in the same spot so many years on, reflecting. Back then, he'd been a broken, hurt young man, wondering what the hell had just happened to his dreams. Now he was a confident detective.

'That's where I pulled up,' Dave told Bob, pointing at the unattractive car park nearly on the beach. The pub across the road was plain and unappealing, even with the windows covering the front wall. Those windows were probably the reason the pub could boast seafront dining, when in reality, there was a car park and roads between the dining room and sea.

Further down the road a bit from where he and Bob were parked now there was a broken jetty and Norfolk pine trees lining the footpath along the beach. A few brave walkers dressed in rain jackets and hats hurried up and down the wet path, occasionally stopping to point to something out at sea.

A sea that was full of white-capped waves and churning, angry water.

'Had no idea what I was going to do with myself when I first landed here. Ate a meal at the pub and booked into the hostel. That's a bit further in that direction.' He pointed towards the outskirts of town, down past the jetty.

'How'd you get a job?' Bob asked, leaning his head against his elbow, which was propped on the window. Across from where they sat, the grey waves slammed into the beach, dragging sand and seaweed into the churning water.

Bob seemed less tired than he had been a couple of hours before. The conversation about Johnny, the kid and Johnny's wife had been difficult, but had relieved him of the secret he'd been carrying for years.

The raindrops fell heavily against the windscreen and Dave turned on the wipers.

'Went to the stock agent's office the next day and had a bit of a yarn to a couple of the stockies. One fella in particular was real helpful and he suggested a couple of places I'd be able to find work. His name was Pete. Can't remember his surname, but he wore a green shirt.'

'If he wore a green shirt, he worked for Wesfarmers,' Bob said. 'Hey, I guess you've heard that AWB has bought Wesfarmers Dalgety Rural Services? They're changing their name to Landmark.'

'Yeah, I'd heard that. Be interesting to see how that plays out. Anyhow, this Pete made a couple of phone calls and teed up some interviews then drew me a mud map.' Dave tapped the steering wheel, thoughtfully. 'Don't know what would've happened if I hadn't come across that bloke. Wonder if he's still around.'

'Probably not, if he was young. They seem to move on once they've done a couple of years, don't they?'

'Yep. Although I always wondered why companies like Elders and Wesfarmers do that. They just get their clientele sorted and they have to move to another town.'

'As I've told you before, son, the stockies need to get as much experience as they can. Same as you coppers. Go to different towns, learn about various areas, build up networks. Meet other people and buyers from all over the state, sometimes nationwide. Stands them in good stead for later, when maybe there's a promotion on offer.' Bob cracked open his window to let the cold air in and stop the windows from fogging up.

He kept talking. 'I hear some of the companies are starting to offer franchises to the blokes who don't want to leave town. Maybe they've got a family there and don't want to upend the kids. I heard the parameters to apply is they have to have a good solid clientele and book. Still something like that gives the stockies a bit of ownership. They're not just working for the company and wages with a bit of commission. It matters because the business is theirs. Reckon it's a top idea.' Bob stretched out his arms. 'Anyhow, your history lesson on Stockdale has been nice, but let's make a beeline for the hotel, son. I'm beginning to feel buggered again.'

Starting the car, Dave glanced at the clock on the dash. If Bob went for a sleep now, how was he going to fill in the next few hours before dinner at the pub? And later at dinner, Bob probably wouldn't eat much and only sip at one beer. Probably not even finish it. Disappointment spread through Dave's gut, although he tried not to let on.

Bob was crook. The chemo was taking a lot out of him, so it didn't matter what Dave wanted, only what Bob needed.

Betty had sent a novel-length text message at lunchtime. He'd started to read it before he realised how long it was. With Bob close by, Dave had decided to finish reading it later, in his room, and answer all of her questions then.

Dave sighed inwardly, finding himself wishing Shannon was here, too. Though, Shannon was probably still smarting from their date and his insensitive words the other night. There was probably no chance she was wishing the same as he was.

At the hotel, Dave grabbed Bob's bag out of the back and hauled it towards his mate's room, while his partner stretched his legs again before taking a few tentative steps from the troopy.

'I get so stiff these days,' Bob complained. 'Don't know why.'

'Not moving about as much, I guess,' Dave answered, opening the door. 'Right-oh, well I reckon I might head out and do a few things. What time for tea?'

Bob looked at his watch. 'I reckon I might skip tea tonight, son. That lunch at Kallygarn was huge!'

Now was not the time to mention how little Bob had eaten at lunch, or that Bob's jeans were hanging loosely from his waist. Instead Dave nodded his okay.

'Better if I get an early night so I'm ready to help in the morning. You don't mind, do you? Reckon you'll find someone to talk to?'

'Of course I will. And if I don't, I'll ring Shannon.'

'If you're going to ring that lovely lady, I think it's a great idea I'm not having dinner with you,' Bob said as he turned away. 'Her name has been conspicuous by its absence.'

'Don't know what you're on about.'

With Bob's gaze on his face, Dave knew he hadn't fooled him one little bit.

'Don't you? Not to worry, we will have this conversation later. See you about seven am then, boss.'

Bob put his finger to his forehead in a salute and turned to go into his room, bumping against the door frame as he did. 'Bloody hell,' Bob muttered, rubbing his arm. He shut the door firmly before Dave could react.

Dave was still back at word *Boss*. He felt sucker-punched.

He wasn't the boss. Bob was. Dave was just filling in. Bob would be back. It would take time, that's all.

Acting Detective Sergeant Dave Burrows. Officer in Charge. The titles sounded foreign to his ears.

Swallowing, he grabbed his bag and then entered his dim, musty room. Looking around at the unattractive space, he slid the curtains open, hoping for a view of the beach to make it better. Instead, he found a grey wall, only a few feet from his window.

'Seriously,' Dave muttered, dragging the curtains shut in disgust then sinking down onto the bed. The mattress felt too firm and, when he fell backwards, the sound of crunching plastic made him groan. The plastic-covered pillows would make his head sweat tonight.

He stared at the ceiling, hands behind his head. Why had the word 'boss' given him such a jolt? What was wrong with him? To be the lead detective of the stock squad had been his goal since joining the force and now the position was finally his.

But it was only by default.

Detective Sergeant Bob Holden was the officer in charge. His mate—that's whose job he'd taken and only because Bob was having treatment for cancer.

Dave felt sick at the thought of being the officer in charge.

Why? a little voice asked. *This is what you've always wanted.*

'Not like this. Not because Bob is sick.'

You want to have been promoted because you were worthy, the little voice told him, *not because there weren't any other options.*

'I wish Bob wasn't crook,' Dave said aloud. 'That's all.'

He picked up his mobile phone and opened Betty's message again.

Hi Dave, hope everything is going well? How is he? Has he been taking . . .

Even though he'd intended to read the whole message now, the words blurred in front of his eyes. Instead he typed out a generic answer.

Hi Betty, everything is fine here. Bob a bit tired but all good.

He threw the phone back down. Then he picked it back up again and dialled Shannon's number.

It took a moment to connect and then he heard the ringtone. Once, twice, three times. It only rang five times before the line cut through to the message bank, so Dave hung up. He wasn't sure what to say to her.

Would an apology fix everything? If he told Shannon his intention had been to say something entirely different from the words that had come out of his mouth, would he hear that soft smile in her voice, the one she used when gently chiding him.

It's okay, Dave. I know you didn't mean it. When are you back? Let's have dinner.

Dave breathed deeply, trying to calm the rush of memories of everyone he loved, exploding in his mind.

Bob, and the first time they sat around a campfire together. Back then Dave had been convinced his new partner was the biggest alcoholic in the force.

Bob's insistence at calling him 'son', and the fierce annoyance Dave felt at the condescending word.

Waking up so hungover after Spencer's funeral, and Dave realising Bob had taken care of him.

Shannon as she dug around a corpse on the beach in one of the cases Dave was investigating.

Shannon looking over her shoulder with a half-smile on her face.

Shannon curled up, asleep in his bed.

Bec holding out her arms to be picked up.

Alice sleeping in her cot.

Melinda's and Mark's cool disdain at Ellen's funeral.

After a moment of feeling sorry for himself, Dave got up and dragged out the bulky police-issued laptop computer and modem and connected to the slow internet. He downloaded his emails, scanning the names for anything of high importance, then picked up his phone to ring Lorri.

'Dave,' she answered after the first ring, 'how's Bob going?'

'Weird trip, Lorri,' he answered. 'But I guess I shouldn't have expected anything else. He's coping but pretty knackered.'

'Chemo does that,' she answered in her no-nonsense, practical tone. 'And being crook in the first place. As long as he's well, that's all you can hope for, I think.'

Taking a deep breath in through his nose, Dave acknowledged she was right. He didn't want to talk about it, though

'How about Parksy? Any news on him?'

'Only that he's taking a sabbatical. Couple of months then back into the office. Word is his wife is upset that he's coming back, so watch this space. My bet is he doesn't make it back here. Happy wife, happy life, yada, yada, yada.'

'Let's hope you're wrong,' he said. 'But, as you and I know, partners do seem to have a bit of sway. Parksy's a great detective and the force will be poorer if he's not here.'

'Hmm.' There was a pause and Dave heard papers shuffling. 'Shit, boss,' she said.

Dave felt that punch to his gut again. How many times did he have to tell everyone he wasn't the boss? He was only filling in for Bob.

'We're snowed under here. Not with cases, although there are reports coming in. It's the phone calls taking up the time. Other stations requesting training days. Has the super said if he's going to send anyone our way?'

'Haven't spoken with him recently. What type of reports?'

'With the uptick in prices for livestock there's a fair bit more information being passed to us by local stations. Sheep allegedly missing. Some diesel. I had one phone call yesterday about a stallion worth thirty thousand who isn't in the paddock he's supposed to be. I'm across that one, though. Anyhow, it's meant a whole lot of requests for you to give some tuition to these officers on how we go about investigating rural specific crimes. They're coming from across the wheatbelt. And there're a few down south, including at Stockdale, so do you want to get in contact with the OIC while you're down there?'

149

'Yep, too easy. I'm looking for something to do this afternoon, so I'll go and find him.' Dave paused, while he searched his briefcase for his diary. 'I'll check with Bob and make sure he's up to it, but if we could get it organised, how about I stay down here a few extra days and implement a training course after I've gone through the abs. Is there anything crazy urgent up there?'

'I'd check with Betty first if I were you,' Lorri said. 'She might not agree.'

'I'll do my due diligence,' Dave told her.

'Right-oh, hang on and I'll just see if anything new has come in.'

He heard her shuffling through paperwork and then the clicking of the keyboard. 'Nooope.' She drew the word out, and Dave knew she was speedreading emails. 'I think we'll be okay if you take a couple of extra days down there but, Dave, you need to get in contact with the super and ask if they can give us another detective. Or even a constable who wants to become a detective. It will get to the point we'll need a hand here.'

'Sure, I'll give him a ring after I get off the phone from you. Oh, and while I think about it, has there been any mail for me?'

Last week, Dave had given up the lease on the three-bedroom house that he'd been renting in the hope his daughters, Bec and Alice, would be allowed to come and stay. The impending divorce proceedings had made him realise there was very little chance of the girls ever coming to stay overnight. A big house had only amplified his feeling of being alone. So he'd found a one-bedroom flat, sold any excess furniture, and had his mail forwarded to the office.

'Yeah, there's a couple but nothing that looks important. Last power and water bill and a handwritten letter with no return address.'

Dave straightened. 'What sort of writing? A kid's?'

'Um, not sure what you mean.'

'Is it a child's handwriting? Lady? Man? You're a detective, surely you can hazard a guess.' He didn't mean to sound so sharp.

'Lady's, cursive, blue pen, looks like it's been written with a medium tip biro. Date mark is ... Damn, can't really read it: twentieth? Maybe twenty-sixth or eighth? The stamp is smudged,' Lorri answered without rising to his tone.

'And there's no sender?' Dave tapped his fingers on his knee. Who could be writing to him?

'Sorry, no. Did you want me to forward it to the motel you're staying at?'

'Probably wouldn't get here in time. Don't worry about that, just put it on my desk. I'll check it out when I get back, thanks.' His heart sank a bit. He would have given anything to see his daughter's large, child-like letters printed on an envelope. The last father's day card he'd received had been from Bec after she'd been at day care one morning. Her attempts at letters seemed to fall off the page as they got closer to the edge. Maybe her writing would be more refined than last year.

151

'Sure, easy as,' Lorri was saying. 'Right-oh, better get back to this paperwork. If I find anything really urgent, I'll ring and let you know.'

'Great, thanks, Lorri. And sorry if I sounded a bit grumpy just then. The kids, you know . . .' His voice trailed off.

'I get it,' Lorri said quietly.

He knew she did. Lorri had been privy to many of Dave's and Bob's conversations in the office, as had the rest of the team. They knew the sorry story of Mel and Dave and his heartache at not seeing his girls.

Their squad was close-knit—like a family—and everyone knew what was going on in each other's lives. They supported and cared about every member, and for Dave, that feeling was almost as important to him as Bob was.

Saying goodbye, Dave checked the time, then flipped through the contents of his briefcase, locked the room and hurried through the drizzling rain towards the troopy. He checked Bob's room—the curtains were tightly drawn. Bob would be curled up under the blankets, his head on the plasticky pillows, sound asleep.

Or maybe he was staring at the ceiling, thinking about his life. About Johnny and his wife.

Perhaps he was . . .

Dave shook his head and gave himself a shake. 'Pull yourself together,' he muttered as he turned the key and reversed the troopy out of the parking bay.

A few minutes later, he drew up in front of the police station.

Outside, he stopped briefly at the flagpole that was at half-mast for an officer who had died in the eastern states, then continued on inside.

'G'day,' he said to the constable behind the desk. 'I'm Detective Dave, ah—' He cleared his throat and started again. 'I'm Acting Detective Sergeant Dave Burrows, from Rural Crime Squad. Just wondering if your OIC is in, please?'

A curious look passed over the constable's face and he looked over his shoulder. 'One moment.'

He disappeared and, after a while, Dave heard voices.

'I tell you, Dutton, I'm sick of out-of-towners. All these extra people they've brought in for that blast at Kallygarn. If they'd just let me sort everything, it would have been much bloody easier. Tell him to piss off. I've got enough on my plate.'

There were murmurings and finally the door opened with more force than needed and a short, heavy-set man planted his feet apart and glared at Dave. 'And what can I do for you?'

CHAPTER 16

'Come on, let me take you out to dinner,' Tom said.

Connie had just finished hugging Aunty Mary goodbye in the street and watched her leave for their house.

Mary had promised to talk to her sister and try to shock her out of her stupor, the way she had with Connie earlier in the day. Connie really didn't hold out a lot of hope for her mum, but she did for herself.

Next year, she would be studying law.

Tom and Connie walked together down the main street. 'You can't go back to the house while Mary is talking to your mum. Imagine the chat that's going to go down there this afternoon.'

'No, thanks,' Connie said. 'Mary was ferocious enough with me! I've had my lecture. I don't want to hear another one.'

'Well, I'm glad Mary's got through to about your mum. I've been trying but you haven't really been listening.'

Tom raised his hand as an old car drove past. His mate leaned out of the window and wolf-whistled at the two of them. Tom changed his wave to the finger and Connie giggled. The sun seemed to be shining brighter today, even though the sky was stained with heavy clouds.

Part of her was exhausted and the other excited. If law school was in reach, she was going to have to get organised. Briefly she wondered where her old exam results were. Perhaps her mum would know.

'You haven't answered about tea. We can go to the pub.'

'There's nowhere else, you idiot!' She smiled and put her hand on his arm. 'Look, I appreciate what you're trying to do, Tom, but I'll have to go home soon. If Aunty Mary gives Mum a bollocking, I might need to be there after she's gone. And if I leave Mum alone in the house, she might ring up the radio and rant about how the police are all bastards. She did that, you know, not long after Brandan died.'

'Did she?' Tom sounded impressed.

'Yeah! She found the number for some late-night show and I woke up to her yelling about how all police were dickheads and murderers.' She groaned, remembering the scene. 'I guess it made for good night-time radio though. The announcer was lapping it up, such great drama.' She gave a mirthless laugh. 'I don't know why they let her on air.'

'Exactly what you said—drama.' Tom nudged her shoulder as they walked.

'I don't disagree with what she did,' Connie said. 'People have to be made aware of what happened to Brandan and how the police were involved. But let's go about it with a better plan.'

'Have you got one?'

Connie gave a coy smile. She hadn't told Tom what she and Aunty Mary had discussed about confronting the police officer. And today wasn't the day. Tom was happy and she was still working through an idea. 'Maybe. I'm thinking about one.'

'Tell me.' He stopped and turned to face her.

Connie kept walking, knowing her secret was playing across her face and she was going to have to improve her deadpan expression if she was going to be a lawyer. 'Nope, then I'd have to kill you and I like you too much for that,' she quipped.

'You're kidding? What are you going to do? Do you need any help?'

'I'm not saying any more, Tom. Just let me sort a few things out and then I'll tell you, okay?'

A heavy shower of rain started, and Connie pulled on Tom's arm so he stayed sheltering under the verandah of the local jeweller's store.

'The pub looks like it's waiting for us,' Tom said, looking out into the rain. 'Have a drink with me. I promise not to ask you anything more about your, ah—' he made his tone rounded '—course of action.' Dropping the pretence, he looked at her pleadingly. 'Come on, just a drink.'

Glancing at her watch, Connie said, 'God, anyone would think you're desperate!'

'Not likely. I've got Hannah coming over later.' It was Tom's turn to give her a secretive look.

'Hannah? Where's Donna gone?'

'Donna who?' One side of Tom's mouth turned up.

'You're a male tart.' Connie spoke loudly as the rain made it difficult to hear, then glanced at her watch. 'Shit! It's nearly five. I hope Mum's okay. I might—'

Tom didn't let her finish. He grabbed her hand, tugging her out into the rain ignoring her squeals.

'Tom! Stop it! What are you doing?' Connie yelled as together they dashed towards the front bar of the pub.

Opening the door, Tom almost pushed her inside. 'You should see your face,' he told her with a grin. 'Bet you haven't been that impulsive for a while!'

Wiping the rain from her face, Connie shook out her jumper and moved towards the fire. 'Geez, Tom, what the hell?'

'Come on, now you're here, you might as well have a drink. What do you want?' He got out his wallet and Connie saw four fifty-dollar notes inside.

Her eyes widened. 'Tom! What have you been doing to get that much money? You never have cash on you.'

Pulling his wallet away, he stared at her. 'Never you mind. You're not the only one with secrets, you know. Now, answer my question.'

'Did you steal it?' Connie asked, eyeing him suspiciously. 'I can't let you buy if it's with stolen money.'

Tom gave her a grumpy look. 'No. It's not stolen. I went to the ATM, okay? I'd planned to ask you for dinner so I got some cash out.' He tapped his foot. 'Come on. A man's gonna die of thirst here.'

She let out an exasperated sigh. 'Just a beer. Thanks.'

'That wasn't so hard, was it?' Tom grinned and headed to the bar.

Connie stood, drying herself in front of the open flames and thinking. Had he really taken that money out of the ATM? She didn't think so. It would be unusual. Maybe he had to take Hannah out somewhere tonight. Or was it Donna? She couldn't remember which way around he'd mentioned their names.

Tom was ordering their drinks, now flirting with the barmaid. The girl's cheeks were flushed so he must've pulled out a Triple T. The Token Tommy Tribute. Telling her that her hair glowed the same as her smile or something ridiculous. How did girls fall for shit like that? Tommy was a charmer, there was no doubt about it, but Connie couldn't work out why the women kept fawning over him when it was common knowledge he never stuck to one.

She was pleased they were friends and he'd never tried his magic on her. Although Connie was also secretly offended he hadn't seen her as worthy of his attention. Still, they'd been mates since primary school and there was a lot to be said for long friendships that didn't turn into anything else.

Moving her gaze, she checked to see who else was in the pub. Months, if not longer, had passed since she'd stepped inside. Nothing was different, the carpet still smelled like stale beer and was stained from spilt food and red wine.

In the corner near the TAB, Connie saw Emily, a colleague from the chemist. She gave a self-conscious wave as she realised the man sitting with Emily was one of the customers they both complained about, saying how rude he could be.

The full-time job she'd been offered at the chemist after Brandan had died had been a godsend. So many businesses hadn't wanted to take her on. One manager had told her that employing someone after a terrible bereavement like she'd experienced wasn't practical. 'You're going to have so much grief still to work through, Connie,' he'd said. 'Can't have personal life affecting your work.'

Unfurling anger hovered in her stomach at the memory.

'Hello, Connie. How are you, dear?'

Behind her, Connie recognised the sugary voice of her next-door neighbour, Mrs Patton. She closed her eyes and clenched her fists. What the hell was that old bat doing here? Wasn't it enough Mrs Patton spent most of her days looking over their adjoining fence and offering advice, which wasn't that at all. It was judgement.

How nice it would be to copy Aunty Mary's reaction to Lisa this morning towards Mrs Patton. Now that would make her feel confident! Still, god help her if she did. The reaction would outweigh Connie's satisfaction. Swallowing and taking a couple of breaths, she turned and gave a fake smile. 'Hello, Mrs Patton. How are you?'

'Oh, just fine. I'm having dinner with my dear son. You remember Malcolm, don't you?' She waved towards a tall man with sandy hair who was looking uncomfortable behind his mother.

'Nope. But how're you?' Connie wished she had some gum to chew so she could pop a bubble in the old woman's face. *Mature, Connie, so mature. Remember you're going to be a lawyer.*

The man nodded and shifted to his other foot while he waited for Mrs Patton to stop talking.

'How's Georgia, love? Gosh, such a bad thing, the way she's gone, isn't it?' she tutted. 'You must be so worried. I know I would be. If only Brandan had known what his death would do to his mother, I'm sure—' Mrs Patton broke off. 'Well, I'm sure he wouldn't have done what he did. Is there anything I can do for you both? I pray every day for you.'

How about you shove your Christian judgement up your arse?

'Mum's going okay,' she said, instead. 'Thanks for asking about her.' Connie tried to ignore how fast her heart was beating. Where was Tom?

To distract herself she shoved her hand in the pocket of her black jeans and rubbed the tissue in there.

'Oh, now by the way, lovie . . .'

Mrs Patton didn't seem at all interested in Connie's answer about Georgia.

'I need to talk to you about that dog of your brother's. Ah, Dougal?'

'Dude.'

'He really is being a bit annoying. Digging under the fence and the like. Maybe you could stop him, eh? Perhaps he needs a little more exercise.' She rearranged the handles of her handbag on her arm, causing deep wrinkles as she pushed it towards her elbow. They gave Mrs Patton's aging skin a crocodile-like leather look. Her teeth and words were just as sharp.

'I know it's Brandan's dog, but someone has to take both that animal and your mother in hand. Not that they're in the same category, granted. That's not what I mean. But someone needs to shake some sense into Georgia. She can't be drowning in grief forever. Your mother wasn't the one who died and it's important she starts to—'

Connie's heart was beating so fast, she thought she might have a heart attack. She really wanted to punch this woman in the mouth, and by the look on Malcolm's face, he could see just how close she was coming to that. Her chest rose and fell with such force, little spots were dancing in front of her eyes.

Maybe she could sue her later for being a cow?

'Hello, Mrs Patton. Don't you look lovely today.'

Thank god for Tom. He'd handle the self-righteous bitch. Connie took the beer he offered her and drank deeply, feeling as if her feet were stuck to the ground. If they weren't she would've run out the door and not looked back.

'Well, now, young Tom, you're looking more and more like your father every day. Gosh, you must be nearly thirty, aren't you? Where has the time gone? I remember when you were born.'

Tom's rich laughter echoed around Connie's head.

'Connie and I are turning twenty-three this year. We were born within a couple of days of each other. Shared the hospital room.'

'How nice. And your mother, how is she?'

'Just fine and dandy. We all are.' Tom glanced over at Connie and seemed to read the signs. 'We'd better be off. Got to find a seat for tea. See you round, Mrs Patton.' He put his hand around Connie's shoulders and started to move her towards a table. But then he turned back. 'Oh and Mrs Patton?'

'Yes, dearie?'

Connie stiffened, half hoping he'd give her a mouthful.

'You should wear that colour all the time. It really suits you.'

Mrs Patton made a gushing noise and her cheeks tinged with pink as Malcolm escorted her towards their table.

'Now why can't you say things like that?' Mrs Patton asked her son, loud enough for everyone in the pub to hear.

'What a fucking—' Connie exploded as quietly as she could.

'Shh,' Tom said. 'Look at me. Hold my hand and look into my eyes.'

'What?' Connie almost snarled at him. 'Why?'

'Just do it,' Tom sounded bored as he took her hand in his and covered it with his other hand. He leaned in and kissed her soundly on the mouth.

For one tiny second, Connie felt the warmth and human touch she craved then the curtain slammed down and she reeled back, staring at him. 'What are you doing?'

'Giving the old bat something else to talk about. "That young Tommy Foster and Connie Phillips were kissing in the pub the other night." I can hear her now.'

Despite her anger, Connie found herself smiling at him. 'You are such a rogue.'

'And you love me.' His eyes darted to the door as three men entered. Annoyance crossed his face. 'Bloody hell, don't look now, but it's the coppers. You want to go? Drink up.'

Connie looked around and a new rush of heat started in her stomach and worked its way up through her chest, her heart, her brain.

The little fat, jumped-up prick—she couldn't remember his name. Only that he oversaw the police station. He was the one who'd come to tell them about Brandan's accident and his care factor had been zero. Only stood at the door and told them in a monotone voice what had happened, then: 'I'm sorry for your loss.'

Five words that he didn't mean, he'd never mean. Now, Connie wanted to spit in his drink.

Instead, she took a breath and brought the beer to her mouth, finishing the drink in one gulp. 'I think I'd like another drink and to stay a bit longer.' Mary's comment was still fresh in her mind: *You find that copper and tell him you're coming for him. Not just you. We, as a family. We're coming for him.*

Well, here he was.

Tom was looking at her warily. He glanced back to the three men who'd ordered drinks and were standing at the bar deep in conversation, then asked, 'You think that's a good idea?'

'It's a free world last time I checked,' Connie said, her attention on the coppers. 'Who's the tall guy? Haven't seen him before.'

'Dunno. Might be one of the out-of-towners. You know, to do with the bombing over in Kallygarn. I heard they were bringing in a heap of other coppers. Good thing. They'll forget about us for a while.'

Connie looked back at him, remembering the money she'd seen in his wallet. 'Forget about you?'

'They'll be too busy to keep an eye on the locals—you know what I mean. They're going to be focused on trying to work out if someone blew up those offices rather than running breatho checks and looking at security footage that might catch some poor unsuspecting local parking in the wrong area.' He winked and took a sip of his beer.

Connie put down her empty glass. 'Want another?'

'Nah, one's enough.' Tom picked up a coaster and turned it over in his fingers.

Connie tossed her head. 'Well, I'm getting one so, since it was you who dragged me here, literally, you can have another, too.' She got up and walked over to the bar, just as the men erupted in laughter.

She stood close, listening to what they were saying, enjoying the confidence the beer had given her. Drinking was never high on her priority list, so between the anger and the alcohol tonight she was buzzing.

'Like I said, Dave, I'm sorry for the welcome I gave you. Thought you were another arseholes from Perth who've got tickets on themselves. Heap of those bastards have been down here throwing their weight around like nobody's business.'

'No worries, Roger,' the taller man said. 'We're sort of used to it, you know. We blow into town and the locals can get their nose out of joint. All with good reason. We're aware we don't have the local knowledge or the lay of the land which is why Bob and I want to work with you blokes, not piss you off. And that's one of the things I talk about in the training course you're wanting me to do. Good relations are the way to get people to open up.'

Connie agreed. That little fucker, Roger, could get a lesson on good relations. She was pleased she'd overheard his name.

'Help you, love?'

Connie refocused on the barmaid and asked for two more beers. She handed over a twenty-dollar note; the woman handed her a few coins and Connie pocketed the change, all the while listening to the men talk.

She took a couple of sips for courage and walked over, standing next to them until they noticed her. Out of the corner of her eye she saw Tom start to move towards her, so she focused on the short, fat man. Roger. Repulse-ful Roger. Was that a word? Who cares, she'd make him a Remorseful Roger by the time she was finished.

When he turned to see who was standing alongside him, his smile fell away.

'How dare you stand here, drinking and laughing, when you killed my brother,' Connie said quietly.

An embarrassed purple spread across the man's cheeks and he glanced towards the other coppers standing with him. 'Now there's no need to be like that, Miss Phillips,' he said. To the others, he said, 'Just ignore her.'

'Oh, I wouldn't do that,' Connie continued. 'All you have to do is admit what involvement your officers have in Brandan's death and I'll leave you alone, but until then, I'm coming for you.' She took a breath. 'The cops killed my brother. One mistake.' She held up one finger. 'He made one mistake and he's hunted and harassed by you lot. You think he was bad inside and out, but it was just one mistake.' Her voice broke. 'He died because you coppers wouldn't leave him alone.' Her voice was louder now, and the tall man stepped towards her.

Connie shot him a look, daring him to come any closer. 'Stay there. You've got nothing to do with this. Just this bastard. 'Cause he's in charge.'

'Now, Connie . . .' Roger put down his drink and held up his hand, taking a small step towards her.

She thought he was going to put his hand on her shoulder, so she flung up her arm to protect her body.

He stopped. 'You're overreacting.'

'Don't touch me, you slimeball. If you do, I'll make a complaint about assault. You and your constables are murderers, and I won't stop until the rest of the state—no, the nation—knows it.' Her voice shook as she emphasised each word.

Tom was beside her now. 'Con, let's go.'

'No, this needs to be said. Brandan was just another notch in your belt, wasn't he? You kill a good man and then you turn up here, have a beer and laugh about it.'

'Look, um—' Dave glanced around '—Con, was it? Con, I'm not sure what you're talking about, and I can really see you're hurting and angry, but this isn't the place—'

'Shut up. Just shut up.' Her voice was louder now. 'If you're a copper, you killed Brandan, too.'

'Miss Phillips, I need you to calm down.' Roger spoke in a no-nonsense tone. 'If you'd like to come down to the police station we can talk about this.'

'What, so no one can hear what you did? Not a chance in hell. Until I can haul you into a courtroom, I'll be doing this publicly.'

Tom shouldered his way in between them and pointed at Roger. 'Bro, fuck off. I'll take her, but you fuck off and leave her alone. Like she said, you're nothing but a bunch of killers.' He grabbed Connie's arm and pulled her away.

'Jesus, you idiot, is this your plan?' Tom muttered in her ear as he pushed her away. The beer spilled over their hands, but neither of them took any notice. Connie tried to turn around and give the coppers the finger, but Tom had too much of a grip on her. 'I reckon I could have come up with a better one.'

CHAPTER 17

I've checked in with Bob this morning and he's okay but not getting up yet, Dave typed out to Betty. The morning was frigid and he clenched his fingers back and forth, trying to keep them warm as he typed. *I think he's staying in bed because it's cold, rather than anything else.*

Voices came down the Stockdale Police Station hallway, and he looked up to see three police officers heading to start desk duty with coffees in hand. Nodding at them all, he looked past the group to see if the constables Roger had suggested he take to the abattoirs had arrived.

His phone dinged back almost as soon as he'd sent the message. Dave looked down at the screen and his stomach rolled in a nervous way. It wasn't Betty's name on the screen, but Shannon's.

To open or not, he wondered.

Hi Dave, sorry, I see I've missed a couple of calls from you. Work is hectic. When are you back? Let's grab dinner.

His shoulders dropped in relief. Okay, so he hadn't blown it completely with Shannon. Thank god for that. Because he'd missed her laugh and their conversations since the balls-up he'd created at dinner the other night. He needed to tell her.

'Morning, Dave,' a voice called out before he had a chance to answer Shannon's text. One of the blokes he had a beer with last night was walking towards him, with a stranger at his side. These would be Constables Brad Cooper and Kane Davis, two new-to-town coppers, who were keen to take a trip with him.

He pocketed his phone, knowing that Shannon would understand that work had intervened, and led them outside to where the troopy was parked.

'How's everything this morning?' he asked. 'Nothing too big happen overnight?'

'Never like to answer that question because if I say it's been quiet that's when something suddenly blows up,' Kane answered, getting in and clipping his seatbelt.

'True story!' Dave answered, checking his mirrors and starting the engine.

'How long have you both been here?'

'Only a couple of months,' Brad answered.

'One for me,' said Kane.

'It's hard when you come into a town and you're trying to get the lay of the land, isn't it?' Dave added.

The road out of Stockdale to the abattoirs hadn't changed one bit since he'd last driven it. Waving in the wind on the edge of the road was tall lovegrass, the easiest-to-spread noxious weed that had ever been introduced into Australia, while other weeds—radish, capeweed and brome grass—lined the table drains.

'I like going to new places,' Brad said. 'It's a challenge getting people to trust you and build up networks but sometimes that's the best part.'

Kane was nodding. 'Yeah, you're coming in fresh. No one has any preconceived ideas about you or the way you police. You can just get on and do the job. I join as many clubs as I can and make friends that way.'

'That's a great way to get to know people,' Dave agreed. 'Tell me why you asked to do this course? Not many blokes have an interest in the rural side of things.'

'I'm from a farm,' Kane spoke up. 'Down the south-west. Bridgetown way.'

'Didn't want to stay there?'

'The farming lifestyle isn't really for me,' he said. 'Bit too laid-back. I enjoy the adrenalin of policing. Being able to help people. There's never a day the same. Always something different, even if the town is small. Farming is like that to a point, but every year is the same. Harvest comes once a year, just like seeding and shearing. Get what I mean?'

Dave nodded and pulled the steering wheel to the right to avoid some puddles left over from last night's rain. He was glad he'd organised a spontaneous training day. The young blokes sounded keen and ready to learn.

'What about you, Brad?'

'Just trying to get as much training and information as I can. I enjoy the job and always want to improve my skills and knowledge. Guess, the way to do that is by increasing my experiences.'

'Agreed,' said Dave, and glanced in the rear-view mirror to see the young man's eager face. 'You were with us at the pub last night, Brad. What was the go with the woman who had a crack at your boss? Roger seemed a bit annoyed with her.'

'Oh that. Yeah.' Brad scratched at his eyebrow and screwed his nose up a bit. 'Bad business all round, really.'

Kane's head swivelled backwards. 'What happened?'

'Connie Phillips is what happened,' Brad said as Kane groaned. 'I feel for her, and her family. It's always awful to lose a loved one, especially unexpectedly. Tragically.'

'And what were the circumstances?' Dave started to slow as the turn-off for the abattoir came into view.

'Her brother, Brandan Phillips, was very well known to the police but a saint in his family's eyes.'

Dave gave a small laugh. 'Normal.'

'Yeah. Can't remember how many times he'd been pulled up and breathalysed. He kept being caught blowing numbers. Last court date he had the magistrate ran out of patience. Told him he'd end up killing someone and slapped him with a lifetime driving suspension.'

Dave let out a long, low whistle. 'That should have been enough to piss him off.'

'Oh yeah, there was all sorts of trouble over it. His boss contacted the station and asked for him to be issued with an extraordinary licence for work. Think he was a brickie. Needed to be able to get to and from the job sites. Roger explained he had to wait twelve months to be able to apply for a licence like that. Still, Brandan wouldn't take no for an answer. He just kept driving. Everyone at the station knew he was, but no one couldn't catch him. So yeah, like Connie mentioned, we went looking for him. It took a while; he was careful and we were never in the right place at the right time. Until we were.'

Dave pulled up in the parking lot and shut the car off, turning around to look at Brad as he finished the story.

He held his hand up in regret. 'Long story short, he was driving on a back road, we tried to pull him over. He did a runner and ended up wrapping the car around a tree. There wasn't a chase, like Connie said. We did follow him with our lights and sirens on, but it was a dirt road and it was wet, so we were extra careful. Our car never went above the speed limit. That accident was his own doing. Regrettable, for sure, but his own doing.'

Dave despaired at the senseless loss of a young life. 'I can understand her anger,' he said.

'Yeah, but it's not aimed in the right direction,' Brad said. 'We didn't do anything wrong.'

'Were you driving?'

It was Kane who spoke up this time. 'Nope, this is the royal "we". Brad and I weren't stationed here then. Roger moved the two blokes who were on patrol that day on to other towns. Said he couldn't keep them here after such an accident. Would just create bad blood in the community, even though there was an inquiry and it found we, as in the police, were not in the wrong.'

'He'd be right,' Dave said. 'Still, there's a lot of hurt in Connie right now and I would imagine she could stir up a lot of trouble if she wanted to. A bit of community policing would help damp that down, I'd imagine . . .' He left the comment hanging. When neither of them responded, he took a deep breath. They were right not to get involved, he supposed. It should be Roger who contacted the family, not two newbies who weren't even here when the accident happened.

'Right, let's chat about what we're here for. What I'm going to show you today is only part of the training course. Quality control in an abs is important. Checking the scale weights and waybills, making sure the stock are exactly what is written on the documentation and—'

Brad broke in. 'Scale weights? They'd be factory issued and weighing correctly when they arrived, wouldn't they?'

'Anything can be changed if someone is wanting to make a quick buck. Just say the abs is having trouble making a dollar. The stock prices have gone up due to lack of stock numbers or the quality is poor, you know, that type of thing. In a case where the owners of the abs were on the shonky side, they could well try to adjust the scales to weigh lighter. If the scales were ten per cent out, weighing less than they should, then the farmer is missing out on ten per cent of his income for every sheep or beast he puts over the hooks.'

'Reckon my missus would be glad if her scales were ten per cent lighter,' Brad said with a laugh.

Dave grinned, too, then saw Kane's confused expression. '"Over the hooks" means killed for meat. The carcasses are hung on hooks and then they go over the scales. So not only do the scales need to be checked, but everything in the line, such as the hooks, has to be weighed, too.'

Both men were nodding now.

'Right, let's check it out.' Dave opened his door, grabbing his notebook as he went.

'Lairage is the first thing that we look at, once we've checked in at the office. I do these unannounced visits so no one can change anything before we get here. I guess it's no different from a raid, but it's a lot softer than bashing someone's door down and turning over their house.'

Brad screwed his nose up as the smell of shit and piss, mud and lanoline hit his nostrils. Dave was used to it, and he loved the smell. Not so much the loud screech of the machines.

'Hup, hup! Get up there,' a woman's voice called as she herded a sheep into the raceway.

'How is this funded?' Kane wanted to know. 'This is so far outside of the parameters of what we would normally police. Do we have to get approval to come here?'

'Me or any of my team have been gazetted by the Meat Industry Authority to come onto any abattoir site and check through the things I've mentioned. Compliance with weights and measures, paperwork and so on.' Dave waved at the man who had come out of the office with a hardhat on. 'Come on, I'll tell you more as we go.' He called out, 'G'day,' walking quickly to the boss. 'I'm Detective Dave—' He faltered as he realised he hadn't given his correct title, then kept going. What did it matter? 'Detective Dave Burrows from the Rural Crime Squad. Just here to do an impromptu compliance check.'

The man looked confused, then concerned, then shrugged. 'Whatever, bro. No skin off my nose. But you'd better sign in.' He tilted his head towards the office. 'Gina can do that and give you all the safety gear. You need escorting?'

'Nah, we'll be fine. Thanks for your help.'

Ten minutes later they were standing with NVD paperwork in hand and Dave was pointing out the stock.

'Okay, this NVD or National Vendor Declaration form here says there's three hundred and ninety-two hoggets from Gindarla Station. Now, I know from my work that's out on the Nullarbor and so the country up there is full of red dirt, grey-green bushes and clover burr. When I see this line of sheep I'd expect that their wool would have a red tinge to it from the dirt.' He swept his eyes over the pens. 'Like these ones here. And see this?' he tapped the drawing on a sheep's ear. 'This is the earmark. An earmark is a unique owner's identifying mark made in the animal's ear when they're lambs. If the animal is sold on from the farm it was born on, then there's a pink tag with the brand of the farm they've gone to. A brand is also a unique form of ID for properties.'

'How the hell do you tell that?' Brad wanted to know. But Kane had hightailed it over the fence and now had a hogget sitting on its rump as he held the ear.

'See this?' Kane said and held the ear straight for them both to see.

'That's right,' Dave said. 'And look, sometimes earmarks are hard to match. There's a bloke on the lamb marking cradle who hasn't done it before and can make a hash of it, tear the ear or similar, but there're other ways to check. Like I said, look at the wool, the sheep. Hoggets can have no more than two adult teeth. There's burr on the belly. See here?' he pointed to the small clover burr that clung, entangled in the wool.

'And this,' now he pointed to the tags in the ear, 'this is the brand that identifies the stock as owned by Gindarla. So, even though, I can't quite make out the earmark, I'm confident this animal is in the right pen.'

Brad looked as if someone had bamboozled him good and proper. 'I didn't know there were so many checks and balances in the agricultural industry,' he said.

Dave nodded. 'There has to be. Lots of reasons why. Disease, theft, ownership arguments between neighbours.'

'Okay, what about these ones?' Kane asked. 'Brand is . . .' He jumped the fence and read out the tag. 'The crimp is finer than the ones we just looked at. Got a dark oily grey-black colour covering the tip of the fleece. I'd say these have come from the south-west or some place where there's a high rainfall.'

Dave nodded. 'Quick study,' he told him.

Kane flashed a large grin. 'Cheers, boss.'

Dave opened his mouth, then shut it.

Sucker-punched again.

CHAPTER 18

George pushed back the bedcovers and got slowly out of bed. At seventy-four, he was still in pretty good shape, but there were mornings when his whole body ached and he found it hard to move.

Today was one of those days.

'Not surprising, Jinx,' he told the black cat who was sitting upright on the chair in the corner of the bedroom. Jinx always seemed to take a dim view of him, glaring as George shrugged into the dressing gown. 'I don't suppose there's many my age who will get into the race with a mob of lambs and needle and drench them. They love to put up a fight, those little buggers.'

Jinx answered with a flick of his tail, and George wasn't sure if she was critical of the person who was put on this earth to feed her, his antics in the sheep yards, or just disapproving in general. Cats never seemed happy about anything, in his opinion.

Despite Jinx's constant disapproval, George was glad for the cat's company. He'd never married and was an only child. From the day his mother had died, he'd been on his own.

Some days he was sad his family name wouldn't live on; other days, usually when the ABC had nothing good to report on the news, he was glad he didn't have any children or grandchildren on this earth.

Slippers now encasing his feet, George went through his morning ritual, as he'd done every day since his mother had died and he'd had to live by himself.

First, he lit the gas stove and put the kettle on. Then he found the cat food and poured a little into Jinx's food tray, before hitting the on button of the remote and bringing up the early morning news on a commercial channel.

The news anchor was dressed far too well for early morning news, he thought. Hair and makeup too perfect, clothes too upmarket. Not that he knew what upmarket was, only that the blouse and jacket looked like they'd be more at home in a boardroom than in his kitchen at five am.

He picked up his coffee mug from the dish drainer and put a heaped spoon of coffee and two sugars in the cup, while he stood at the bench, watching the news.

'And now to our reporter, who is in the township of Kallygarn, with the latest details on the explosion at the shire offices. Tania, what a catastrophic thing to happen to a small country town. Do you have any updates?'

George's head whipped up at the sound of the town's name and he tightened his grip on the spoon. The young

178

reporter was dressed in a heavy coat and gloved hands, which were wrapped around a microphone. She was staring straight down the barrel of the camera, right at George.

'Thanks, Monica. Yes, dawn is yet to break here in Kallygarn, yet the site is very active with more police and a fresh forensic team.'

The camera panned around to show floodlights lighting up the rubble and many people still combing through the debris.

Jinx wrapped herself around George's legs and he reached down to pat her, not taking his eyes off the TV.

'It's taken some time to get a statement from the police, but last night Senior Sergeant John Campbell, Officer in Charge at the Kallygarn Police Station, came forward to issue a statement.

'Now, Monica, what's interesting about Senior Sergeant Campbell's statement is that he is not in charge of this investigation. As you'll hear, Major Crime, along with other police units, are heading up this inquiry, but they've appointed Senior Sergeant Campbell as the spokesman. This statement came through last night and we'll listen to him now.'

The kettle let out a shrill whistle and continued until George leaned over and turned the gas off with a grunt.

'Evening, everyone, I'd like to update you with the proceedings of this inquiry. At approximately two thirty am on Monday, an explosive device was triggered at the Kallygarn Shire Council offices, resulting in the destruction of the building, due to the blast and subsequent fire.' Senior Sergeant Campbell looked at the camera and shuffled his papers, while journalists jostled for prime position to best hear his words.

George poured water into his cup and stirred, before taking it to the kitchen table and sitting down, his eyes never leaving the screen.

'The investigation is ongoing, and we are still assessing the crime scene. There has been a large amount of collateral damage to surrounding buildings. In total fifteen premises have been affected, being both business and residential and with varying amounts of damage. A radius of five hundred metres surrounding the shire building has been impacted.'

Jinx was now on the table and George leaned forward and gently picked up the cat before dropping her on the ground. She let out a loud yowl in protest.

'Shh,' George told her. 'I need to listen. There might be something important here.'

'Fortunately, no injuries have been reported although many people are shaken by this event, and it will leave a long-lasting imprint on our small community.' Now the senior sergeant straightened and looked into the camera and through to everyone in their houses. 'This was a deliberate attack.'

The pause was so long, George didn't realise he was holding his breath, until the police officer spoke again, and he had to drag in more air.

'A deliberate attack,' he reiterated. 'And as a result, the Major Crime Squad along with the Bomb Squad, Forensics and local resources will be continuing the investigation over coming weeks. The specific target of the event is yet to be established as the building was occupied by a number of government agencies.'

The jostling on the TV screen became more intense and he stopped, waiting until everything had died down before he continued.

'Motive remains to be established and we are requesting anyone with any information to come forward to police here in Kallygarn or contact Crime Stoppers. People with information may remain anonymous if they wish.'

The senior sergeant hadn't moved his eyes from the camera, and George felt the weight of his stare. He squirmed in his seat.

'Questions?' Senior Sergeant Campbell asked as the reporters were recovering from his words: *This was a deliberate attack*.

The first journalist shot her hand in the air and yelled out at the same time. 'Has a reward been offered for information?'

'Not at this stage.'

The next journalist leaned forward with a microphone. 'Has anyone claimed responsibility?'

'Not at this stage.' The police officer looked uncomfortable, George thought, as he shifted from foot to foot while microphones kept moving in front of his face.

'Is there a dollar figure on estimated damage?'

'That's yet to be determined. Now if there's nothing more?' He waited less than one second and then turned to go just as another question was fired at him. The voice was loud, but respectful so the police officer stopped.

'Senior Sergeant Campbell, as far as I can establish, the only other bomb blast Western Australia has ever had that was similar to this attack was the car bombing last year that killed a retired police officer and his friend. Is it possible the two are linked?'

George sucked in his breath. He was staring so hard at the screen it felt like his eyes were coming out of his head.

Senior Sergeant Campbell seemed to consider the man's words, then shook his head. 'We have found nothing to connect the two.'

'I imagine you wouldn't have had time to assess all the evidence. Would it be fair to say, you could still find a link?'

Now Campbell held up his hands. 'That's all,' he told the press firmly. 'You'll be notified when we have more information.' He turned his tall frame against the cameras and the further barrage of questions that were hurled at him as he walked away.

The shot brought Tania back into the frame. 'So, as you've heard, Monica, the police really have very little to go on, other than that it was a deliberate act. Let's hope someone from the public can help. If you do have information, please call the number on your screen. Back to you.'

Monica smiled benignly. 'Thanks, Tania. On to another highly contentious issue . . .'

George took a sip of his coffee, absentmindedly stroking Jinx, while he stared into nothingness, replaying the interview.

A few minutes later, he got up, dressed and walked out to the ute, putting his hat on as he went.

The ute started on the third attempt. Sometimes the poor old vehicle was a bit like him these days—it needed longer to warm up than the average Joe. She was younger than George, by about twenty years, and she rattled and clanged a bit, but, as he said to Cheryl last delivery day: 'Reckon she'll see me out. No point in getting a new one. Wouldn't know how to work the computer engines and CD players and the like. Much easier when we could fix an engine with a bit of elbow grease and knowledge.'

Cheryl had agreed, but she was only a young thing. Fifty if she was lucky, he guessed, so it wasn't likely she understood.

The road followed a straight-lined fence that headed north–south, and the sun was about to peek over the horizon, so he pulled his sleeves down. Coldest part of the day was just before the dawn and that was now.

Gee, these crops were looking good. As long as there was one more rain, probably about another half inch, they would finish off nicely. Then there were only the frosts to worry about as they could cause a decrease in yields. After living here all his life, he knew they'd come, as they did every year. It wasn't if, rather when, and how much damage.

He leaned his elbow out the open window and breathed in the icy air as he drove.

Just before the shed, he stopped and got out of the ute, leaving the engine running while he walked out into the crop that was nearly mid-calf high. Not as thick or lush as the wheat crops down south. This was marginal country: twelve- to fifteen-inch rainfall in the old language—enough to grow a profitable crop, just so long as the rain fell within the growing season.

Yep, these crops looked good, and they were all seeded without any of the new mod-con equipment. Just his little sixteen-run combine and 866 International tractor. Not that any of the young ones would recognise his machinery.

Tugging at one of the wheat plants, George inspected the roots, then the rest of the plant. This was his sixty-fourth crop. Sixty-fifth if he included the year his dad passed. He was only nine when his old man had died in his sleep, and even though too young, he'd wanted to shoulder some of the responsibility and help his mum with seeding and harvesting that year. School had made that difficult and there had been only one way to fix that.

George left school the following year and been on this farm ever since. Who knew how many seasons were left for him? That was in the lap of the gods. But what George did know was that no one would make him leave his farm until he was dead. He was born in the house he lived in now and he would die there, too.

Oh, there were people who laughed at him. His machinery was small and old, but he could fix every problem himself and he didn't want to learn about this GSP or PGS or GPS system, or whatever the hell it was called, that the young fella from the machinery dealership had turned up to tell him about the other day.

'You don't have to steer the tractor, it does it for you,' he told George with glee. 'You've just got to turn it at the end of the run. The rest of the time, the GPS will keep the machinery in a straight line. Once it's all been mapped from the satellite of course.'

To George, the young man had been speaking gobbledy-gook.

'And why would I want to have a "whatever" to steer the tractor, when I'm perfectly capable of doing that myself? Been doing it a while.'

'No, no, you just have to be there to turn it around at the end of the paddock and head it back from where you started.'

George had harrumphed and seen the boy on his way.

His seed and fertiliser came in small bags instead of the massive triple road trains. Bulka bags held one or two tonnes, but even that little amount of fertiliser in one hit was too much for him, so he used his very small auger, that still had the engine on the top of the barrel rather than underneath—another old piece of equipment—to move the fertiliser from the two-tonne bulka bags, into the smaller, more manageable twenty-five kilo ones. They were a little on the heavy side for him now, but with a bit of effort, he could still get them onto the back of the combine and empty them into the fertiliser box and that's the way he'd always sowed his crop and he wasn't about to change.

Happy with the way the wheat was looking, George headed to the super shed. This was where he kept of the fertiliser.

He pulled up in the ute, leaving it running, while he looked at the door. Nerves trickled through his body, before he gave himself a good talking to. 'Come on, man. When has anything ever been solved by not tackling the problem head on.' Still, he sat in the ute. 'Let's go,' he said to the windscreen.

This time George convinced himself to open the door.

The loud, high-pitched screeching from the unoiled hinges sent pigeons, which had been roosting on the roof, high into the morning sky, cooing in fright. They didn't bother George.

Holding his breath he peered into the dimness. Pinpricks of light cut through the murky shadows from the gaps in the tin. There against the back wall, covered in a heavy tarp, was the fertiliser he'd augered into bags back when seeding was underway.

He stood in the silence, waiting for what? The answer?

'I don't know,' he muttered to himself. 'Not convinced.' George ducked inside.

Last week he'd driven by and seen the doors open and tarp flapping. With rain forecast, he'd stopped and secured it yet again. Somehow, during the winter months, the gusts continued to howl through the spaces and force the doors apart. Wreaking havoc by causing the tarp to lift in the wind and not protecting the bags enough. The super shed had floor tilt cemented the wrong way, thanks to some shoddy workmanship about forty years ago, meaning the water could flow inwards.

One thing he'd learned as a young bloke was that fertiliser and water mixed together turned into one great hard lump, rendering it useless. The stuff was expensive and hard to come by to have that happen.

There had been whispers that fertiliser companies were phasing out ammonium nitrate in favour of urea.

Ridiculous!

According to the salesman, that type could be used to make bombs, and with the way society is these days, well . . . Then he'd gone onto say all the trucks which carted fertiliser were GPS-tracked now. There was that bloody acronym again—the one George wasn't too sure about, but he thought it meant that the people in the office knew exactly where the truck was all the time. What was the need for that? A call to the driver on the VH radio would tell the office exactly where the truck was!

Although he supposed if someone wanted that fertiliser and hijacked a truck, and then used the fertiliser to make a bomb . . .

Bombs like the one on the TV this morning.

He lifted the tarp now and jumped a little as two mice scurried out from underneath, heading towards the old twenty-tonne silo that held grain for their breakfast.

Bags full of ammonium nitrate were lined up just as he'd left them after he'd finished seeding six months earlier. In rows of five and lines of ten. Six months is a long time to remember back to when you were seventy-four years old, he told himself. Perhaps there had always been forty-five bags, not fifty. Making a mistake was absolutely on the cards.

The other question was who would know that he kept this fertiliser here, around the back, out of the weather, in an old shed, under a tarp? Almost one hundred kilometres from the closest town?

'No one,' he said aloud. 'Absolutely bloody no one. You're being ridiculous. Letting your imagination run with the fairies as dear old Mum, god rest her soul, would have said.'

Counted the bags again, coming up with the same answer. Forty-five. Well, he could be sure that number hadn't changed from yesterday when he'd checked.

Were five bags enough to blow up a shire office? He doubted it. The things he knew about explosives could be counted on one hand—they were used to bust up rock in the paddocks or blowing through deep layers of rock when a dam was being built.

A while back, George had tried to shift a granite boulder with a stick of gelly he'd conned a mate from the mining world into giving him. Like about sixty years back. Hadn't worked, and he'd put it down as bad luck, never trying again.

Jinx appeared and jumped on top of the tarp with a loud meow.

'What do you think?' he asked the cat, unsurprised at her appearance.

Not answering, she only glowered at him through her yellow slit eyes.

'You're right, Jinx,' George told her. 'You usually are. I didn't have fifty bags left over. Only forty-five. I'd forgotten. Going senile in my old age. Better not let Cheryl know. She'll have me in aged care before I know what's happened and you'll have to find a new home.' He pulled the tarp back over the bags and fastened it down with bricks and heavy lumps of wood.

Grabbing Jinx, he threw her gently inside the cab. The way she flicked her tail, told of how beneath her the cat thought the action was, but she jumped to the back of the seat when George got in.

'We'll check those ewes and lambs I needled yesterday, Jinx,' he told her.

Curling her tail around her feet, Jinx sat on the seat and carefully watched out of the windscreen.

A strange feeling settled in George's gut. The part he relied on to help him make good decisions. Was it fifty or forty-five?

Uncomfortable, he pursed his lips, sure that he was, in fact, remembering correctly.

There had been fifty bags at the end of seeding.

CHAPTER 19

Darryl grunted as he lifted a twenty-five kilo bag—the label letting everyone know that it was mineral supplements for the ewes—onto the tray of the ute. There were five in all and once out in the paddock, he'd stack them in the pump shed.

No one except him ever went out there.

In the distance, the motorbike engines were revving and fading, revving and fading. One of the bikies—the bloke's name had been weird Spook or Spock?—had come to see him yesterday to say they'd be leaving.

Spook or Spock handed five hundred-dollar notes from the inner pocket of his leather jacket. 'Thanks for letting us camp here, mate. Nice spot you've got.'

Darryl's eyes had gleamed at the cash, stopping himself from snatching at the notes. 'No trouble,' he'd said. Holding up the money, he'd told Spook or Spock to 'Come back any time.'

With the motorbike running, Spook or Spock, had winked from behind his helmet and revved the accelerator taking only seconds to leave Darryl alone once more.

Now the bike engines cut across the clear, still air. Noise travelled long distances easily when the atmosphere was unmoving and cold.

His phone chirped. Jasmine.

Are you coming home for smoko?

Be there soon, he typed. *Checking the ewes.*

At the end of the driveway, out of habit, he checked for traffic. Not that he expected any. It was a rare few who ventured this far from Chapman Hill. On the Hubler Track there wouldn't be tourists unless they were lost. This was a road for locals, because the road finished where George's driveway began. Beyond that nothing but Crown land and bush, and no roads.

Darryl loved the isolation. No one was looking over his fence, telling him his stock were underfed, or had flies. The closest farmers minded their own business, even though they were vaguely aware what their neighbours were doing.

Like the other morning—Darryl knew George had gone into Chapman Hill about eight thirty. It was his ute with its rattles, bangs and loud exhaust that told everyone the elderly man was on the move, way before they saw him.

Talk around the locals was they were all glad of the noise because if the ute was going, the owner had to be driving, which meant George was alive and, at seventy something, that was always good to know.

Darryl stopped at the mailbox and checked inside, there would be nothing—mail day had just been. It was more of an excuse to make sure the bag he'd left out had been collected, which it had.

His phone rang this time; his lawyer's name showed on the screen.

''Ello,' Darryl answered.

'Darryl, it's Greg Bales. How are you?'

Sucking in a breath, Darryl tried not to let his anxiety rise to the surface. He reached in through the window and turned off the ute, leaning against the warmth of the bonnet.

'Greg,' he acknowledged, 'I'm sure you're not ringing with great news because I've already made an appointment to come and see you next week.'

'Yes, my secretary has told me. Look, you need to know a couple of things. I'm aware both you and Jasmine have been concerned about a gaol sentence. For some time, I had been hopeful to avoid this via the amendments to the Environmental Act under Section 51C. Because you're an individual, there was a chance to reduce this to a fine. A sizeable fine of two hundred and fifty thousand, but—'

An invisible fist punched Darryl in the stomach. 'I can't pay that,' he stuttered.

'Well, none of this matters because the assessor has been in contact—' Greg paused as Darryl's heart kicked up a notch. Then another, and another. 'There has been a more thorough investigation of the creek system in question.'

Darryl wanted to ask if that was allowed to happen, so far into proceedings, but his mouth was too dry.

'They are now claiming that you've caused environmental harm to the land.'

'What the hell?' Darryl straightened up. 'I haven't been near the creek. The area they're talking about isn't even a creek, more like a tiny fall in the land. Sometimes, if there's a deluge, a bit of water might run. How can they say I've caused . . . What did you call it?'

'Environmental damage. Look, Darryl, it doesn't matter whether you've done this or not nor whether it's a creek, stream or waterfall. The fact is environmental damage means the penalties change. Of course, I'll be doing my best to get them dismissed. I must inform you, however, with all this talk about damage to the environment, well, it is a very touchy subject and the law is looking for people to make an example of.'

Darryl looked skyward. The blueness was still there, when really, it should be under his feet because his world has just turned upside.

'Are you there, Darryl?'

A white cockatoo flew overhead and glided off to perch in a tree. Oh, to be so free!

Darryl didn't want to be here, listening to Greg tell him about the penalties. If only he'd never chanced the dream, believed he could make a go of being a farmer. Believed he could build a house. Nothing good had come of his goals, despite his promises to Jasmine, his hard work and effort.

If only he'd taken a different path. He could have been a mechanic or fitter and turner. Worked in the mines. Anything but a farmer, and a useless one at that.

If only . . .

'Darryl?'

'Yeah, uh, sorry. Couldn't hear you, the cockies are pretty loud.

'Did you hear me say the penalties have changed?'

'Yeah. Yeah, I did.' Darryl looked at his boots. The red sock he put on this morning was peeking out at him from where the sole had pulled away from his boot. No wonder he'd got wet feet when he was loading the bags. 'What do—' He took a breath and looked at the sky again. It was still where it should be. 'What do they change to?'

'There's a big difference. If serious harm was caused with intentional or criminal negligence, the fine is half a million dollars or a five-year gaol sentence.'

'What the fuck?' Darryl exploded. 'What the actual fuck? There was nothing intentional about what I did. I cleared twenty hectares so I could build a decent house in a nice area for my wife, who now, incidentally, is terminally ill. How do these bastards live with themselves? Do they think they're going to change the world by locking up normal, hardworking people? I mean, is this jerk going to come and look after my wife when his handiwork has got me locked up? She'll probably be dead or in a nursing home by the time I get out.'

'Darryl,' Greg said patiently.

Darryl blundered on. 'What did you call it? Intentional or criminal negligence. Which one is it? How do they work that out? And what is so fucking important environmentally that I should go to gaol for? Is it more significant than

194

looking after my wife? What about the livestock I have here? Who's going to look after them while I'm in the clink?' Darryl slammed his fist into the bonnet of the ute twice, leaving a deep indent. Pain ricocheted through his hand. 'And the other bloody question I have is how come they get to tell me what to do when I own this land?'

'Of course, Darryl,' Greg said calmly, 'we will fight this, but it's imperative you understand what you're up against.'

'Fine,' Darryl snapped. 'My question still stands—where are the property owner's rights? I bought this farm with my money. I've paid the interest and principal loan amounts every year with money I've earned from this land I'm standing on right now. Where are my rights?'

'It was native vegetation you cleared without a permit, Darryl. You don't have any rights.'

CHAPTER 20

Bob and Dave were both glued to the lunchtime news report on the TV. The earlier press conference at Kallygarn was playing in the motel restaurant.

The question about the bikies and the bombing had caused Johnny's welcoming face to close over. One reporter had kept throwing questions, until he shut down the media conference.

Once the reporter had thrown back to the anchor, Dave looked over at Bob, who was dabbing his mouth with a serviette.

'There we are. Deliberate. That's what we've been waiting to hear. I thought Lorri might have rung to tell us,' Dave said, putting a piece of tomato into the sandwich he was making from the lunch buffet.

Bob stirred a packet of sugar into his cup of tea.

'Lorri mightn't know yet, especially if she had to head bush. When did you talk to her last?'

'Yesterday, after we got here. Lorri said it was busy and there were a few reports that needed attending to. There were also requests from rural police stations wanting training days, similar to what I just did with Brad and Kane.'

'Hmm.' Bob lifted his cup of tea and took a sip.

'Your mate Johnny speaks pretty well.' Dave added a piece of cheese and put another slice of bread on top. 'Did you do media training when you first started?'

The stubble on Bob's chin cast a dark shadow across his pale face. Dave was nervous about how Bob was feeling today since he'd spent the few days they'd been in Stockdale in his room.

This morning, Betty had suggested it was time to head home. Dave had put her off, knowing Bob's reaction to any interference wouldn't be pretty. Perhaps he'd been too hasty.

'Yeah, and Johnny came in at top of the class. He's never been short of a word.' Bob took a breath. 'Told you he had the gift of the gab. Better him than me. Some people are comfortable in front of a camera, and I'm not one of them. The media have their uses such as when we need public assistance, but more often, they're an annoyance and a distraction. As you know, I've never willingly set foot in front of a camera.'

'Funny, not something anyone would realise when you're talking to them. You'd think they're always your best mates!' Dave said.

'Well, you attract flies with honey, not vinegar, son,' Bob said.

'True. Anyhow, I've learned a heap from watching you deal with the media.' Dave took a bite of his sandwich. 'Did you notice the interesting question about the bikie?'

Bob nodded then took a sip of his tea. 'I've been waiting for you to mention that.'

'Who was the journo?'

'Didn't recognise him.'

'Wonder if there's any drum around that line of enquiry.'

Bob looked at Dave. 'Is there a line of enquiry around the bikies? Reckon we would've heard if there was.'

'I guess you're right. But if the media—' Dave stopped speaking as a couple walked past, heading to the buffet.

'Yeah, if they've come up with the same idea as you, it'll be in a paper or on the news somewhere for sure,' Bob said grimly. 'Not sure how helpful that will be, son.'

Bob's hand shook and Dave pretended not to notice, once again hearing Betty's voice from their phone call.

Bring him home, Dave. I know he wants to be out there with you, but he's got more treatment next week. It's important to have a proper rest before he starts.

Shifting uncomfortably in his seat, Dave changed the subject. 'Anyhow, the visit to the abs went well. No problems at all. They've got a tick. And the two constables were very interested. Asked lots of good questions. One of them was brought up on farm. He'll be able to re-explain the nuts and bolts of what we talked about if needs be.'

'That's good.' Bob put down his cup and spilled a little of the hot liquid over the side and onto his hand. 'Bloody hell!' The words burst from him causing another couple at a table to look over.

Dave grabbed a serviette and started to mop up the mess. Practical help when all he wanted was to hug Bob, say it was just a bit of tea and he'd get him another cup. He was sorry this was happening to the strong, fit man he'd known only five months before.

Bob wouldn't like any of those words.

Now, the silence between them felt like a yawning black hole. So deep it could swallow them both.

'I'm done.' Bob got up and walked away.

Dave let him go. There was nothing he could do to make this better.

Putting Bob's knife and fork together on the plate, Dave dabbed again at the stain, feeling like the whole restaurant was staring at him or following Bob's slow walk through the dining room.

What were they thinking? A father and son argument?

Sick to the stomach, he took another sip of his coffee, closing his eyes. He'd never had a friend hurting so badly.

His mobile phone rang, and he reached into his pocket. *Shannon.* A smile spread across his face.

'Hey,' he said quietly. A quick glance around the dining room, showed that no one was frowning at him. Mobile phones had become a bit of a contentious issue around meals.

'Hey, yourself. How are you?'

'Going okay. Everything is fine,' he repeated, almost to convince himself. 'Thanks for your text. I'm glad we can have dinner. I'll probably be home sooner than I thought.'

'Is Bob not holding up?'

Dave's smile fell away, and he rubbed his forehead. 'He's not good, Shannon. I don't think he's sick. Not sick enough to go to a doctor at least, but . . . I don't know, maybe it's the chemo making him tired and shaky.'

'It could be. Are they the only symptoms you've noticed?'

Her concern made Dave swallow. 'He's really tired all the time. Doesn't want to come into the pub for tea, and he wasn't up to the abs visit this morning. It was the reason why we're here. Normally you wouldn't be able to stop him. I—' He broke off as a lady from another table gave him a frown over the rim of her coffee cup. Turning his back to her, Dave lowered his voice even more. 'Betty thinks we should head home. I spoke to her this morning.'

There was a muffled noise and Dave realised it was Shannon's hair brushing the phone. 'And have Bob cranky because you've gone behind his back? You told me he wanted to go bush. You should let him make that decision, not anyone else. He's still got all his faculties!'

'Cranky would be an understatement. I'd be happy with whatever decision makes him feel better.'

'Dave, while he's going through this treatment, nothing is going to make him feel better. I don't know much about chemo—thankfully, no one in my family has had cancer of any sort—but I'm sure they'd be hitting him really hard. The chemo will make him tired. It'll make him not able to focus, he'll lose his train of thought in the middle of a conversation and lots of other horrible things. There will be symptoms that he'll never tell you about. Like, have you noticed anything about his fingernails?'

'What? No.' Dave picked at his sandwich and ate a piece of cheese he pulled out.

'Check and see what they look like. I'll bet you they'll be cracked at the very least. And his fingers might be a bit swollen. Has he had any trouble with his balance? Stumbling or anything?'

'Ah . . .' Dave couldn't think.

'Chemo mucks around with your muscles so people can experience problems with balance and coordination. A side effect that you wouldn't put down to this treatment if you didn't know. Bruising is another.'

A memory slammed into Dave. Bob had side-swiped the door on the way into his hotel room yesterday. Dave assumed he'd overbalanced holding his bag, or misjudged where the frame was. Everyone did that from time to time. But the chemo was causing it? There was nothing good about this treatment.

'You know how chemo works, right?' Shannon asked.

'Only that it's supposed to kill cancer cells.'

'Yeah, but it annihilates the good ones, too. Unfortunately the drugs aren't sophisticated enough to discriminate between the two.'

There was a lump in this throat and he had to work at not crying.

'I know this is a stupid question, but are you okay? What can I do for you?' Shannon's voice was gentle, and the softness made Dave want to run to her. Draw her in to him and feel her care.

Instead, he cleared his throat a couple of times. 'I don't deserve for you to ask me that question,' he told her honestly.

It was Shannon's turn to be silent.

'I'm sorry,' Dave said. 'I'm sorry I hurt you the other night. I didn't know I was going to say what came out. That sounds stup—'

'Let's talk about this when you get back, Dave. Not on the phone.'

He tried to read her voice. She was speaking softly, with kindness. The same voice Shannon used when she blew him a kiss from the car. There was always a wave and a smile goodbye.

How different from Mel. Her expression had been sullen when he left for work.

He refocused. 'Okay. But I'm sorry. I think I stuffed up.'

Laughing a little, Shannon quipped, 'Think?'

Dave closed his eyes. 'Shit, sorry. I *know* I stuffed up.'

'Tell me how you are, Dave.'

Pushing his plate with the sandwich to the other side of the table, Dave rubbed his free hand over his face. 'I don't really know. Pretty sad. Wishing it wasn't happening. All that sort of shit.' He paused. 'There's a hell of a lot of responsibility having Bob with me and that makes me nervous, too.' He cleared his throat again. 'Um, that's the best thing to do, Shannon? I'm sorta stuck here.' His words sounded a little desperate, panicked even.

'The best thing you can do is to talk to him. Ask him what he needs.'

'Ha! You really think he's going to tell me?'

'Better than following Betty's request without his knowledge. Bob would lose his trust in you. This would be the lesser of the two evils.'

Her words had made Dave feel much lighter. 'You know what, Shannon? I reckon you're all right.'

'All right, huh? Gosh, high praise from the great Dave Burrows.' The teasing made Dave smile.

'I'd better go. Um, Shannon, can I please call you later?'

'Let me know how you get on.' Shannon hung up.

⁓

Dave stood outside of Bob's door and took a nervous breath. Tentatively, he tapped. 'It's me,' he called, probably unnecessarily. 'Can I come in?'

There was no answer.

'Bob?'

The sound of the toilet flushing and another door opening. 'Yeah, I'm here. Come in.'

Inside the dim room, Dave saw Bob's bag on the bed, packed and ready to go.

'What time do you want to leave?' Bob asked, standing with his hands on his hips.

Dave read defiance. Especially when Bob didn't wait for an answer.

'I think we should head up the highway towards Coolgardie and do the run back in to Perth that way.'

Dave assessed this piece of information and decided against saying no. 'Quicker to go back the South Coast Highway, the way we came down, isn't it?'

'Yeah, it is. No need to go rushing back, though. You said yourself that Lorri had mentioned there was nothing pressing. The country police stations will wait for your workshops.' His words were short and clipped, daring Dave to disregard his comments.

Bob didn't pull rank often, but when he did, there was no point trying to change his mind.

This time was different. Dave might have been an unwilling boss, but he was the boss just the same.

'What about we start heading back to Perth?'

'Didn't I just say that's what I wanted to do? The long way.' Anger flashed across his face. With a decisive step towards the door, he said, 'Come on, let's get on the road.'

Dave looked around, wishing Shannon was next to him. She'd know what to say. Pussyfooting around wasn't working; it was time for something to change.

Dave took a breath. The words came out, hitting Bob fair in the chest.

'What the actual fuck, Bob? You're crook. Even a blind man could see that. If you back to Perth like this, I'll be in more trouble than ninety men. Let's get one thing clear. I don't want to take you back home either. It should be you and me on the road like we always are. To go into the bar and have a few beers. Shoot the shit with the locals. But, news flash. You're not up to it, and the sooner you realise that the better. You're my responsibility and I want you to be okay.' Dave's chest heaved with emotion and heat stung his eyes as he tried make Bob understand how worried he was.

How much he wanted Bob to be all right.

How much he loved him.

'I want you to be okay.' The words had a different meaning when he whispered them now.

Bob sank onto the bed, his throat moving in time with his jaw as he clenched and unclenched his teeth.

He said nothing and Dave waited.

And waited.

And waited some more.

Shit, had he overstepped the mark? He should've just kept his mouth shut and not listened to Shannon.

'Bob?' he said quietly. 'Mate?'

Then his stomach plummeted, and he didn't want to be in the room.

A muffled noise.

Bob was crying.

Fuck. Dave put an arm around Bob's shoulders. The situation was crap, and it wasn't going to change any time soon. Even if Bob responded well to the chemo, recovery would take months, if not years, to get over the long-lasting effect it was having on his body.

Dave leaned his head against Bob's and held him tightly. 'If I could change this, I would,' he said.

Bob nodded and took a couple of breaths before getting control of himself again. He cleared his throat. 'Sorry, son.

I didn't mean . . .' He clapped his hand over Dave's and patted hard.

'S'alright. What can I do to help?' Dave asked, hoping that's how Shannon would've asked Bob.

His friend gave a helpless shrug. 'There's nothing really. Except to keep me out of the city as much as possible.'

Dave opened his mouth then shut it again. He'd asked and Bob had told him. Just because he didn't like the answer, didn't mean he should say no. Bob's wishes were the ones that should be adhered to. But could he do what his mate wanted?

'Look, son—yeah, this bloody treatment is knocking me around. You can see that and I'm feeling like shit, but—' he grabbed hold of Dave's hand and looked him in the eyes again '—I can't give up yet.' His voice was as impassioned as Dave's had been only moments before. 'I can't give up yet,' he repeated. 'This—' he waved his hand towards his bag and Dave '—it's not about the work. It's about me. About normality. Because normal makes me feel as if I'm still alive. Which let me tell you is good, because there are some bloody days I wish I was dead.' He shuffled around on the bed. 'I'm a cop. A detective. That title means everything to me. Everything, son. It's who I am. I've got—' He cleared his throat and took a deep breath in through his nose. 'I've got to be here. Can you try to understand? Please?'

Dave could, but not if it was going to kill Bob in the process. He told him so. 'If you keep going the way you are, you'll have to go home. There won't be a choice.' He tried to inject some humour into the conversation. 'I mean, seriously, can you imagine how Betty would react if I delivered you back to her like you are?'

'I'd really like to stay out bush a bit longer.'

Running his fingers through his hair, Dave shook his head, unsure of what to do.

The alarm on Bob's phone beeped. A stark and shitty reminder of what they were talking about.

Blowing out his breath, Dave said, 'I'm sure you do. As I've had to tell my daughters when they're having a temper tantrum, we don't always get what we want.'

Giving a small smile, Bob reached into his pocket and took out the two plastic vials. He shook out a few tablets and popped them into his mouth then took the glass from the bedside table.

'Look, son.' Bob was back in control now, his voice stronger. 'This might be difficult to understand, but this can't be the end. Here, in this dingy motel room. I want to nab some bastard for cattle stealing, or find a bloke who's got a load of sheep and no paperwork. He sighed as if all his energy had seeped into the dismal brown bedspread he was sitting on. 'If I go back to Perth, I'm going to be at home and I'm real—' The shakiness was back. 'I'm real scared I'm gonna die there.'

'No,' Dave said, forcefully. 'That's not—'

'I can fight this, Dave.' Bob grabbed Dave's hand. 'I can and I will. Look, I know I get tired, and I can be a pain in the arse. But, hey, you should be used to that. I'm staying.' He shrugged as if putting an exclamation mark on the end of his words.

Silence.

'Right,' Dave said. 'If that's the way it's going to be, I'll carry you as much as I can. But Bob,' he leaned forward and spoke quietly, 'before we leave, you are going to the hospital to get the all-clear. There's no argument. If you check out okay, then, we'll make tracks to Coolgardie. You gotta meet me halfway here, mate.'

Bob smiled. There were no tears anywhere in sight when he said, 'If I'd ever had a son, I'd have wanted him to be like you, Dave. And since I don't get any damn choice, and this is a battle I have to fight, knowing you are going to be there means more than the world.'

The air left Dave's lungs as he looked at Bob, who was now getting off the bed with a new purpose.

'Let's get on, son. We've got things to do.'

CHAPTER 21

It was the ideal night. Dark and rainy just the same as when the first explosion happened.

Perfect conditions to blow things up.

As he stood at the window, he imagined how the night would play out.

The streets of Kallygarn empty, quiet; the houses dark. Of course, the streetlights would still be on; he didn't have control over them, more's the pity.

What he did have control over was the ignition and the aftermath. That excited him.

Outside, a soft, moist breeze was meandering down the street. The call of an owl broke the silence. Jerry cans heavy in his hands, he kept to the shadows, sneaking towards his target.

The stick of gel was in his pocket, and he hoped he would have time to get back home before it exploded.

He wasn't sure if he'd feel the heat or debris as it rained down across the town. Would he smell the burning? He might feel the ground shake while on high alert, waiting in anticipation.

Ideally, before the blast happened, he'd be back home, in bed. If that was the case, he'd be able to join the rest of the town as they collectively asked why. What could have happened to cause another explosion so soon, in a tiny country town, where nothing ever happened?

'Bullshit,' he thought. There was always something illegal going on. He'd caught Gavin Freat in the parking bay on the outskirts of town selling weed a few weeks ago.

Weed! In his town! The ownership he felt over Kallygarn had started from when he was a boy and he'd tried his darndest to protect it and its occupants from any scum who tried to settle here.

Gavin had believed him when he threatened to let the cops know about his little side business. Of course, Gavin had given up the greens and begged him not to tell his parents. Good. The little snot was scared.

He'd taken the stash, threatened the bastard within an inch of his life, then walked away, knowing he'd have something to smoke a bit later on that evening. Do as I say, not as I do.

It had been hard not to enjoy the power trip.

What Gavin didn't know was that he would never go to the police. The useless cops in this town weren't even worth pissing on if they were on fire. He handed out his own punishments.

About three weeks ago young Jenny Osborne had caught his attention. It had been pure luck he'd seen her slip two packets of snacks and some biscuits into her backpack while she walked the aisles of the supermarket. Jenny hadn't known he was observing her. She'd looked over her shoulder and made sure no one was watching before she'd walked out nonchalantly, her backpack slung over her shoulder.

A few minutes later, he'd found her and two friends in a back lane, laughing about how stupid the woman on the till was. They were just about to open a packet of cheese Twisties.

Again, he threatened them with the police unless they handed everything over.

A few frightened 'sorry, sirs' before they scuttled towards the netball courts for training. That's where they should have been in the first place. Playing sport and keeping out of mischief.

Kallygarn should be thanking him. Especially for the punishment he'd handed out three years ago. Gee, he was most proud of that one. Tristan Michaels was a mongrel and probably should have been reported to the cops, *if* they could do their job properly.

His crime? Spying on girls in the netball court change rooms through the skylight. He was a sick puppy.

One afternoon as he'd closed his office he'd noticed Tristan laid out flat on the roof of the change rooms. There was nothing unusual about that—he was an air-conditioning mechanic and he must've servicing the club's air-conditioner.

But then he had noticed Tristan in the same spot three weeks in a row. A visit to the change rooms later that evening, after the reserves had finished training, had confirmed his suspicions.

The people of Kallygarn had different opinions of him and some people thought he was a loose cannon. Someone who acted on impulse. A reactive fella.

The town's people really didn't know him at all.

What he was, in fact, was incredibly patient. Five weeks later—the week before the grand final—he'd found Tristan eating his lunch in the park. Alone. And he'd pounced.

Oh, that conversation had given him such satisfaction. Kallygarn didn't need the cops when he was here.

'Tristan,' he'd said as he strolled up to the bench seat and sat alongside the sleazy fucker, 'how's the business going? Busy?'

Tristan, surprised at his appearance, had said g'day. It hadn't taken long to get him talking about himself—everyone's favourite subject was themselves.

'And tell me . . .' he'd finally begun, when Tristan had stopped yabbering on about air-conditioners, coolant, filters, and other shit he really didn't give a toss about. 'Tell me when you first worked out that you liked to watch little girls in the change rooms?'

Tristan had just about choked on his sandwich. 'What the hell?'

'Oh yeah, I've seen you. The last few weeks. On the roof. Come on, Tris, you know what I'm talking about. Don't need to play the innocent with me. We can talk man to man. It's okay, mate.'

The confusion on Tristan's face had been marvellous.

He'd smiled sweetly, in control, and cocked his head to the side, waiting for Tristan to answer.

'I'm not sure what you mean.' Guilt had been written all over Tristan's face, and he'd looked a little green around the gills.

'Pretty sure you do. You're a sick bastard, aren't you?' he'd said. 'Now, Tristan, I've got a proposition for you.'

Tristan's expression had been hopeful.

Then he'd dealt the killer blow.

'How about you get the fuck outta my town or I get the cops involved. I'm sure they'd be very interested to hear what I could tell them.'

Spluttering, Tristan said, 'You can't prove it. The cops wouldn't believe you. Johnny's one of my good mates.'

'Do you really want to test that theory?' With an insincere smile, he'd got up from the park bench. 'You've got a week, Tristan. Get out of town in a week and I'll say no more. You don't? Well, you won't want to know what's coming your way.'

Three days passed before he'd heard from a lady on the street. 'That nice young man, Tristan, you know, from the air-conditioning business? Well, he's up and left! Gone interstate apparently. Just like that. His mother is very unwell so the rumours say. Not supposed to last the month and he needed to be with her. Such a loss to the town.'

He'd nodded and tutted and agreed, yes, it was a loss. And, no, he didn't know who would service all the air-conditioners in Kallygarn now.

Keeping the law and order in this town was his mission. It didn't bother him that nobody else knew. The town's people were safe under his watch and that was enough.

Unaware of his work were the police, just as they were of the underbelly of Kallygarn. And, yes, there was one. Sure, Johnny's squad picked up the drunk drivers or the mums who were going a bit quick through the school zones. Small things. The stuff that was minor.

It had been him, not the police, who had ensured that Gavin wouldn't supply weed, nor Jenny steal again.

He was damn sure Tristan *would* sneak another look at young girls.

But not in his town.

A little pat on the back before he refocused on tonight. There was a family who needed to be removed from his town, and the blast that had levelled the shire council building had given him an idea.

See? He was patient.

His alarm had sounded at midnight. Before getting out of bed, he ran through the checklist. The weather site still showed rain was due. He needed at least a few millimetres to wash away any footprints but not so much it affected the blast.

He dressed in black tracksuit pants and a black jumper. A black ski mask was in his hand, ready to pull over his face before leaving the house. Another glance at his watch. He'd scheduled half an hour to get to the site, then another fifteen minutes to set the bomb.

It was nearly time.

Tonight's mission was important. The multinational companies had been buying into country towns. This was unacceptable for many reasons. One being locals weren't employed by these companies—they preferred to bring their own staff in. Secondly, the money didn't go back into the local community.

Disappointed and annoyed had been an understatement when he'd found the new service station had a family in from out of town managing it. A family he hadn't liked on first meeting. Although, to be fair, when they first arrived he'd tried to give them a go.

He'd refuelled his car there one afternoon. Yes, the diesel had been adequate. A bit cheaper than the other service station in town, but not enough to make a huge difference to anyone's weekly budget.

Inside the servo, he'd chosen a sandwich and some hot chips to test their takeaway options. The ham and tomato sandwich hadn't been impressive—brought in on a truck and made somewhere in a capital city. He guessed the bread was full of preservatives so it stayed fresh. The chips were greasy and there had been dirt on the floor inside the kitchen! Obviously tracked in by a staff member. Food left

215

out on the counters. All the kitchen was missing was a few flies. His stomach had churned.

Even worse was the sullen, greasy-haired young man behind the counter who had rung up his items without smiling or talking to him. How did this family think they were going to fit into Kallygarn if they didn't talk to the locals? Keeping to themselves wouldn't help.

A week later he'd called in again, just to make sure he hadn't caught them on a bad day. He'd rolled into the restaurant, smiling and jovial. This time wanting to introduce himself and welcome them to Kallygarn.

It was a different teenager behind the counter this time, but the response was the same. No smile, no talking, no interest.

That was when the anger had burst through his chest, and he'd asked to use the toilets. He had to calm down in private, before he left.

Inside the toilets had been pure filth. The build-up of dirt made it seem as they hadn't been cleaned since the family had arrived.

He considered himself a fair man, but Kallygarn was not a third-world country. It was unacceptable the toilets in the town's service station had stains in the bowl, a strong smell of urine and sewage, and paper towels screwed up on the floor. He'd taken one step in and three steps out of the room quickly, his hand over his nose.

That day their fate had been sealed.

He started to play with ideas on how to remove them from town. So far their crimes were filthy toilets, substandard

216

food and refusing to integrate with the community. More appeared over time.

The town would thank him later. When they realised he had saved them, he would accept their thanks with humility and gratitude.

CHAPTER 22

'I've got the all-clear.' Bob told Dave.

'Thank fuck for that!' Dave couldn't hold in his relief.

'Yep,' Bob slammed the door of the troopy and grinned. He almost bounced in his seat like an excited child. That was when Dave realised Bob had been as concerned about himself as he had.

'Right, we've got the clearance from the hospital, I'll take you for a drive around the tourist loop before we go,' Dave made sure he kept the words light.

'Good idea. Reckon last time I was in Stockdale must've been when I was chasing a group of fellas who'd been releasing goats and pigs in the national park east of town,' Bob said. 'Didn't get to do anything touristy.'

'Do we ever?' Dave asked.

'Not really.' Bob was interrupted by his phone ringing. 'Here's my girl! Hello, love.'

Dave flicked on the blinker, listening to Bob's side of the conversation with Betty.

'Yeah, love, Dave's looking after me real good.'

'No, love, you don't need to be at all worried.'

'Yeah, getting enough sleep and taking my pills.'

'I understand that you're worried, but everything's going really well. No need for any concerns. I know you think I need a rest before the next round of chemo and I promise that will happen.'

It was the old Bob—not completely up to his usual standard of larrikinism, but nearly—and the knot in Dave's stomach shrunk a little.

'It's not raining,' Dave said.

'And thank god you're a detective,' Bob quipped.

Surprised, Dave let out a laugh. It felt good. 'What I was meaning was I'll stop up here and you can walk over to the lookout for a squiz. Even though it's cloudy, the water's always vividly blue. Something to do with the sand apparently. Might even see some dolphins, they're always putting on a show.'

'It's different country from what I'm used to, that's for sure,' Bob said, looking out the window.

'Yeah, I prefer the red dirt to this sandy plain dirt, too, but the sea is kind of nice for a change.'

The car park was empty save for one couple. The woman was dressed in tight tracksuit pants and a sports shirt while the man had on shorts and a singlet. They were both bending over, trying to catch their breath. A dog was stretched out on the bitumen, puffing hard, too.

'Oh, see there,' Dave said, pointing to the woman wearing the black top. 'She was in the pub last night. Con, I think her name was. Man, has she got some anger towards the cops. I reckon Roger might have to watch his back with her.'

Bob looked over at her, interested. 'Oh yeah, what's she upset about?'

'Brother was killed in a car accident and she's blaming the police. I tried to suggest to Brad and Kane that a little community policing wouldn't go astray, but I don't think I got through.' Dave turned off the troopy and looked over at Bob. 'I feel for her, but at the same time, she's got something very defiant about her, so I'm a little wary.'

'Serious? She's one of them?' Bob leaned forward and opened the car door. 'What do you think she'll do if she sees us here?'

'Probably nothing. I doubt she'd even remember I was there, because she was really giving it to Roger. But I've got the background now, so if she does say anything, I'm prepared.'

Grey clouds were gently drifting across the sky and, even though the rain had gone, the wind had a chill level that was icy.

'Glad it's not pissing down,' Bob said, putting on his beanie and jacket.

'Stockdale is known for four seasons in one day,' Dave reminded him. 'The sun might make a bit more of an appearance this afternoon. Or the rain might set back in.'

'Let's be on our way by then if it's gonna rain,' Bob said, shuffling towards the stairs leading to the top of the lookout. 'I'll just go slow.'

'Sure.' Dave leaned against the troopy's bull bar and watched his friend take the first step then the next and the next. He marvelled at the change in Bob. That was just what Dave had been hoping for.

'I remember you from the pub. What the hell are you doing here?'

Dave turned and saw Connie standing off to the side, a little way away, like she was too frightened to come any closer. He fought the urge to tell her Australia was a free country and that being aggressive was the best way to put people off your cause, but he already knew that wasn't going to get him anywhere.

'Hi,' he said. 'I remember you from the pub last night, too.'

'You were with those prick coppers.'

Dave held up his hands in a peace gesture. 'Look, Con . . . it is Con, isn't it?'

'Connie. Connie Phillips. My brother, Brandan Phillips. Go look him up and see why he died.'

'Connie, come on, let's go,' the man called out, not coming any closer to them.

'Just wait, Tom.'

Dave jumped in quickly. 'Connie, after you left, I got the background on why you were so upset last night.' He was giving her his full attention, hoping she would listen. 'All I can say is, please don't judge all coppers by that one event. Police officers want to help people. If you ask any one of us why we joined the force, you would hear it's because we want to help people and—'

'What a load of shit.' A red stain spread across her cheeks and neck as she took a step closer. 'Helping people. Seriously? The copper made me furious. I don't usually drink and rarely raise my voice. I was brought up better than that, but you lot—' Disgust flared in her tone. 'You lot are nothing but scum. I felt much better after I'd told Roger that last night.' She flicked her head to the side and gave a nasty smile. 'And now I feel better for telling you. I'm going to make the police force wish they'd never heard my name.'

The man called Tom came to stand next to Connie and put his hand on her shoulder. 'Come on, Connie. Let's head off, yeah?'

'I haven't finished yet,' she said and turned back to Dave. 'Mark my words, you'll wish you'd never met me.'

Dave glanced over to where Bob was, at the top of the lookout, staring out across the blue southern sea. He seemed oblivious to what was going on below.

'I'm only trying to explain that we have a job to do,' Dave said calmly. 'It's not always a great job, but we still have to do it.'

'Your job is to chase people in vehicles until they die? Really? My god, I didn't know that was a job description.' Her mouth curled up in an unpleasant smile. 'You arseholes harass good people getting on with their lives, trying to earn enough money to look after their family. Brandan is just one example. Hear me? Just one. There are plenty more and I'll find them, too. Bring a class action against the police. Just wait and see.'

Dave's heart clenched as he looked into the face of this angry young woman. Death and grief were awful things to experience at the best of times, let alone when there was a whole lifetime ahead of feeling the way Connie did now. Tragic, unexpected deaths were even worse. The shock rippled through people in ways that no one could predict. He wished he could say something that would take away her pain.

'I understand the loss of your brother—' Dave started but he was quickly interrupted.

'Lost a brother to a high-speed car chase, have you? No, I didn't think so. You understand nothing.' She turned to leave then stopped, as Bob made his way down the stairs. 'What about you, old man? You got an excuse as to why your lot killed an innocent man?'

Bob looked up at the shouted words and hesitated. Dave could see him assessing the situation.

Don't come down, he thought. *Just stay there and let me deal with it.*

Tom put his arm around Connie and pulled her towards the car. 'Connie, this isn't you. You've got to stop.' He looked over at Dave. 'Sorry, mate, she's just real upset.'

Dave nodded. 'That's okay. There's nothing wrong with being distressed. Connie, all I'm trying to say here is that we're not as bad as you think we are, and if you hold on to that anger, it will destroy you.' He gave a small smile, hoping to defuse the situation.

Connie broke out laughing now and crossed her arms tightly across her chest. 'Destroy me, you reckon?' She assessed him for a moment. 'What do you think your mates did to me and my family already, then? They've ruined my life, my mum's life, when they forced my brother off the road.

'My mum hasn't been outside the house since Brandan died. She sits in her room and cries. Or writes him letters. This woman—' She broke off and brushed tears away. 'Actually, it doesn't matter. Nothing I say will bring him back, but I will make sure you fuckers are held responsible.' She smiled nastily again. 'And you can take that as a threat.'

'Come on, Connie, you've said your piece. We need to go.'

Connie shook Tom off, just as Bob took the last few steps from the stairs and started towards them.

'Let me tell you one thing,' she said, her words full of venom, 'I wish every single one of you coppers, your families and all of your mates were in the building over in Kallygarn when it was blown up. That would have been the greatest gift to the world—to make sure none of you could hurt someone else.' She shook her finger at Dave now. 'I'd shake the hand of the person who blew the building up, if I could.' This time she left without looking back.

Tom waited until Connie was out of earshot. 'Sorry,' he said. 'It's the anniversary of Brandan's death this week, and

224

she's suddenly got all angry.' He turned, clearly wanting to leave immediately.

'What's your name?'

'Tom Vincent. Look, I gotta go.' He looked over his shoulder and back to Dave, clearly wanting to go to his friend.

'Well, Tom, Connie has a good friend in you,' Dave said.

Tom nodded and jogged over to Connie and the dog.

Bob went to the troopy and got out a water bottle, drinking deeply, before looking at Dave. 'Looks like that went well.'

Shrugging, Dave stretched and shook his head. 'I just wanted her to understand she needs to let go of the hate. Yeah, it's tragic her brother died, but holding on to so much hurt and anger is just going to eat her up. It'll make her bitter and twisted. Plus, from the way the fellas told it to me this morning, they didn't chase him. He was killed when his vehicle hit a tree.'

'Of course they didn't chase him. If the coppers had been involved in a high-speed car chase down here, I would've known about it and so would have you. You know as well as I do, son, that sort of event goes through the force like a goddamn tidal wave.'

Dave opened his door and started to get inside. 'I know. Still, she feels like she needs to blame someone and we're the closest thing.'

'That's how it goes. Another reason why us coppers have to have broad shoulders. You shouldn't let her draw you into her fantasy world. Some people are just made for bitter and twisted.'

'No argument there. Connie's only young, though, and there are better ways to live.'

He waited until Bob had got into the car before starting the engine. With the window down Dave took a couple of deep breaths of salty air and closed his eyes. Maybe Bec and Alice would like to visit here. He could imagine them splashing in the waves and laughing and screaming at the chilly water.

Or perhaps Shannon would like a weekend away. She liked the sea—they'd made love on a beach once.

Bob was talking to him again.

'Sorry, what?'

Bob threw him an exasperated look. 'I said, you can want people to accept situations gracefully all you like, but she's the only one who can change her way of thinking, and,' Bob sounded thoughtful now as he looked over at Dave, 'the more I look at life, I realise sometimes all people have is hate—that's what they need to hang on to get through. Hating is much easier than love and forgiveness.'

Dave smiled and nodded at Bob's wise words as they headed out of town.

'You know what I find interesting?' Bob asked.

Dave had his blinker on to indicate he was turning on the highway towards Kalgoorlie. The open road was calling him. That, and the next job he and Bob could do together.

'What?' he asked.

'I find it interesting that you should be having this thought process about hanging on to anger.'

'Why's that?' Dave looked over at his mate who had a smirk on his face. He had a feeling he was walking into something, but he had no idea what.

'Let me throw one word at you. *Mark!*'

Dave blanched. 'But that's—'

'Different, is it? Really? How?'

Thoughts whirled. Mark, his father-in-law, the bloke who had stopped him from seeing his kids. The man he'd willingly throttle with his bare hands. He sniggered. Bob was right. 'Still different.'

Bob nodded slowly. 'You keep telling yourself that, son. Just keep on telling yourself that.'

Dave picked up a single light coming towards them and made sure he was well and truly in his lane so the motorbike could pass without getting too close.

The engine noise was loud. Even with the speed, Dave noticed the logo on the rider's helmet and momentarily froze. 'Was that . . .'

Another roar of a bike. Then they saw two abreast. The bikes flew past, headed to Stockdale, while another two came around the corner.

'Two, four, five.' Bob counted. 'And there we are, six, eight. Twelve bikes. And they've all got the same logo on their helmets.'

'The Sinners,' Dave said, his eyes on the rear-view mirror.

'They're a long way from their home turf. Wonder what they're doing down here,' Bob said thoughtfully.

'Want to turn around?'

'Hmm, don't think so. Probably just out for an overnighter somewhere. If they've come from Kal, maybe there was a two-up tournament on, or the like.'

'Maybe.' Dave didn't sound convinced. 'Only a couple of hours to Kallygarn from here.'

Bob turned in his seat and looked at Dave. 'I know you've got them pegged for that explosion, but there's no evidence or reasoning. Nothing that's solid, anyway, even though you seem to have made your mind up on it.' Bob reached out and clapped Dave's shoulder. 'I really thought I'd got through to you that assumptions don't work in this business. Gut feelings, yes. Assumptions, no,' he said, kindness in his tone. 'Now there is no possible way I can die yet because I still have so much to teach you.'

CHAPTER 23

'Get around!' Darryl yelled at the black and tan kelpie, Magpie. The dog pinned back his ears and took off like a greyhound, around the mob of sheep, who had been grazing quietly near the scrub.

Blue skies today, but that didn't mean it wasn't cold, and Darryl blew on his hands as he watched Magpie's path.

'Good boy! That's right, way back.' He let out a piercing whistle and then put the ute into gear and followed around, pushing the sheep towards the yards.

The sheep settled into a mob and trotted slowly along their path, knowing the gate was ahead. To the ewes, a gate usually meant fresh pastures and they'd be happy to find that open gate and go through it without help.

Unfortunately, today fresh pastures weren't on the agenda. Darryl had to draft them, because he'd spotted five or six of his neighbour's sheep in among his own. He'd get them in and take them back to George. As much as Darryl liked his neighbour, he didn't like his sheep because they often had lice. Not that he'd tell the old man that. No farmer told another farmer how to do his job. If he criticised, then someone might mention Darryl's ineptitude. Then he'd have to agree with them.

The angry phone call with his lawyer, the day before, played on his mind. Fury had been the only emotion present when Greg had spoken of the punishment that could be coming his way, and it was fresh. Even though he pretended it wasn't. Darryl was getting on with his daily jobs without being distracted.

'On channel, Darryl?'

He picked up the two-way mic and answered Jasmine's call as he watched Magpie direct the sheep through the gate and into the yards. Hopefully, this wouldn't take long.

'I'm putting in an order to the shop, do you want anything?'

Gritting his teeth, he pressed the button in and answered no.

Two years ago, Jasmine wouldn't have ever considered using the two-way for something so trivial. Now she forgot things and had to call him and ask questions he'd really rather weren't put out over the public channel.

Yesterday, she'd asked if he'd paid the lawyers.

Channel three was their own personal two-way channel but if anyone was passing and had their radio on scan, they would have heard the question. He hated other people knowing his business. He'd always been private, whereas Jasmine was the opposite. There wasn't much she didn't mind talking about. If they had lice, they had lice, so what? Better for people to know in case some of their stock had strayed.

If budworm or red-legged earth mite, or some other kind of insects had infested their crop, then she was all for letting others know. 'Tell the community, Darryl,' she'd always said. 'If we've got it, someone else might, too. If they check their crop and find they've got the same, they can do something about it. Farming isn't a secret society, you know!' She'd smiled up at him then, and his heart had melted.

The trouble was, he had grown up in a family that didn't talk. His father was the strong, silent type, while his mother had been busy looking after Darryl and his three siblings. She hadn't had time to talk!

Darryl had never heard his father discuss anything farming, unless it had been the basics about weather, with anyone. Following suit, Darryl kept quiet because that was all he knew. He wished Jasmine felt the same.

Now, slamming the ute door with extra force, he went to the gate and closed it behind the sheep then pushed them towards the raceway.

Fifteen minutes later, his ewes were headed down the laneway and back to their paddock while the five escapee weaners from George's place were still in the yards.

'Speak up,' he told Magpie, pushing them towards the crate he'd loaded on the back of the ute and tied down. With a clattering of feet, the weaners ran up the loading ramp and inside the crate, stopping with confused expressions as they found the back of the ute. Too late they realised they couldn't go anywhere else. They spun around, looking for a way out, but Darryl slammed the gate shut and was latching it before they could escape.

'Fuckers,' he muttered, before turning to Magpie. 'Good boy,' he told his dog, who lay puffing at the bottom of the race, even though the temperature was below ten degrees. 'Now, go home. I'll be back soon.' He raised his voice. 'Go home, Magpie, go home!'

Magpie heaved himself up and started back towards the house. The dog was ten and beginning to show his age. Darryl wasn't sure what he was going to do when Magpie was too old to work. He'd been his constant companion and friend for so many years.

He should invest in a new pup, but something was holding him back. Maybe it was the court case. The fear of going to gaol and not being here to look after and train a new dog. Jasmine certainly wouldn't be able to look after an excited puppy who would be jumping around. It could knock her over.

He started to breathe faster as he thought about gaol and Jasmine. He was angry enough to kill someone. Or at least hurt them badly.

Arsehole was the one he should be gunning for, although anyone in the government would be okay. Start with one and work his way through everyone in the shire council.

He caught himself. *You're being an idiot*, he thought. Arsehole was only doing his job. True, but Darryl *couldn't* go to gaol! Greg would just have to work out something. Could they do a plea bargain? He'd heard of that happening.

Maybe Greg could think of something. He must be able to. That's what he was being paid for.

Would Jasmine's disease help? Could Greg cite family illness? Would that stop Darryl from ending up behind bars?

Deep down he knew that no matter how sick Jasmine was, her illness wouldn't stop the government from sentencing him. Darryl would have to handle this himself.

His watch showed it was nearly time for smoko. Maybe George would like some company. He made sure the crate gate was closed tightly and then drove towards the road.

As he passed the house, an image of Jasmine lying on the cement came to him. That could easily happen. A wrong step, her muscles giving out. She could lie there for days if he wasn't on the farm to check on her. Did the government have a duty of care?

The two-way call showed that Jasmine was up, even with the curtains still tightly closed.

Five years ago, that wouldn't have been the case. She would have been in the garden pottering or hanging clothes on the line. Sometimes she would have been in the ute alongside him.

The passenger seat in the ute was empty now.

Jasmine hadn't been raised on a farm. They'd met in the pub on the weekend of the football grand final. Darryl had been playing in the reserves, and they'd lost. Badly. It had been a wipeout.

The team, upset with their loss, were downing as many cans and stubbies as they could when Jasmine had walked into the bar. As the strapper for the other team, to talk to her was cavorting with the enemy. That hadn't mattered to Darryl. He'd had been captivated from the moment he saw her.

Ignoring all the comments about defecting to the other side, Darryl had spent the night listening to her talk. Watching her mouth and the way she laughed. He'd been struck down with lust that had turned quickly to friendship, then to a deep love. How cruel life could be that Jasmine would be snatched away from him, before either of them were ready.

Darryl flicked the blinker on and drove past George's mailbox and into his driveway.

The crops were looking pretty good, he thought, heading slowly towards the house. For someone who didn't use the new technology and machinery, George should be happy. They were better than Darryl's anyway.

Again, Jasmine crossed his mind. They hadn't been able to have kids and that had always played on her mind. Being childless hadn't bothered Darryl as much, because he'd never had to share Jasmine with anyone—he knew that sounded weird, or controlling or something that meant he was an arsehole, but he'd never meant it like that. He just liked it being the two of them.

George hadn't even married. Surely living by yourself out here made for a deep loneliness.

The familiar ute, the one that made the racket whenever it drove down the road, was pulled up next to the verandah, so he parked next to it and beeped the horn to let George know he was there.

The weaners ran around the crate, still trying to find an escape route, causing the ute to rock to and fro. He ignored them and waved to the man who'd come out onto the verandah.

'Cup of tea, mate?' George called.

'That'd be great. Cold enough for you?'

'Oh yeah, it was chilly enough yesterday morning, let me tell you. I went to check the crops just as the sun was rising and there was a real bite in the air. Today isn't much better. Still, we should expect that. It's winter and it's been the same every year I can remember!'

'True.' Darryl took off his muddy boots and followed George inside, thinking how painfully irritating it was that he'd never managed to build Jasmine a house and yet George was living in a three-bedroom house with an internal bathroom and laundry. No twin-tub for him! And there was only one human inside.

Darryl knew the house had been built by the previous generation, but the fact only George lived here alone didn't seem fair.

But what about life is fair?

'Thanks for bringing those rogues back,' the old man said. 'I had a bit of a look along the fence line today but I can't see where they got out. I'll have another look this afternoon. Try to find what I missed.'

'Might have just pushed through, mate,' Darryl said. 'Thought the grass was greener and all that.'

'You'd have to wonder why with all the feed that's around. Still, weaners never surprise me. The teenagers of sheep.' George smiled. 'So tell me, what have you been up to, young man?' He put the kettle on the stove. 'Did I hear motorbikes a few days ago? Thought there was a thunderstorm coming, then I realised it was engines. Did you hear that as well?'

Darryl nodded, pulling out a chair and sitting down. He glanced around, reacquainting himself with the house. No photos, green threadbare carpet and a fawn-coloured benchtop. At least their home had family photos of their parents and siblings.

'Yeah, a mate rang and asked if some of his friends could camp out for a few nights. They were looking for somewhere out of the way. Send them up towards the break-away country near the top of my place. They were happy, so I showed them where to go and left them to it. 'Bout twelve or so blokes. Boys having some time away by the sounds of it.'

'Good on them. I never saw the bikes, but they sounded pretty flash. There were a few bikies in town the other day. Hec and I were having lunch at the pub. They were there when we arrived. Rough-looking crowd.'

Darryl ignored the comment about rough. 'Yeah, there must've been a few dollars tied up in all the machines.'

'How're your crops looking? I haven't been out the back past your place for a little while. Everything going along all right?'

'Yeah, I'm pretty happy with how everything is going.' Not that Darryl would tell anyone that things weren't great on his place. That sort of information, he wouldn't ever share. 'It's nice to have a season that isn't hand to mouth. Especially after last year—wasn't that a shithouse season?'

George poured the tea, nodding. 'Last year was a killer. Glad that last rain topped us up nicely.'

Darryl removed the sugar bowl lid, which was a light pink with faded green gum leaves painted on the side. He smiled. 'My mum had one of these. Same colour and everything.'

Sitting down, George twirled his cup around a few times. 'I think they were popular way back when.' He fixed Darryl with a stare. 'Mate, I need to ask you something and I'm a bit nervous about it because—' He broke off, but then looked up.

Darryl didn't move. Surely, George wasn't crook and needing a hand. He had more than enough on his plate without having to babysit his farm. *Fuck's sake*, he thought.

Still, a small buzz of excitement had also started. Maybe George wanted Darryl to buy his farm . . . Actually, how good would that be? He could buy some extra ewes and—

Reality bit mid thought. Jasmine. Court case. Jasmine. Court case. There would be no purchasing of any farms with that going on.

'Don't need to be nervous. What's the problem?' Darryl stirred some sugar into his black tea and leaned forward, trying to be encouraging. He'd rather smash something these days than have a conversation that might require him to have some compassion.

'Well, I'm wondering. Have you seen anything out of the ordinary going on around here? Other than your bikie mates, I mean. Strange cars or lights late at night? I don't know what I'm hoping you have seen, but—' George stopped, sighing. 'Anything, I guess.'

'What do you mean? Has someone been up here bothering you? Or have you been hearing weird things at night?' Darryl sat up straight, giving the old man his full attention.

'No, no, nothing like that. But—' He stopped again as if unsure whether to continue. 'Anyhow, doesn't matter. Only thought I'd ask.'

George seemed vulnerable, sitting here at the kitchen table, but there was still a strength about him.

'Well, look,' Darryl said, 'I haven't seen anything that's made me concerned. I'll keep an eye out, though.'

'That'd be good, lad, thank you. Now, like I said before, old Hec and I had lunch the other day. In town. You know old Hec?'

Darryl nodded. 'I've seen him at Anzac services.'

'Great old fella. He got a soldier settlement block after the war. On the other side of town. He was telling me this is the wettest year he can ever remember.'

'Nice to be under the rain cloud. Got to jag it sometime.' Darryl gave a small laugh.

'Yes, you're right. It's nice when we do.' George put the teaspoon down and took a sip of tea. 'In fact, he was the one who told me about the explosion at Kallygarn. I'm sure you've heard?'

'Bloody oath.' Darryl put his cup down, too. 'Terrible!'

'I heard it was deliberate but nothing about if there was a suspect. Have you?'

'Nah, I haven't seen the news for a few days.' Darryl ran his hands along his jeans and leaned back in his chair. What a strange thing for George to bring up. 'Is that explosion bothering you?'

ABC radio played quietly in the background, and Darryl heard the music signalling the ten o'clock news.

'Not bothering me as such,' George said slowly, 'but I would be very interested to know what type of bomb it was. Hec used to muck around with explosives in the war, see? And he was interested, too. We had a bit of a chat about it over lunch.'

'Can't help you there, sorry.' Darryl looked towards the door. It might be time to leave. The old man was getting all het up about something he couldn't do anything about.

Before he could make his excuses, George seemed to decide something and started to speak. 'Look, Darryl, this is going to sound odd, but I think I'm missing some bags of fertiliser.'

Shifting in his chair, Darryl reached for his cup again and took a sip, thinking quickly. 'Missing as in stolen?'

'Well, that's the trouble. I don't want to mention it to anyone else because I'm not sure. Maybe I counted incorrectly when I finished seeding this year. But I'm sure there were fifty bags and now there are only forty-five. Perhaps I've forgotten.' George gave a little laugh. 'When you get to my age, sometimes you forget things.' He paused, his face changing to a look of worry. 'See,

Darryl—' swallowing hard George chewed the inside of his lip before speaking again '—if I tell anyone, I'm worried they'll think I'm losing my marbles and want to put me in a home. But . . . what if someone knew the fertiliser was here and had the skills to make a bomb? It's my responsibility to tell the police, isn't it?' He looked miserable.

'Ah shit, George, you're not losing your marbles. Don't be silly. You're the fittest seventy-plus-year-old I know. Don't worry about it. I can't remember where I put the spanner and screwdriver half the time. I'm sure all your fertiliser is there. Who would take it anyway?'

'That's the silly thing! I can't think of anyone who would, but that explosion . . . You can use this stuff to make those bombs. And I don't think I could forgive myself if it came from here.'

This time Darryl laughed aloud. He got his hankie out and patted his forehead. That fire George had going had a bit of heat to it.

'Right-oh, so let me get this straight. Someone, persons unknown, has driven to the back of bumfuck, because that's where we live, George. We're not close to anywhere.' He grinned at the old man who was starting to smile now. 'And snuck onto your farm and found your fertiliser. No prior knowledge or any reason to be here, but they've found your stash.

'Can I point out that I'm your neighbour and I don't even know where you keep it.' He held up his finger. 'Then they've proceeded to steal it, make a bomb and blow up the Kallygarn Shire Council offices.' He shrugged. 'With

Kallygarn being about five hours away from here—yeah, I could see how that would work.'

'Get away with you,' George said, humour in his voice. 'When you put it like that, it does sound strange.'

'And that's exactly how it is,' Darryl said. 'No need to go to the police, even if you're unsure if you're missing a few bags. They'll just say the same thing I have.' Darryl took another sip of his tea, then took a deep breath. His mood shifted from slight mirth to low-grade fury. 'But I'll tell you something if you want a reason to worry.'

George frowned. 'Jasmine no good?'

'Nah, bastards have upgraded the charges for that land I cleared. The lawyers say I could go away for five years. Or they'll whack me half a mil in fines. Pricks.'

'For what? Clearing that bit of scrub up the back of your place? No, surely not.'

'Yeah, the bit over near the Crown land.'

'How bloody stupid! That land is better cleared and being used than not. Not worth anything the way it was.'

'I know, I know. They're bastards. I'm out here working my guts out trying to make a go of things and that's what they do to an honest fella.'

'Geez, mate, I'm really sorry to hear that. How did they even find out about it? That bit of bush is way off the road.'

'I think it goes back to some conservationists doing a wildflower survey. I saw a few cars out in the bush when I was spraying a while back. Guess it's obvious that it's been cleared and they didn't like it. What's the bet that I've stopped some nearly extinct orchid from blooming or some shit like that. Anyhow, I reckon it was them who dobbed me in. Then the government went and checked the satellites and they could see the change in the land.

'Now I'm not denying I've done it. Never have, but for god's sake, it's my place!'

'Bloody greenies need to mind their own business, that's what they need to do.' George put his cup down with a bang. 'They've got no right coming onto someone's land and passing judgement. Dobbing them in. Goes against the Australian way.'

'Well, mate, all I know is that it's got Jasmine pretty worried. She's frightened that I'm going to gaol and she's not going to have anyone to look after her.'

'Gawd, mate, I'm sorry she's going through that. And you, too. People who are that sick shouldn't have any extra stress on them. Especially something as worrying as a court case.'

'Tell me about it. If I knew who to contact inside the department I'd give 'em what for, I tell you. All these stupid bloody laws about what I can do on my own land. Those bastards need to understand they're ruining people's lives.'

CHAPTER 24

The mobile phone sitting on the dash rang and Bob leaned forward to pick it up. 'It's Lorri,' he told Dave.

'Better answer it then.' Dave saw the sign for the hotel and flicked on his blinker, checking the rear-view mirror before he put his foot on the brake to slow. The motel had weeds growing through cracks in the cement and a couple of windows were boarded up.

Coming to a stop in front of the reception, he kept the troopy idling, wondering if he should make a quick getaway before the bed bugs came out of the weeds to bite them. 'You think it's okay here?' Dave asked.

Bob waved him on as he answered Dave's phone, so he picked up his wallet and went over to the door.

The bell on the door tinkled, and he waited at the counter, wishing whoever was coming to serve him would hurry. What would Lorri have to say? He was hoping she would have news on the Kallygarn shire bombing.

Dave kicked at the carpet, a faded green with brown swirls. The walls had old photos of Chapman Hill in its early days. Black-and-white stills of steam trains, mines and men standing together with picks and shovels over their shoulders. Chapman Hill was still a mining town, helped along in the early days by the train line that connected Kalgoorlie to Perth.

A few minutes later, an old man came out from the back. He was stooped and his stomach was showing through the gaps where his buttons had popped off his shirt. 'Help yer?'

Introducing himself, Dave said, 'I booked two rooms for tonight.' He handed over his credit card.

'Oh yeah?' A gnarled finger ran down a handwritten bookings column and tapped when he found Dave's name. 'Room twenty-two and twenty-three. Missus put the milk in the fridge. We're getting a bit too old to do this job, so everything is a bit rundown, but I guarantee the rooms are clean.'

Dave hoped what he was hearing was right.

'Leave the keys in the rooms when you leave and be out by ten am. Questions?' The man found the keys in a pigeonhole and passed them over.

'No trouble,' Dave answered. 'Best pub for a feed?'

'Commercial. Two streets over. Need a receipt?'

'Please.'

The old man laboured over a handwritten tax invoice before disappearing into the darkness behind him. Dave heard the sound of the TV starting up before he'd even left the reception.

Outside, he saw that Bob was out of the troopy, pacing around, still on the phone.

Looking at him curiously, he mouthed, 'Right?'

Bob used his hand to cover the phone and spoke softly to Dave. 'Another explosion at Kallygarn.'

Dave's eyes widened. 'What!'

Getting back in the vehicle, Bob told him to wait while he kept talking to Lorri as Dave drove round the back and found the car parks in front of the rooms. He listened to the conversation, trying to work out what had happened.

'Okay, well, we can be there tomorrow if they want us.'

'Aha. Yeah, sure.'

'No worries. I'll let Dave know.'

'Mmm. Good. Right-oh, Lorri. Thanks. Dave'll ring you back.' He hung up and blew out his cheeks.

Dave raised his eyebrows, waiting.

'Some fucker has blown up that service station on the outskirts of Kallygarn.'

'When?'

'Early hours of the morning.'

'Same person or persons as previously?'

'The squads had headed back to Perth, but they've turned around now. We'll know more tomorrow.' He looked across at Dave, smiling. 'They're looking for an extra pair of hands. And that's us. Apparently, Johnny asked for us directly.'

Dave returned Bob's stare, unsmiling. 'You up for this? There won't be any going back if we say yes. How long before your next treatment? Jesus, Betty will kill me.'

Bob burst out laughing. 'You right there, son? You just had three different conversations with yourself.'

'Well!' Dave shook his head as if to say, what on earth do you expect?

'I told you this morning, Dave. I need to do this, all right? I might not be as quick as I used to be, or on deck all the time, but I'm needed on this investigation. My treatment isn't until next week and we can be back by then. And don't worry about Betty, she'll kill me first, and that might not be a bad thing. Any other questions?'

It was good to have Bob sort of back to his old self. Dave got out of the troopy and unlocked Bob's motel door, before putting his mate's bag on the bed inside.

'What else do you know?'

Bob sat down on the bed and held up his hand. 'Two secs, let me take my tablets and have a drink.'

Dave wanted to pace the room impatiently, instead he took a breath and went to grab his own bag and lock the car. He had to keep moving. Adrenalin had kicked in and he was keen to get information, so they could start working through what had happened at Kallygarn. Find out who the people involved were. Why they had targeted both the shire council offices and the servo. He frowned, thinking about the two different settings. What was the link or connection between the two places?

Inside his room, he checked the fridge, found the milk and plugged in the kettle. He'd kill for a beer now, but not until he knew what was going on. From his bag he got out his toiletries and put them in the bathroom, placed his briefcase underneath the mirror on the bench, clicked it open and looked inside.

Then closed it again.

Surely Bob had finished doing what he had to do by now. Yanking open his door, he rapped on Bob's and walked in without waiting for him to answer. 'So, what's the drum?' Dave asked.

Bob was coming out of the bathroom with a towel over his shoulder and he was wiping his face. 'Okay, at oh two hundred the police were woken to another blast on the outskirts of Kallygarn. No need to make any phone calls because the coppers woke at the same time as the rest of the town did. Same thing happened last time.

'Johnny was first there, followed by two other constables and the fire crew. Took four hours to contain the blaze— petrol, diesel and so on had to burn down before the firies could do much.

'There were a few smaller explosions as the fumes started to leach out, but the destruction was contained to the service station itself. Luckily, it's on the outer edge of town, so there were no houses or buildings to harm. And early morning meant the service station was closed, therefore no cars, trucks or vehicles of any sort. No collateral damage.'

'What about the people who run it? Any injuries?'

'They live about three blocks down. No injuries or fatalities.'

'How bloody lucky is that? Two explosions and no one has been hurt either time.' Dave refocused on Bob. 'Same type of bomb?'

'No word on that yet.'

Dave nodded and ran through everything he knew, which was very little because he hadn't been briefed about the first bombing. Then a conversation Johnny had had with them while they were having lunch came back to him. 'Johnny said he wanted to get some CCTV up in the main street— did you hear him say that? Wonder if they were installed before this incident.'

Bob frowned. 'What do you mean?'

'Maybe you weren't there, then? Johnny said he wanted to position cameras up at either end of the main street because we know the perps like to come back and look at their handiwork. He was hoping to get them put in place ASAP, but there was the issue of permission from Perth first.'

'Hmm, that would make sense,' Bob mused as he lay back on his bed with his eyes shut.

'You want a rest before tea?'

'Better do, I reckon. Give me a couple of hours and I'll be ready, son.'

'Sure.' Dave got up and left, closing the door quietly. He stood on the verandah looking out across the hotel car park. It was as unwelcoming as the old man behind the counter. Some dead weeds were poking out from an empty flowerpot, and a line of small shrubby bushes hid the rooms from the main road.

The traffic from the highway was constant, loud trucks and clanging trailers. Far in the distance, Dave heard the high-pitched yells and squeals of kids at footy practice. He checked his watch and felt the surge of frustration again. There would have been time to get to Kallygarn tonight. But the extra driving wouldn't have been any good for Bob, and Dave needed to focus on keeping his mate as fit and able as possible. Maybe Bob's illness had been sent to teach Dave some patience. He could hear Shannon telling him something along those lines.

A young mum and daughter crossed the highway, heading towards what Dave thought was a deli set back from the road. The little girl's ponytail bounced in time with her strides. She reminded him of Bec, the way she'd walk with purpose when she was in a huff with him.

At times like that Bec used to bounce around the house, her arms crossed and mouth in a pout, until Dave picked her up and turned her upside down over his shoulder. Then she'd squeal with delight and put her chubby arms around his neck and kiss his chest, all the while telling him he wasn't to be naughty again. Dave smiled. He used to tell her that she was the one who'd been naughty; Dads weren't.

The sun was on the downward slide, casting long shadows across the ground. The kids would be heading home, and by about ten that night, the trucks would begin to slow down, too. Being on the main highway from the eastern states to Perth, the road was always going to be busy.

Back in his room, he switched on the light and got out his computer. A few moments later he heard the wave and piano sounds as MS Windows opened the home screen. It was a laborious task connecting the modem to the computer. To fill in time, he paced the room, thinking about Bob.

Bob's health couldn't hinder the case.

Dave had just seen what could happen when the adrenalin kicked in for Bob. The thrill of a new investigation seemed to give them both energy. Once Bob had had his kip, he'd be a new person, chafing at the bit to get started on the inquiry.

Even a half-dead copper couldn't stop the rush when there was a new case. But his body still might hold him back. Dave was a little worried his partner might forget or not pick up on something important. Shannon had told him that the chemo could make his mind a bit muddled.

'Mate, you've got to stop this,' Dave told himself. 'You've never not trusted Bob before, there's no reason to start now. He hasn't done one single thing to cause you to distrust him.' If worst came to the worst, Dave would take control of their part in the investigation. Easy fixed. He was supposed to be in charge anyway.

Checking the computer, he realised everything was connected, so he hit the email icon and waited.

From next door, through the thin walls, came Bob's loud snoring. Normally, Dave would have found this comforting, but not today. There was too much at stake.

Scanning the emails, he stopped when he saw his lawyer's name. *Grace Sumpton.* He stared at the email from her, wondering what it could contain and if he wanted to open it. He hovered the mouse over the message then double-clicked before he could stop himself.

Dear Dave,

In relation to divorce proceedings between Melinda Burrows and David Burrows, I would like to advise a court date has been set for 23 November 2002.

You are not required to attend this session. It will be attended by myself and a paralegal.

Please note, the financial settlement is still in negotiation, and we hope to have an offer to you within the week.

The letter was signed with Grace's signature.

Dave realised it wasn't just the word 'boss' that could sucker-punch him. It was the words 'divorce', 'Melinda' and 'Dave' all in the same sentence.

He swallowed hard and put his hands over his mouth. That was it. The end of his marriage. There was a date for it now—23 November 2002.

There was no more Melinda and Dave, or Dave and Melinda.

They were finished.

Done.

He'd never thought his children would be raised in a one-parent family. If he had his way that would never have happened, but Melinda, Mark, life . . . They had a different idea. Dave had been left pining for something that could never be fixed.

His stomach felt hollow as he re-read the email. Bec and Alice, the loves of his life. What he wouldn't give to hug and kiss their heads. Melinda had them now. She had them.

He didn't.

Clicking the reply button, he typed out one word: *Roger.*

There was nothing more to say.

He would tell Bob about the email tonight and feel justi-fied as Bob ranted and raged against Mark on his behalf and told him it wasn't Dave's fault. Or maybe he wouldn't. Maybe Bob would give him the 'let it go' lecture as he had done earlier in the day.

Deciding not to mention the email, he closed the message.

A gust of wind howled around the outside of the motel, causing the bathroom window to rattle loudly.

Dave tried to shove the thoughts of divorce from his mind. Maybe he should go for a run. His stomach felt queasy though and he wasn't sure a run would help.

From his wallet he pulled two small photos, one of Bec and one of Alice. He stared at them for what seemed like an eternity. 'I'm sorry,' he whispered. 'I wanted to change this for you. I did try.' His voice broke. 'But it's beyond fixing now. I love you both so much.' If only Bec and Alice could hear his impassioned words. He wished he wasn't speaking in an empty motel room.

About to shut the computer down, Dave had a thought. Bringing up the weather website, he checked the conditions for the previous night. Especially at two in the morning. According to the bureau at two am in Kallygarn the temperature was three degrees. The wind direction was from the south at two kilometres per hour and there had been three millimetres of rain, indicating cloud cover.

Dave lay back on his bed, the computer resting against his raised knees. Those conditions sounded similar to the weather on the night of the first explosion. Dark and rainy. Perfect weather for hiding.

He googled Kallygarn Shire Council and found the address for the offices. The temperature and events that were on in Kallygarn during the week were listed on the website. He could click on the tab to find the shire president, councillors, and the CEO and persons of note. Dave wasn't interested in any of them.

He changed his search settings to the office's street address, and found a photo of the office building. Dave leaned forward to try to read the sign hammered into the lawn at the front of the property.

Kallygarn Shire Council.

Department of Transport.

Department of Conservation and Land Management.

Department of Agriculture.

The Kallygarn Pound.

Centrelink.

Post office.

Then, next to the sign there was a new one that said: *Police station.*

So many departments in one building. Who had been targeted? And what was the motivation to target the service station? Was it the same kind of bomb?

Dave pushed his computer to the side gently and got up. It didn't matter what questions he had. The Bomb Squad, Forensics and Major Crime would sort all of this. He was only there to help interview people and create Investigate Serials, files of interviews and information which would probably hold the key to why the shire council building and service station had been blown up, and who had done it. All those snippets of data Dave would glean from the probing questions he would ask.

With any luck it would be him who found the links and information, because he really wanted to solve this investigation. Bob had dismissed his bikie theory as had Johnny. But Dave's view was the opposite and he wanted to prove that right.

CHAPTER 25

To Dave it seemed like Bob was putting in an extra effort that evening. The pub was rowdy, full of men, dirty and dusty as if they had come straight from work, and Bob was in among them, talking and laughing. It was a far cry from the man who had been too tired to eat with Dave the other night.

Dave was happy but he wondered what tomorrow would bring for Bob. Exerting so much energy tonight might cause him problems later.

Looking at the menu, he decided the steak and chips with salad was what he needed tonight. He waved the menu at Bob, hoping he would decide what he wanted to eat soon. If Bob didn't need an early night tonight, Dave did. He wanted to think further about the little bit of local knowledge he'd managed to get off the Kallygarn website.

And 23 November. The divorce, and his daughters.

Looking around the pub, Dave saw an older man dressed in a flannelette shirt and jeans, his large Akubra hat on the floor beside him. He wasn't speaking with anyone else, but like Dave he was watching people, sipping his beer and listening to the conversation around him.

Dave caught his eye and nodded, raising his beer in acknowledgement—they were two men by themselves in among the hordes. The old man nodded back.

Before he could stop himself, Dave got up and located Bob, who was still laughing and talking with the men. Once he was sure his mate was all right, he went across to the older man.

'G'day, I'm Dave,' he said, holding out his hand.

'George,' the man answered with a smile. 'What brings you here, Dave? A fella all by himself, in among this rabble.'

'My mate's over there talking to all the other blokes. He likes to make himself at home. Can I buy you a beer?'

'Wouldn't say no,' George answered.

'I'll be back.' Dave elbowed his way to the front bar, ordered and waited. Listening to the conversation he realised that most of the men were either part of a road-contracting team or had been working at a silo construction business. According to the bloke next to him, the grand final was going to be won by the West Coast Eagles this year, but his mate had bet him two grand that it would be the Adelaide Crows.

'Bullshit! Gary Ayres hasn't got the ability, tactics, or know how to get them to the finals.'

'See, mate, you just don't understand the coaching method Gaz has got.'

Dave grinned to himself, thinking how people believed the players and coaches were their friends. AFL either won you or lost you friends, depending on the outcome of the grand final.

Finally, two beers were put in front of him, and the woman held out her hand. Dave gave her a twenty-dollar note, waited for his change then picked up the glasses and went back to George.

'Here you are. Fair bit of talk about the grand final over at the bar. It's still weeks away. Here's cheers.' He held up his glass and George did the same.

'Follow the footy, do you, Dave?' he asked.

'Not as closely as I should being a West Aussie. I know enough of what's going on, but I'm never around to go to games or watch it on the TV, so sometimes a couple of weeks go by before I catch up on the winners and losers. What about you?'

'Yeah, can't say it's ever been a big priority for me. I'm more of a tennis watcher. Can't play, mind, but I do like watching it on the tellie during the summer months when it's a bit hot to be outside.'

'Ha!' Dave grinned and pointed his finger. 'So it's just a good excuse to stay home under the air-conditioner?'

'Could be something like that,' George admitted with a grin. 'I haven't seen you around here before. Just passing through?'

Dave took a sip of his beer and nodded. 'Yeah, here for work. Headed out tomorrow.'

'It's a quick trip to our little town of Chapman Hill. You look like you could be a stock agent, or a farmer. Tell me, what do you do?'

'I'm actually with the stock squad, or as it's known now the Rural Crime Squad,' Dave answered.

'Ah, a copper?' George replied. 'I bet that's an interesting job. Now I understand you can't explain to me why you're here, but surely you could tell me a bit about what goes on behind closed doors?'

Dave liked this old man and he smiled broadly before replying: 'My mate, the one I was telling you about before, he's a bit crook, and he's my boss, and I needed to get him out of the city for a while. We decided to take a run down to Stockdale and do a compliance check on a few businesses through that area. We finished that, and now we're on our way back to Perth.'

'Sounds mighty fascinating. How often do you get to go out bush?' George took a sip of his beer and leaned forward to make sure he heard Dave's answer.

'Most of the cases require us to go out to the scene and have a look. See if we can find some evidence, talk to the people on the ground. You know, that sort of thing. It's pretty important to eyeball people and talk to them face to face when you're trying to solve a case. But it's hard when the investigation is four or five hundred kays away, because it takes time to get there. Sometimes by the time we arrive, evidence that we really need has been destroyed. Whether it

258

be seasonal conditions, or just time, being based in the city can be a bit of a drag at times.' He took a sip of his beer and leaned back in his chair. 'What about you, George? I'd put twenty bucks down that you're a farmer.' He took another sip of his beer and pulled a coaster out of the pile, then pushed it towards his companion for his glass.

George let out a delighted laugh. 'Hit the nail on the head,' he said. 'Yeah, I've got a block right at the end of Hubler Track. My farm is the last one before the Crown land.'

'Geez, it would be pretty isolated up there,' Dave said. 'You must really love it.'

'Yes, siree, I *really* do. Lived out there since I was born and still love it just as much as the day I was old enough to go out on the tractor for the first time.' He gave a happy sigh. 'You know, I worked out that this harvest will be my sixty-fourth.'

'Bloody hell, mate, you must've seen some changes in your time. And you still love farming?'

'That I do. I always joke they'll have to carry me off the farm in a box.'

'As any good self-respecting farmer would say,' Dave said, laughing. 'What do you run up there?'

'Got a few sheep, bit of crop, and I like to make hay every second year, if there's enough rain to put the oats crop in. The type of land up there is different from down the coast. It's easy to farm down there when you get lots of rain. But up here, we have to assess the season. Watch the weather and make decisions around what mother nature is giving us that year.' George wagged his finger at Dave and spoke earnestly. 'These young fellas, they've just got it in their mind that they have to seed a crop come hell or high water. They've set out their program in January, when they're doing the budgets up for the bank, long before the rains have come and they never make the adjustments they need to.

'They don't read the season, which means they make costly mistakes. You might have to make the call that there's not enough moisture to start with and you can't sow a crop in that year. Sometimes there's more money to be made by keeping your seed and fertiliser in a silo than in the ground. You hear what I'm saying?' George took a sip of his beer.

'You sound like my grandad,' Dave said. 'He was all about watching the seasons and mother nature. The hard thing about what you're saying is finding the money to buy extra livestock for the year ahead.'

'Agree, hard agree. You were from a farm?' George asked.

'Yeah, out of Northam. But there wasn't any room for me at home, so I joined the police force.'

'And a noble occupation that is.' George nodded and took another sip of his beer. Then he leaned forward. 'I don't want to put you in a tricky situation, Dave,' he said, 'but do you know anything about that explosion at Kallygarn?'

Dave shook his head and wiped at the condensation ring the beer had left on the table with his hand. 'Not a whole lot. Is there a reason for your question?'

George seemed to be considering his words. Dave waited, letting George figure out what he was going to say. The noise of the bar rose around them and a song started on the juke box.

George said something, but Dave couldn't hear, so he motioned for his new friend to lean forward. 'What did you say?' he asked. 'Did you have a reason for the question?'

'Not really,' George repeated. 'Only it's a curious thing to have happened.'

'Certainly not great.'

'Dave! Dave!' Bob was waving him over. 'Let's order.'

Dave held up his hand in an 'I'll be there soon' gesture. Quietly taking a sip of beer, he waited to see if the old man said anything else.

'I was in here earlier this week,' George finally said. 'The lady who brings out the mail was crook, so I came into town to collect it. To be honest it was nice to have an excuse to come in. I don't get too lonely out there, but a meal that's cooked for you is always nicer than the one you cook yourself.'

Dave nodded. He understood exactly what George was saying.

'Anyhow, a heap of bikies came into the pub just after I got here. Haven't seen bikies here before and I've been around for a while.' He stopped and let Dave absorb what he'd just said.

'What day was that?' Dave asked. He blocked his ear closest to the noise and concentrated on George's words.

'I reckon it was the day after the explosion.'

'Did they bother you?'

'Nah, just a bunch of bullies if you ask me. One had a bit of a crack and I told him that the behaviour he was displaying would make sure he didn't get a warm welcome in this town. There were other places to be. Funnily enough, it turned out they were all camping just up the road from my place.'

Dave raised his eyebrows. 'That's an interesting coincidence.'

'See here's the thing, Dave. I don't believe in coincidences. Do you?'

'I've always been taught not to.'

'Hmm.' George nodded. 'That grandfather of yours was a clever man.'

'Actually, it was my previous partner. I used to work at Barrabine, not that far from here, so I know the area pretty well. Spencer was the one who taught me to trust my gut and that coincidences didn't exist.' Dave took another sip of his beer and realised it was nearly empty. He didn't want to interrupt the conversation with George, but he could also see, out of the corner of his eye, that Bob was trying to get his attention.

'You know what my gut instinct is telling me now, George?' Dave asked.

'You tell me, mate.'

'I think you've got something to tell me, and yet, you're not sure. So, how about I get you another beer and buy you dinner? Bob looks like he's ready to eat. How would that be?'

'Sounds like a good plan.' George nodded and tipped his glass back, drinking until it was empty. He held it out. 'I'll have a parmi, please.'

Dave noted he didn't even need to look at the menu. He collected the glasses and left the table.

'Who's the old fella?' Bob asked as Dave came up next to him.

'George. Nice old bloke. We're going to have dinner with him.'

'Are we?' Bob narrowed his eyes. 'Any reason?'

'Yup. I reckon he knows something about something, but I haven't got a handle on what yet.' Dave could see Bob was beginning to fade again. 'I don't think it will take long.'

'"Knows something about something." God, I really wonder who gave you that badge you're carrying. Right-oh, well, let's see what we can get out of him. Don't bother to get me another beer. Water will be okay. And maybe a chicken and salad or something light.'

'Leave it with me.' Dave went to the bar and ordered, then turned around to see Bob and George already with their heads together.

He picked up their drinks and headed back to the table in time to hear George say, 'Isn't it interesting there was another target at Kallygarn again today? I heard about it on the news.'

'Yeah,' Bob said. 'Have you been there much? Or know anyone?'

'Nah, never venture too far from home. The pub and supermarket are about as far as I go. Had to go to the big smoke a few years back, to have some medical tests, but they turned out all right and I don't need to go back there again soon. Not really my cup of tea.'

'Yeah, it's a rat race, for sure.' Bob looked up as Dave put his water down. 'Thanks, son.'

George's eyes flicked between the two men as if assessing their relationship and seemed to settle on an opinion. He accepted his beer from Dave and thanked him.

'Dave said you're crook, Bob?' George nodded towards the glass of water.

'Yeah. Got the big C. But I'm okay. Not going to let it get me if I have a choice in the matter. Being out on the road is just as good therapy as the chemo, I reckon. And Dave here, well, he's real good. Looks after me, makes sure I'm not doing anything stupid. Isn't that right, son?'

'You look after yourself,' Dave said. 'I have no say in the matter.'

They both grinned and shared a fond glance.

'I haven't got any family,' George told them. 'Must be nice to be mates like you are.'

'Got to be that way,' Bob said. 'As coppers we have to trust each other one hundred per cent. And we do.'

Dave felt a twinge of guilt for his earlier thoughts about Bob. To cover it, he turned to George. 'So the bikies stayed up your way, you were saying.'

George nodded slowly. 'They were.'

'And did this concern you?'

'Well, no. At first, I didn't realise they were staying at Darryl's place. It was only when he came over to drop some weaners back and I asked whether he'd heard any motorbikes roaring around. That's when he told me they were camped at his place. Darryl's my neighbour, by the way.'

'Does he often have bikies stay with him?'

'Nah, this is the first time. But it is unusual they showed up now.'

'Why's that?'

George looked a little embarrassed. 'I mentioned my concerns to Darryl and he made me realise that what I think could have happened is really ridiculous. To be fair, I'm not sure what I remember . . .'

Dave leaned forward as the old man's words dried up. He was talking in riddles and Dave didn't want him losing his train of thought.

'Nothing is ridiculous, and every little piece of information helps. We just agreed coincidences were not a thing.'

George looked from Dave to Bob and back again, then said, 'I reckon I've had some fertiliser nicked and my understanding is that there are some types of fertiliser that can be used to make bombs.' George took a breath and looked at them both. 'That's why I've been trying to find out whether the bomb in Kallygarn was homemade or not.'

CHAPTER 26

Bob and Dave stared steadily at George, until Dave broke the silence.

'What type of fertiliser is this?'

'Ammonium nitrate.'

Bob blew out a whistle. 'How much are you missing?'

George looked embarrassed again. 'Well, this is where the problem lies. I'm not sure.' He explained how he couldn't remember what had been there at the end of seeding. 'And I don't want to stir up trouble. If I used five bags more than I thought, then I've caused all sorts of issues for lots of people. Probably me included because some well-meaning old busybody, like Cheryl the mail lady, will reckon I've lost my mind and want me off the farm. Not to mention getting you coppers excited. Especially if none of this is true!'

Bob looked at George sternly. 'I promise you that won't happen, George. There's nothing about you that makes me think you've lost your memory. And busybodies are easily dealt with.'

They were quiet as the waitress appeared and put their food down. They were all waiting until she was out of earshot before speaking again.

George shifted uncomfortably in his chair. 'I don't want to put you out of your way.'

'If you hold the key to what's happened at Kallygarn, George, you won't be putting us out of our way, I can assure you,' Dave said. 'You'll be the man of the moment.'

'How about we get you a room in town tonight? And then we'll head out to your place first thing in the morning. Have a look around. Would you be comfortable with that?' Bob asked.

'You really think you need to come out to my place and have a look?'

'Yes,' Dave said, without conferring with Bob. 'I think we do.'

George shook his head. 'I can't believe this. Darryl, my neighbour, made it seem so silly, and I really felt he was right. And Kallygarn is such a long way from here.'

'You still must have had some concerns, though, because you brought them up with us tonight.' Bob put his knife on the plate. 'Look, mate, you didn't come down in the last shower. If something is feeling off, then it's feeling off.'

'We're really glad you've spoken up,' Dave said. 'I'm just going to duck out and make a few phone calls while you finish up your dinner. Then we'll grab some shut-eye and head out to your place first thing in the morning. Be back shortly.'

George cut himself another piece of parmi while Bob put his fork down. As Dave slid his chair backwards and left the table, he realised that Bob had eaten little, if anything, of his salad.

Weaving his way through the busy pub, and trying to avoid elbows and beer glasses until he was outside, Dave eventually found the door and headed into the quiet street. Digging out his mobile phone he dialled Lorri's number.

'Evening,' she answered on the first ring. 'How's Bob?'

'Much better tonight,' Dave replied. 'Thank bloody goodness. We got the all-clear at the hospital, so we're good to go to Kallygarn if that's where we're needed.'

'Everything is still quiet here. No more reports, only stations wanting your expertise, so you've got the all-clear.'

'Has there been anything come across your desk to say the bomb at the shire council offices was homemade?'

'Not that I know about,' Lorri told him. 'If you want up-to-date information you should ring Kallygarn.'

'Fair enough, will do. Have you had any reports of stolen fertiliser recently? Ammonium nitrate in particular?'

Lorri sounded bemused when she answered. 'No. Nothing like that.' She paused. 'Why, what's going on? Have you heard something?'

'Well, yes and no. We got talking to an old fella, George, at the pub tonight—we're in Chapman Hill and I just happened to start up a conversation with him. He's not sure but he reckons he's had about one hundred and twenty-five kilos of ammonium nitrate stolen. The fertiliser was in twenty-five-kilo bags so they'd be pretty easy to shift. Just chuck 'em on the back of a ute. And five bags in the back of a ute wouldn't raise anyone's suspicions. What I'd love to know is whether that was enough to blow the Kallygarn Shire Council offices to smithereens.'

'Woah, are you serious?' Lorri sounded incredulous.

'Sure am.' Dave pulled his jacket tighter around his shoulders and changed hands, shoving his cold fingers into the pockets.

'Well, let's find out,' Lorri said excitedly. 'What are you going to do?'

'Head out to George's place first thing in the morning. And I'll give Kallygarn police a call and see what information they'll give me. I think it's worth following up, even if it comes to nothing.'

'Absolutely.'

'Cheers, Lorri. Thanks for your help.'

'No trouble. Be safe, boss. Say hi to Bob.'

Dave registered the word boss, but he was too busy planning to let it bother him now. He grabbed the phone book he kept in the troopy's glovebox. Flipping through the pages, he found the number he wanted and punched it into his flip phone. He waited while it rang and rang.

'Kallygarn Police.' The voice sounded tired and annoyed. Probably sick of all the journalists trying to get a statement.

Dave introduced himself and asked to speak to Johnny.

'Dave, good to hear your voice, mate. It's me, Johnny.' His tone relaxed as he spoke.

'How's things down there, mate? Sounds like you've had a bit more action.'

'We have. Geez, I'm not sure what the hell is going on, but it's certainly got the locals rattled. Us coppers included. We didn't sign up for this sort of shit out here, I can tell you.'

'Look, Johnny, just wanted to touch base and see if there have been any new developments there. Do you know if the Bomb Squad has worked out what the explosive was made from or how it was detonated?'

'Hoping for that information later tonight or first thing in the morning.'

Johnny sounded cagey.

Dave paused. 'Ok-aaay,' he drew the word out. 'What if I told you I've been speaking to a bloke who thinks he's had some ammonium nitrate stolen.'

Dave heard Johnny draw in a breath.

'I'd be very interested in that, as would the Bomb Squad. Whereabouts?'

'Bob and I are currently at Chapman Hill, and the farm in question is approximately a hundred kilometres north from here.'

'Bloody long way from Kallygarn. You don't really think it's related?'

'Well, mate, I know it's a bit of a longshot, but there's enough here with the evidence you've got to check it out, don't you think? Ammonium nitrate makes bombs and we've had two bomb blasts in very short succession. And then the other interesting piece of information is the Sinners

270

have been here. Staying up near George's farm. On his neighbour's place.'

'There's nothing to indicate bikies are involved, that much I can tell you.'

'No, but you and I both know that bikies like to blow up things or shoot people. Not too much in between. I've been telling Bob this since the first blast happened.' He felt like a broken record. Still, if he kept at it, surely someone would listen to him.

'Right. Look, I don't think the bikie theory works, but . . .'

There was silence and Dave waited, looking at the stars above—pricks of silver in black velvet. In the background of Johnny's office, the radio chatter was constant.

'I don't know, Dave,' Johnny said after he'd obviously assembled his thoughts. 'I still don't think the bikie link feels right to me.' His voice was more certain now.

Dave waited again. 'Is one hundred and twenty-five kilos of fert enough to total the offices the way that blast did?' he finally asked when Johnny wasn't forthcoming with anything else. He repeated the amount that had been taken and the fact it was in smaller bags, not bulk bags. 'It would've been easy to shift.'

'I reckon one hundred and twenty-five kilos would've done the job,' Johnny agreed. 'I'd have to confirm that but mix the fert with some diesel and make a slurry then pack jerry cans around the slurry . . . say, it was in a drum— yeah, I could see that working.

'But how heavy would the bomb have been? It's sounding like it could've been heavy. We didn't find any forklift tracks or anything like that. Whatever was used had to be light enough to be carried. By how many people, I don't know, but it was certainly carried by hand.'

'Any woman or bloke who's reasonably fit would be able to carry twenty-five kilos. And that's what was in the bags.'

'Hmm.' Another silence.

'Have the Bomb Squad found a fuse or anything to say how the bomb was detonated?'

'They think it was electronically.'

'And there weren't any cameras?'

'No. But there are now.'

That stopped Dave. 'And were they up in time for this last attack?'

'Yes. We've got some footage.'

'Geez, have you?' A thudding in Dave's chest, which he knew was adrenalin, hit him hard. 'Do you know who it is?'

'We're working on that. Look, between you and me, we don't think it's the same person or people. One of the blokes found a safety fuse in the wreckage of the service station today, and that doesn't fit with the way the other explosion was detonated. Two different devices we think. For fuck's sake don't repeat this to anyone because it isn't confirmed yet, but we think the service station blast was from a stick of gel. But we can't be sure yet,' he reiterated.

'What was last night's then? A copycat?'

'Maybe they're just being clever and giving us the run-around. Hang on.' Johnny's voice was muffled as he answered a question from another person in the station, then came back to Dave. 'Now, where was I? Oh yeah. The whole feeling of this second explosion is different from the first. The first one was meticulously planned. There's hardly any evidence left, which is why it's taken so long to get any answers. Everything has been totalled and that was the perps' intention.

'This other one . . . well, it feels a bit haphazard in some ways, although not in others. Jury's out.'

'I don't understand why Kallygarn was the target.'

Johnny blew out a breath that muffled the phone line for a second. 'I would give anything to know the answer to that question. Fuck me dead, I've had phone call after phone call from the locals, wondering if it's still safe to live here. I know of ten families who have left to go and stay with relatives. Just pulled their kids out of school and hightailed it out of town. Can't say I blame them. I might, too, if I wasn't in the job.'

'You don't have any indication as to why—'

'Nope. If we can work that out, I reckon we'll find who set the bomb off. At first, I thought it must have been aimed at someone in the shire council offices. Or a department. But if the service station has been done over by the same people, then that blows that theory out of the water, because although the servo is a multinational company, the franchise is owned by a family who have moved to town to manage it. They have no connections to Kallygarn at all.'

'But if you look at them both individually . . .' Dave waited again.

'You've got one government building and one multi-national company.'

'Who stands to benefit from the service station going up?' Dave opened the door and climbed in to get away from the chill. His breath was still coming out in white bursts.

'Well, again, no one . . .' Johnny paused. 'Unless someone wanted to have a crack at a multinational. But why would you? So many faceless and nameless people inside those businesses, you can't get to the person you're trying to hurt. Especially using a town as small as Kallygarn.'

'Anyone local who might benefit?' Dave asked.

'Not really. I mean perhaps Dan Hinderkin might but only for a short period of time until the fuel station was rebuilt. Do you remember him? The shire councillor I had to have a word to when you were here the other day. He owns the other servo in town.'

'Are you looking at him?'

Johnny burst out laughing. 'What do you take me for, a fool? We've given him a once-over, but no, Dave, he hasn't got anything to do with this. Look, I know he sounds like a wanker, and he is, but he's also full of hot air. Plus, he's not that clever. I had a chat to him this afternoon and he said he was away last night. His alibi is still to be verified, but he was at a meeting in Perth, so there will be plenty of people to authenticate his whereabouts . . .' Johnny paused again. 'Hey, *mate*, are you wanting to come and head up the investigation?'

Dave realised he'd pushed too far and questioned Johnny's ability. 'Sorry, I'm just trying to get my head around what

I might find tomorrow when I get to Kallygarn, and also to see if there could be a link between this fertiliser and your bomb. It really doesn't sound like there is.' Dave took a breath, not wanting to say the next words, but knowing they were important. 'Sorry if I upset you.'

'I'll ring you as soon as I hear back from the boys in the Bomb Squad,' Johnny said. 'You go and chat to your farmer tomorrow and let me know how you get on. Sound like a plan? I do think that link is worth following up.' His voice had relaxed back into his usual jovial tone.

'Sure. I'll let you know as soon as I've got something to report.'

CHAPTER 27

'Daddy! Daddy!' Bec's voice filtered through the fog of Dave's sleep and he jerked awake.

'Bec?' He threw the bedclothes off and jumped out of bed, ready to go to her side. Then reality came crashing down.

Neither of his daughters were here and he was getting a divorce from Mel. He flopped back onto the bed and tried to plump the pillow, eyes wide open. Bec's voice in his dream had made goosebumps form on his skin. She had sounded so real. All he wanted to do now was pick Bec up and hug her. Hug Alice, too.

The clock read two am. Dave got up and went into the bathroom then ran back to bed. The air was freezing and when he'd tried to turn on the reverse cycle air-conditioner earlier, it hadn't worked. Not that he was surprised.

To add to his list of complaints, the bed was lumpy. It all reminded him of the reasons why he hated these small country motels. He'd rather be in his swag and camped next to a campfire.

Through the wall, Bob was again snoring loudly. A similar noise came from George's room on the other side.

Dave hit the pillow in frustration, then lifted it over his head. If there was one thing Dave hated it was not being in charge of an investigation. It was frustrating trying to help Johnny without having access to all the information and interviews.

There was a silver lining tonight, though. By the sounds of both of his charges, they were alive at this point. He wasn't sure he could guarantee their safety until morning, especially if they kept snoring like they were! He pushed thoughts of Alice and Bec aside and turned over, closing his eyes, trying to go back to sleep.

Something was niggling him since he'd hung up from Johnny, but he couldn't quite put his finger on it. He had said something Dave wanted to follow up on, and because he hadn't had his normal notepad with him, it hadn't been written it down.

Detonators, explosives, evidence.

It wasn't any of those.

Suspects.

He frowned into the pillow. The first bomb at Kallygarn was unusual. Again the question he'd kept repeating to himself over and over was why would anyone attack a shire council office? In a small town? Who were they trying to send a message to? That had to be it. Someone in Kallygarn was being sent a message. But who and why?

Sighing, he now threw his pillow across the room and got out of bed once more. Padding across to the bathroom, he cupped his hand under the tap and drank thirstily, hoping the freezing water would help clear his brain.

'Has anyone left town recently?' he asked aloud, turning off the tap. In the bedroom he rummaged around in his briefcase and brought out a notebook and pen. Whatever questions there were, Dave would need to be careful how he phrased them to Johnny.

Had the service station refused to refuel someone? Perhaps the family hadn't paid a bill? Who owns the servo building?

Who owns the shire council building for that matter? The council?

Did anyone have links to organised crime or bikie gangs?

He knew none of these questions would give him a straight-out answer, but they might throw up some extra information when put together. A common name would be a help.

This was the way Dave knew to solve a case. Answer a question, which would lead to another, then answer the next question, and the next. Finally, there would be enough knowledge and facts to lead to the end of the case. Solving a case was like a jigsaw puzzle, you had to get all the pieces in the right spot, then you would be able to see the big picture.

Could anyone in Chapman Hill have links to Kallygarn? Dave wrote that question down, too.

He'd asked George whether he had any family in Kallygarn, but he'd shaken his head.

'I was an only child and I never married. If there are any family around, I don't know about them. When I die, I'm pretty sure the family lineage ends.'

Dave had felt the stick of regret in his stomach as George had told them his history. How sad to be the only one left. Even though it was unlikely, he hoped that never happened to him. Bob seemed to be having the same thoughts because he also looked sad at George's comments. And he was already in a similar position to George, except he had Betty.

Dave's thoughts had flown to Betty as that conversation had come to an end. She had rung him, which was unusual, and Dave hadn't answered because he was in the car with Bob.

Then the text message: *How is Bob?*

Pretty straightforward text, but a loaded question. Dave hadn't been sure how to answer. Bob was okay today. But he hadn't been yesterday and the day before. Maybe the chemo from the last round was wearing off and he was feeling better. The clearance from the doc had sure taken a load off Bob's mind.

An amount of time passed before Dave had been able to text back: *Better than the last few days.*

What would come of that answer?

Surprisingly, nothing. The phone had stayed silent.

He was half relieved until he'd wondered if she was rallying the troops and planning to come looking for Bob.

Outside, Dave heard a vehicle's engine so he went to the window and opened the curtain a crack. It was late for anyone to be arriving at the motel.

A ute with a canopy on the back pulled into the motel and shut its lights off, the driver getting out of the car. He went to the door of a room, and bent down, inspecting the lock.

The old man must have left a key there for him because the door swung open. Turning on the light before he motioned for his companion to come in. Dave waited until another person, wearing a heavy, thick jacket, hiding their gender, was safely inside the room and then let the curtain fall. He went back to his musings.

A moment later his computer dinged with an email and Dave wiggled the mouse to bring it to life. The message was from Johnny: *Here's some light reading for you.*

'You're keeping late hours, Johnny,' Dave muttered.

Intrigued at how the copper would have found his email address, and what he had sent, Dave clicked on the attachment and stared. Why had Johnny sent him an interview that the police had conducted straight after the first explosion?

He took the computer back to the bed and sat cross-legged under the sheets then started to read.

Interview with Shire President, Mr Bruce Lowe, 56.

Dave began reading the interview. 'JC' he took to mean Johnny Campbell. 'BL', Bruce Lowe.

JC: Can you tell me where you were last night at the time of the explosion?
BL: At home, in bed with my wife.
JC: And Laura can verify that?
BL: Of course! What are you asking, Johnny?
JC: Just answer the questions, Bruce. I've got a bloody big day in front of me. Has anyone threatened you recently?
BL: No. I would've reported it to you if they had.

Dave read on. Johnny had interviewed all the shire workers; thirty-five people questioned and there didn't seem to be a single piece of information that was helpful. No one knew anything.

How could no one in a small country town not know something?

Dave yawned and checked his watch, but his eyes were tired and he couldn't read the hands properly. If it wasn't for the excited fizzing in his stomach, the sort he got during a case, he'd try for a bit more sleep.

The next page showed names of the local residents.

JC: Mrs Fletcher, where were you last night when the explosion happened?
Mary Fletcher: Well, I'd not long been home as I'd gone to Stockdale that day, doing my shopping. I stopped to have tea with my family, too. I've got a sister and a niece over there.
JC: And what time did you leave Stockdale?

MF: Not sure, but after nine pm. I should have been home by eleven, but I got a flat tyre just before the one hundred kay mark. Took me a while to change it because no one stopped to help.

JC: Did you see anyone on the road?

MF: Only trucks. And they wouldn't pull up to help a damsel in distress! Just got to keep those wheels turning, you know that, Johnny.

JC: And what time did you arrive back in Kallygarn?

MF: I'm sure it was close to one in the morning, but I didn't look at the clock. I was wanting my bed.

JC: Can you remember if there was anyone out on the streets?

MF: Well, I wasn't looking so I can't be sure, but I think the answer is no.

JC: No, you can't remember, or no, there wasn't anyone out that night? Think carefully, Mary, because you seem to be the only one in this town who was out of their house close to the time the bomb went off. Was there a car parked in a strange spot? I don't know, perhaps there was a dog walking down the street that wouldn't normally be out . . . anything?

Dave sympathised with Johnny. After eight hours of interviews he would have been knackered, and although Dave wasn't listening to the recordings, he could read in Johnny's words that he was ready for a break.

MF: I'm sorry, Johnny, if I could help I would, you know that.

JC: Okay, one last question. Who is your sister in Stockdale so I can verify you were there.

MF: Georgia Phillips.

JC: Do I know that name?'

MF: I'm not sure. She's lived there for years. Her boy was killed in a car accident last year. His car slammed into a tree. She's taken his death very hard.

JC: And a niece you said?

MF: Connie Phillips.

JC: Right, well thanks for coming in, Mary. Appreciate it.

Dave rubbed his eyes and closed the computer. He wasn't sure if Johnny was baffling him with bullshit for his insolence on the phone earlier, or if there was useful information in these interviews. Still, tiredness was beginning to overtake him.

Pulling up the covers and turning on his side, Dave checked both George and Bob were still alive and snoring before he let his eyes close.

~

The alarm went off at six am and Dave started, then groaned. After his early morning exploits he didn't feel like getting out of bed. Morning noises filtered through. One of his charges was still snoring and he realised it was

Bob. Of course, George, being used to early mornings, would already be up and keen to get going.

Dragging himself out of bed, Dave thumped gently on the wall, hoping it would wake Bob, then headed for the shower, without waiting to see if there was an answer.

Minutes later, when Dave flung the door open to the outside, George was sitting on the cement path outside the motel rooms, a cup of tea in hand. His legs were stretched out in front of him as if he was sitting around a campfire.

'Morning. Sleep all right?' George asked.

Dave shook his head. 'Bit of a restless one, I'm afraid.' He looked hopefully at George's cup of tea. 'Any coffee?'

'Only what's in the rooms.'

There wasn't a chance Dave would drink that instant stuff if it was the last coffee on the planet. There must be a bakery close by and they would have a proper machine.

Bob's door swung open and he greeted everyone with a hearty hello. Only Dave knew he wasn't feeling great today. He hadn't shaved.

'If you'd like to follow me, I'll take you past the bakery so you can get some breakfast,' George offered as if reading Dave's mind.

Bob didn't even look at Dave as he said, 'Let's just get on the road. Quicker we get out to George's, the quicker we'll find the information and work out what we have to do.'

'Wouldn't mind a coffee,' Dave said.

'You'll be right, son. Be back in town by nine and you can get one then.'

George watched the exchange and then got up, tipping out the dregs of his tea. He put the cup back inside, closing the door gently. 'Follow me,' he said and got into his old ute.

When he turned the key a rattling echoed across the parking lot and it reminded Dave of the late-night visitors who had arrived last night. He hoped they wouldn't wake at the noise.

Dave looked at Bob, who was already in the troopy, and jumped into the driver's seat, following George out onto the road.

The country was different from Stockdale. Even though the crops were still green, they weren't as high or as thick, and the trees grew tall with broad, salmon-coloured trunks. The canopies of leaves and branches shaded the ground. There was a bit of native bush on the side of the road, but mostly it was clear and made spotting for kangaroos very easy.

Twelve mailboxes later, and with no conversation between Dave and Bob, George indicated to the right and turned into a driveway that had a well-maintained road leading up to a house on a hill. Dave followed him past the house, around the sheep yards and to the back of an old shed.

George pulled to a stop and got out, pointing at something.

'What's that?' Dave wound down his window and leaned out, but Bob was already out of the troopy, looking at the ground.

'What is it?' Dave felt like his head was full of cotton wool. Tired and grumpy from the previous investigation efforts and the fact he hadn't been able to get a coffee had made him cranky. Now Bob and George were talking and looking, interested in something at the front of the shed. He chided himself for thinking that Bob was going to be the one who wouldn't be helpful today.

Outside was cold and the fresh air helped clear his addled mind. George's yard looked like an antique machinery yard. Dave clocked the old twenty-tonne silo, twenty-litre chemical drums and the Chamberlain sixteen-run combine seeder.

George had been right when he'd said his gear was old. Dave's grandfather had worked with machinery like this and Dave had grown up driving some of it. He'd never forget when his dad had bought a new tractor and his brothers and he had fought over who was going to drive it first. That year Dave hadn't minded seeding.

'Get the camera, Dave,' said Bob, hurrying towards the troopy. 'And see if you can make a cast of the tyre tracks.'

'Sorry?'

Bob looked impatiently at him. 'Get the camera. See here? There're tyre tracks. They're fresh since the rain.'

Suddenly the pieces fell into place. 'Has there been more fertiliser stolen?' he asked, heading towards where George was squatting down looking at some more tracks next to the flapping tarp.

'There's been rain overnight,' George said. 'These tracks aren't mine and weren't here when I left yesterday. I can guarantee that.'

'Where's your fertiliser kept?'

'In that shed there.' He pointed his gnarled finger to where the tarp was lying flat on the ground. 'Now I know there were forty-five bags in there the other day. I counted them. They were there.'

'And now there are none,' said Dave.

CHAPTER 28

'They've taken forty-five bags, Johnny,' Dave said into the phone as Bob took George's statement. 'Forty-five freaking bags. You know what that means, don't you?'

'They're going to set off another bomb. And it's going to be bloody massive. Shit!'

'We've got to find them.'

'Dave, we don't even know it's a them. It could just be a him. Or a her, I guess.' Although Johnny's voice sounded doubtful. 'This is like looking for a needle in a haystack because we can't answer the first question—the why. How the hell can we know who it is if we can't narrow that part down? There're no clues as to where to start.'

'Whoever this is they'd have to be pretty strong to shift that number of bags by themself.'

They were silent, both thinking of the ramifications if they didn't find the person—or people—who had stolen George's fertiliser very soon. Next time there could be deaths.

'Stuffed if I know what to do,' Johnny said. 'But I reckon I'm going to ring Perth and request they get some eyes in the sky. I don't know what we're looking for, what vehicle even, but we'd better get searching for something suspicious. With any luck, they'll find a vehicle parked off deep in the bush somewhere.'

'Good call. We'll finish up here and then head towards Kallygarn. We can only make an educated guess that's where the perp is headed.'

'Sure. I'll let you know if we come up with anything.'

Dave hung up and went back to Bob and George.

'I'm very sorry this has happened to you,' Bob was saying to George, 'but we'll do our best to get to the bottom of it. Now here's your report number. Make sure you give that to your insurance company and they'll be able to put the claim through for you.'

George touched his fingers to his forehead. 'Thanks very much, fellas,' he said. 'I really wish I hadn't been right. I hope whoever has taken the fertiliser doesn't use it for what I think they might.'

'Us too, mate, us too,' Dave said grimly.

They shook hands and left in the troopy, Dave silent, waiting for Bob to tell him what he'd found out.

'Reckon we'd better call in at the neighbours, son,' Bob said once they were nearly out on the road.

Dave slowed and wound down his window, looking at the vehicle tracks that turned out of George's driveway and followed the road. 'You think we might be able to track them?'

'Nah, other vehicles have driven over the top of them. Namely George and us, but that can't be helped now. We didn't know. There's decent enough casts of the tracks near the shed. Hopefully they'll give us something when we find a vehicle to match them to.'

'We do need to talk to the neighbours and see if they heard or saw anything. George said that no one except locals come this far up the track, so if they saw any cars they didn't recognise in the last couple of days, we might have a lead that is worth following.' Bob tapped his fingers on his knees.

'Any lead is a good lead at the moment. George tell you much about the neighbours?'

'Only that they're a nice couple doing their best. Seems like they've had a fair bit go wrong for them, though. The wife is crook and that's making life pretty shithouse.'

'Unfortunately the husband is in the middle of a tangle with the law, too. Got into trouble for clearing some land. Let's just pay them a visit. Might not get much, but you never know. We'd better get some of the local coppers out here to interview all the farmers on this road.'

'Johnny wants us down there as soon as possible,' Dave said. 'He's worried, as I am, that another bomb is going to go off in Kallygarn, and this time it'll be a huge one.'

'Yes, I agree that's logical, as is to link the other two bombings in Kallygarn. However, information is going to be king in this instance. If we can find the reason the bombings occurred in the first place, we'll find who planted them,' Bob said calmly. 'So, let's bring the locals in.'

'Needle in a haystack,' Dave repeated Johnny's words to Bob.

'Which is what we're good at solving, because being Rural Crime Squad officers, we know a bit about hay. Turn here.' Bob indicated the mailbox and long driveway heading towards a shed in the distance as Dave rolled his eyes.

Dave's stomach rumbled and he put his hand over it. 'Sorry,' he said. 'God, I'd love a coffee.'

'Apologies for this morning,' Bob said. 'I just wanted to get out here. I should've known that something like this would happen and we wouldn't get back to town for ages. Murphy's Law.'

'I've got some muesli bars in the back. Do you want one?'

'Thanks. I'll get one when we stop.' Bob didn't speak for a second as he assessed the farm. 'Shit, do you think they live in the shed?' he asked.

Dave searched the horizon. 'Can't see anything else. And look, there's sort of a garden leading to the door.'

Pulling the troopy up next to the fence, Dave turned off the engine, before leaning over the seats and grabbing out a box of chocolate-chip muesli bars.

Bob raised his eyebrows. 'Chocolate chip. Nice.' He put his hand out.

'They were Bec's favourites,' Dave said, handing him one, 'so I keep buying them. Just in case she ever comes to stay.' He bit into a bar and opened the door. 'Let's go.'

Moments later they were rapping on the aluminium door that led into the shed.

'Don't see this anymore,' Bob said quietly. 'When country was being opened up years ago, it wasn't unusual to find farmers living in a shed. But not these days. I suppose we're in the right place.'

'Hello?' Dave called out. 'Anyone home?'

Finally, the door swung open and a man in his late forties stood in his boxer shorts and singlet. 'Sorry, mate, I'm not buying,' he said. He moved to shut the door.

Dave caught it before he did, grinning. 'That's lucky 'cause I'm not selling. Detective Dave Burrows from the Rural Crime Squad. This is my partner, Bob Holden.' As he said the words, he wondered how many more times he'd get to say, 'my partner'.

The man crossed his arms and stared at them. 'What the fuck do you want?'

Raising his eyebrows, Dave pursed his lips. 'Nothing that will take long, Mr . . .' He trailed off, waiting for the man to answer.

'I don't have to answer any of your questions. How about you get off my property?'

'We're not here to antagonise anyone,' Bob spoke now. 'We wanted to ask you a few questions. Do you think we could come in?'

'Ask your questions here.' The man leaned across the doorway, blocking the entrance. 'My wife isn't well,' he added as if that was going to stop them from asking anything hard.

'Yeah, George told us. And your name?' Bob wasn't mucking around now.

The man must have sensed that because he answered straightaway. 'Darryl. Darryl Wilson.'

'Right, Mr Wilson.'

From just inside they heard a soft voice. The man turned towards the sound. From where he was standing, Dave could see a frail woman, swaying on her wasted legs.

'Love, you need to get back inside,' Darryl said.

'Invite them in for coffee,' the woman said. 'You can't not.'

'We'd love a coffee, thanks, Mrs Wilson,' Dave said before Bob had a chance to say anything.

With a furious glance towards them, Darryl took his wife's arm and together they walked slowly through the shed, then opened another door into a kitchen.

Pulling out a chair for his wife, Darryl helped her sit, before putting the kettle on.

The woman smiled at both Bob and Dave and indicated for them to sit down, too.

'I'm Jasmine,' she said. 'Find it . . . hard to . . . talk.' She indicated to her lungs.

Dave introduced both of them. 'Thanks for inviting us in, Jasmine, and you too, Darryl. How's the season treating you?'

'Fine, but I had a very late night. A few ewes having trouble with lambing. Coffee for you both?' he asked.

'Please. You lamb late, do you?' Dave pulled out the chair at the end of the table and sat down, Bob following suit.

Darryl seemed confused for a moment then answered Dave's question. 'Few stragglers that must've got tied up with the ram after they should have. Can you tell me what this is about?' He heaped coffee into mugs and put the sugar on the table, along with a litre bottle of milk.

Dave smiled and nodded. 'Of course.' He turned to Jasmine. 'Is there anything I can do to help you?'

She blinked, then frowned. 'I'm . . . fine.'

'Jasmine's got, um, she's got muscular dystrophy and finds it a bit hard to talk sometimes.'

'But I . . . can still . . . do lots . . . of things,' she told them. 'Still have . . . lots of . . . independence.'

'Fiercely independent, I can see that,' Bob said with a smile. 'I understand that need. And the desire to still be treated normally. I've got cancer and I get pretty annoyed when people try to help me. Even when they've got the best intentions. I see it more as them trying to control my life than helping.'

'Yes . . . exactly,' Jasmine said.

Darryl put a cup on the table loudly and stood at the opposite end from Dave, his arms crossed again. 'So what do you want?'

Readjusting his gaze, Dave frowned and got out his notebook. The gesture was to let both of them know that, even though these questions weren't at the station, the situation was serious enough that they would be taking notes.

Bob did the talking. 'Well, Darryl, this morning we have been across to your neighbour's farm. George came and spoke to us last night about some missing fertiliser. He mentioned that he talked to you about it, too?'

'Yeah. The story sounds ludicrous to me.'

'Maybe not so much. We decided it was worth heading out there this morning to have a look and we found the area empty. What was left of his ammonium nitrate was missing. Now, we believe it has been stolen. In this current climate, with the bombings in Kallygarn, we're concerned that the fertiliser might not be used in the best interests of the public.'

Darryl's mouth dropped open, and he stared at Bob and then Dave. 'What the fuck are you bastards saying?' He dropped his hands on the table and leaned towards Bob, his voice low and furious. 'That I had something to do with it? I dropped some weaners back to his place yesterday and he told me he was missing five bags. But he wasn't sure, so I didn't take a lot of notice. He's forgetful and doesn't always make sense. This whole story of his is fanciful.'

'Darryl,' Bob said, copying Darryl's action but in reverse, 'did you just hear what I said? The rest of the fertiliser is gone as well. There is nothing ludicrous or fanciful about George's story. It's the real deal.'

Dave stood up and walked to the end of the table. Pulling out a chair, he indicated for Darryl to sit down.

'How about you calm down and listen to what we've got to say,' Dave instructed.

'Darryl, sweetie . . . Calm down . . . This has . . . nothing to do . . . with us . . . Don't worry . . . Just answer.' Jasmine reached out her hand to her husband and he took it, gripping her tightly as if holding on to her for strength.

'We're just making some inquiries today, Darryl,' Bob said evenly. 'We believe the fertiliser was taken between two pm Wednesday afternoon and when we arrived at George's this morning at seven thirty am. Now, if you were up with a lambing ewe, is there any chance that you saw anything last night that was unusual? Lights on the road perhaps?'

Taking a breath and using his spare hand to pat the one of Jasmine's he was holding, Darryl swallowed and looked at Bob. 'Ah, no. I can't see the road from where I was in the paddock. So, if there had been lights or a vehicle driving along it, I wouldn't have known.' Contrite now, he threw Dave an apologetic glance and then brought his gaze back to Bob.

'Okay, but you didn't hear any vehicles or dogs barking or anything that was unusual? In fact, do you have a dog?'

'Yeah, Magpie, but he was with me helping catch the ewes and he didn't act differently.'

'Right-oh. What about any chatter on the radio? Do you have a two-way?'

Dave reached for the milk, poured some into his coffee and gratefully took a sip. Darryl, who had let go of Jasmine's hand was rubbing the tablecloth in between his fingers.

'Look, yeah, I have a two-way radio. That was quiet as a church, though. There was a bit on last night. It's not easy birthing twin lambs and being caught up in making sure they were both alive.' He gave a shrug. 'Don't think I can help you. I'm really sorry that George had this happen to him, but I sure as hell didn't take the fertiliser or know who did.'

'Like I said, Darryl, we're just making some inquiries. It's a lot of ammonium nitrate to have gone missing in one hit,' Dave said.

Bob looked towards Jasmine, who was pushing her hair back from her face. Dave could tell his partner hated that he had to ask these questions of her. They could both see the deep, dark circles beneath her eyes and the agitation in her movements.

'What about you, Jasmine, did you hear anything?'

'No ... I take ... medicine ... Makes me ... sleepy.' Giving Darryl a fond look, she continued. 'Hard for Darryl ... He's got ... to do ... all this ... work by himself ... Comes home ... Finds me asleep ... Not very useful ... anymore.'

'Hey, stop that,' Darryl said, touching her shoulder. 'Doesn't matter. This is our lot and we're handling it the best we can. And I don't mind, you know that.'

Bob and Dave sipped their coffee, taking everything in.

'Have either of you heard about the explosion in Kallygarn?' asked Dave.

'Yeah.' Darryl turned back to them. 'That's terrible. But it's a long way from here. Does anyone know who's responsible yet?'

'Still under investigation,' Bob answered this time. 'I wonder if you know that the type of fertiliser George had on his farm can be used to make a bomb?'

Raising one shoulder, Darryl tipped his head from side to side. 'That's been happening for years,' he said. 'How do you reckon the older farmers got rid of the rocks from their paddocks when they were opening up the country?'

Dave wrote that down.

'Anyway, no one was hurt in the blast,' Darryl said, 'so I can't see that it's a major problem.' He shrugged again. 'They can just rebuild the offices.'

'No one was hurt in either blast,' Dave said.

There was a silence at the table as Darryl and Jasmine looked at each other.

'Either blast?'

'You haven't heard? The service station at Kallygarn was also damaged in an explosion. That happened a little over twenty-four hours ago.'

Jasmine nodded, suddenly understanding. 'No power . . . since yesterday morning . . . No TV . . . or radio.'

'You think they'd do something about it, wouldn't you?' Darryl said. 'But no, we seem to get forgotten up here.'

'But the power's on now?'

'Yeah, came back on about four o'clock this morning.'

'That must make things much more comfortable for you both,' Bob said, smiling at them. 'Does anyone else live here with you?'

'No, it's just the two of us,' Darryl said.

'And do you have any family or friends in Kallygarn?'

'No, no, I don't know anyone there,' Darryl said.

Jasmine shook her head. Her chest was rising quickly from the exertion of speaking so much. Dave decided it might be time to leave. Give Darryl a chance to calm down and Jasmine a break.

Dave finished his coffee and slipped his business card from his pocket, placing it on the table. 'Well, thanks for your time, Darryl and Jasmine. We might have to pop back and ask more questions over the next few days, but we appreciate you talking to us this morning.'

They pushed back their chairs and stood, making their way towards the door.

Bob stopped and turned back, eyeing the couple. 'I just remembered, George said you've been having a bit of trouble with the Department of Conservation and Land Management. Can you tell me a little bit about that?'

'Not much to tell,' Darryl said darkly. 'Cleared a few hectares over near the boundary where the Crown land hits my land and they pinged me for it. The bastards are taking me to court.'

'How much land did you clear?' Dave asked.

'Not enough to cause anyone any trouble,' Darryl said. 'I just wanted to clear the area where I thought we could build a house. Then some nutter has come along and decided I've done something very bad and charged me for it.'

'When's your court date?'

Darryl's gaze slid to Jasmine. 'In two weeks,' he said quietly.

'What?' whispered Jasmine. 'You didn't . . . tell me.'

Pushing his chair back, Darryl got up and stood next to where his wife was seated. He took her hands in his and looked her in the eye. 'I didn't want to worry you,' he said. 'They've upgraded the charges. I spoke to Greg the other day.'

'You didn't . . . want to—' Her voice broke off in distress. She dropped his hands then put her own hands up to her face and covered her eyes. 'No,' she muttered, her shoulders heaving now. 'No. Oh, Darryl . . . What are . . . we going to . . . do? Who will . . . look after me? And you . . . What about . . . you?'

'Jasmine! I didn't want to worry . . . Look, I would have told you soon, probably today, but these guys beat me to it. I'll work something out, I promise. You won't be here by yourself. I've . . . I've got an idea.' He glanced towards Dave and Bob and then back at Jasmine. He squatted next to her and held her hands again, trying to make her look at him. 'I've got an idea,' he whispered.

'It's actually . . . happening, isn't it?' She raised her eyes to his. 'How did . . . we get here?'

Dave took a step forward to ask if he could help in any way, but that was also the moment Darryl exploded.

'This isn't my fault, Jasmine,' he yelled. 'It's the fucking government!' He stood up and turned away from her shocked expression. 'They're the ones who are tearing you and me apart. Not me. Not you. The fucking government. How can they possibly think that charging me or putting me in gaol with you as sick as you are is all right? Yet nothing I say will make them drop the charges. If I go to gaol, Jazzy, you're gonna be by yourself and there won't be a bloody thing I can do about it.' He stopped now and ran his hands over his face, brushing what Dave thought were tears away.

'But I think I've got a plan,' Darryl whispered again.

CHAPTER 29

'How do we find out if the person who's issued the charges against Darryl is from the Kallygarn Conservation and Land Management office?'

Dave and Bob were parked at the front of the motel rooms they'd stayed in last night. They'd already collected their bags and packed the troopy. Johnny was on open speaker and both men leaned towards the phone, listening intently.

'I can ask around. Someone will know, but we haven't got access to any paperwork now,' Johnny said. 'Because it's all been burned. It's unlikely though because it's too far outside their designated zone. Chapman Hill to Kallygarn is four hundred kilometres. These guys stick within the shire boundaries.'

'Surely there would be some pencil pusher in Perth who would know about this? Maybe the fella who followed it through moved shires,' Dave said. 'And Darryl said something about his lawyer, so we can follow it up that way if we can't find out through your records, Johnny.'

'Sure, I'll put some feelers out. Reckon it's a long shot, though.'

'I'm not convinced it is, Johnny,' Bob broke into the conversation. 'He's the neighbour of the fella who's had the fert taken. That's a pretty big coincidence in my book.'

'Yeah, but I still don't see how there's a definite connection to Kallygarn.'

'Maybe he was just trying to make a point by blowing up a government office—any government office,' Bob said. 'And maybe he thought some random office hours away from where he lived might mean we're less likely to come knocking on his door.'

Johnny still seemed sceptical. 'Has this bloke got any knowledge of how to even make a bomb?'

Bob harrumphed. 'Anyone can learn anything if they ask around enough.'

'I guess so, but I'm still not convinced.'

'Actually,' Dave broke in, 'Bob's comment makes sense. If Darryl blew up the shire council offices here in Chapman Hill, we'd be looking a lot closer to home. That would put anyone in this shire in the frame. But if you blow up something a long way away, Darryl would assume there's less chance of getting caught.'

'He's certainly pissed off with the department that has charged him.'

'And scared,' Dave added.

'Doesn't mean he wants to make a statement,' Johnny said. 'Tell me again why he's been charged and with what?'

'No one in the state is allowed to clear any sort of native bush without a permit, and they're just about nigh imposs- ible to get these days. He's gone in and bulldozed a heap of native bush, which is illegal. Sounds like they're going to chuck the book at him.'

'Right, and his missus is crook?'

'That's where a fair bit of the angst is coming in,' Dave said. He told Johnny about Jasmine's condition.

'Shit, that's a bit rough. I can understand why he's pissed off.'

'Sure, but he was the one who broke the law in the first place, so really, he's the one who has to wear it,' Dave said.

There was silence down the line as Johnny thought through all of the information.

'Okay, well, look, I've got to go,' Johnny finally said. 'Sounds like they're calling a briefing. See you when you get here.' He took a breath. 'God, I'll be pleased to have a couple of fresh hands and eyes. I can't see the wood for the trees I'm so stuffed.'

'Catch you later,' Bob said, while Dave hit the button disconnecting the call.

'I've just got to run to the motel office and get a receipt,' Dave said. 'He only gave me a handwritten receipt last night and I need an Eftpos one.'

'I'm not going anywhere, son. Although don't mind me if I'm asleep when you get back.' Bob put the seat back a little, wriggling to get comfortable, then dropped his sunglasses over his eyes.

Dave felt a rush of protection for his mate. He looked small and frail in the front seat. But there wasn't time to think like that. He jogged across to the reception.

Inside, the bell tinkled again as he walked through the door. And, just like yesterday, no one was around. He looked for a bell to ring on the desk.

'Hello?'

Still no one. Dave leaned against the counter, and tapped his fingers impatiently, while he looked around for another way to attract some attention. The guest register, filled with handwritten notes, was open on the desk.

Dave looked for his name and then down the list to see who the late arrivals from the night before had been. Their dual cab had been gone by the time he and Bob got back this morning.

Dave stilled as he read the name.

Tom Vincent.

Tom Vincent? Why was that name familiar?

Tom. Vincent . . .

He tapped his fingers harder on the desk, his heart beginning to thump. That was Connie Phillips' friend from Stockdale, wasn't it? He closed his eyes and recreated the scene at the lookout.

A man, woman and dog.

'What's your name?' Dave asked.

'Tom Vincent . . .'

'Connie has a good friend in you.'

Yes, Tom had been with Connie.

What would Tom Vincent be doing in Chapman Hill?

Connie Phillips hated the police. Was Tom following them? Was he trying to avenge Connie's brother's death for her?

Dave shook his head at how random that thought was. Ridiculous!

There was nothing to link Tom or Connie to what was going on here.

Except that Connie really hated authority. His brain niggled.

There'd been two people in the ute last night, he remembered. A bloke, the one who'd got out of the dual cab first. Then a smaller framed person, who had been cloaked in a heavy coat. Yes, that person could have been a woman, but if he'd been asked to swear in court, Dave wouldn't have been able to.

Connie?

The elderly man from yesterday came through the door and stared at him without recognition.

'Help yer?' he asked.

Dave leaned over the counter and tapped at Tom's name. 'This bloke, when did he arrive?'

'I can't give you that sort of information.' He looked hopeful. 'Not unless you want to pay for it.'

Dave pulled out his ID and flashed it at the man. 'Tell me everything you know about this person.'

The man's mouth opened and closed like a goldfish for a moment, then he blinked. 'I don't know anything about him. A woman rang to book the room, but she put it in his name. Said they were going to be really late and could I leave a key out for them. That's it in a nutshell. The bloke dropped the key back this morning before they left, but he never said nothing.'

'Did you see the woman he was with?'

'I don't make a habit of spying on guests. I've seen enough over the years to know not to do that.'

Dave glared.

'No. She never got out of the car.'

'Did he say where they were headed?'

'No.'

'Or why they were here?'

'No.' The man crossed his arms.

'How did they pay?'

'Cash.'

'Damn!' Dave banged his hand on the counter.

Tom and Connie had been right here! Dave couldn't explain why, but he didn't think it was just chance that these two were near where George's fertiliser had been taken from.

Logic started to creep into his thinking and the same question came back: why Kallygarn? Brandan's accident, as far as Dave knew, had happened in the Stockdale shire. It didn't make any sense to hit up Kallygarn.

Or did it?

And then why would both the shire council building and a servo be targeted? Brad and Kane had told him the police officers involved had been moved on, which Dave had thought was sensible. He would have done the same if he'd been in charge of the Stockdale Police Station. Had they been transferred to Kallygarn?

Dave thanked the man and jogged back to the car.

'Did you hear that late-night arrival?' Dave asked Bob, as he got into the driver's side.

Bob grunted.

'Bob!' Dave said loudly and his mate woke with a start.

'What's wrong?' He snorted then shifted in his seat so he was sitting upright.

'Last night, I couldn't sleep. I was awake when a couple turned up in a dual cab with a canopy on the back. They were really late. I reckon it was after two am. Tom Vincent and Connie Phillips.'

'And who are they when they're at home?'

'The girl I was talking to at the lookout. The one whose brother was killed—'

'—in the accident and blaming the police for his death,' Bob finished.

'Yeah. Tom is the bloke who was with her.'

'Chapman Hill is a long way from Stockdale.'

'George's farm is a fair drive, too.'

Concern crossed Bob's face as Dave started to make more notes in his notebook. 'You think she knew where the ammonium nitrate was? Why? I thought you had Darryl pegged for this.'

'I don't know if I've got either of them pegged, but there's something bloody strange going on. Darryl's pissed with the government, we saw that. His temper is something to behold, isn't it? And Connie, well, you heard her go off about the coppers. She's able to get hot under the collar, too. And,' Dave stopped writing as he remembered, 'I didn't tell you this, but she threatened Roger in the pub that night. Said she was coming for him.'

'Stockdale. Kallygarn. Two hundred kilometres between the towns,' Bob said gently. 'And Roger isn't heading up the police station in Kallygarn.'

'I know, I know!' Dave rested his head on the steering wheel, trying to get all of this information straight. 'Unless . . .' Dave voiced his thought about the officers involved in Brandan's accident being moved to Kallygarn.

'Geez, Dave, I think Johnny would've mentioned that to us, don't you?'

'You've got something better?' Dave started the car and reversed out of the parking lot then drove towards the highway.

'Nope.' Bob lapsed into silence.

Out on the road, Dave began tapping his fingers on the steering wheel when he remembered something. 'Can you get my computer out?' he asked Bob. 'Johnny sent me some files last night, some interviews, and there's something in there, I just can't think . . . I need you to read them to me.'

'Which part?'

'Not sure. Can you just open it up and read through the names? I think it was in the locals, not the shire council workers.'

Bob put his glasses on and reached in the back for the computer. After a few moments while they waited for it to start up, Dave directed him to where he had saved the files and Bob scrolled slowly through.

'Not the shire council president? He didn't seem to have much to add. Hmm . . .' Bob scratched his head. 'What about this one: *Mary Fletcher.*'

'Is she the one who got a flat tyre on the way home from Stockdale?'

Bob skim-read the page. 'Yeah. Got home about one am, she thinks.'

'Okay, can you read the whole interview to me?'

Bob started to read and then he gave a little huff.

'What?' Dave asked.

'Hang on.' Bob re-read the interview to himself and then took his glasses off and looked at Dave. 'Well, there you go. I think the bit you're wanting is this: Georgia Phillips is Mary's sister.'

Dave started nodding. 'Yeah, yeah! That's it. Georgia Phillips is Connie's mother, right?'

'Need to confirm the connection officially, but her son died in a traffic accident according to Mary. One and the same.'

'Why Kallygarn?' Dave asked again, thumping the steering wheel.

'Damn it, I'm sick of that question.'

'Only because you don't have the answer.'

Both lapsed into silence now. They turned off the highway and headed south on the dirt road towards Kallygarn.

Dave gave a snort and pointed out the window. 'I've always wanted to show the kids this fence,' he said. 'Why do you reckon someone decided to hang one shoe there and then other people have come along and added to it?' They drove past a kilometre of fencing covered in all types of shoes.

'Better than the one over east that has bras and knickers on it.'

'They'd rot too quickly. At least shoes won't do that.'

Back to silence as they both thought about the scenario in front of them.

'How's this for a plan?' Bob finally broke the silence. 'Obviously Johnny will have to give us the all-clear, but Mary needs to come back in for questioning. We don't know if Connie and Tom have stolen the fertiliser, but it would be prudent to put out an alert for them. Darryl isn't clear-cut either. What we have is a lot of circumstantial evidence indicating they're all involved. Yet there isn't any actual proof, meaning this could all be a happy coinci—'

'I'm sick of that bloody word,' Dave snapped. 'My gut is telling me we're on the right path.'

'Sure you don't just have an upset stomach?'

Dave ignored him and said, 'Johnny has issued a press release asking for the public to get in contact if there is anyone acting suspiciously in the Chapman Hill area.'

'Unfortunately, the link between Darryl, Tom and Connie is very tenuous. Two people, Connie and Darryl, who are very angry with authorities. What's Tom's beef?

'Until we eyeball the fertiliser, without being dramatic, the whole state is in danger. If our theory is whoever has the bags—Connie and Tom, Darryl, or persons still unknown—is going to set a bomb off, potentially a long way from here, then any town in the state could be the target.

'None of this is good, son. I bet the powers that be are shitting bricks right now.'

'I'm doing one hundred and thirty.'

'Better to get there alive than dead,' Bob told him and Dave lifted his foot slightly.

'I have another question, if it's Connie and Tom, how do they know about explosives?'

'Anyone can learn anything these days. We've talked about that. I bet they've got books on them or maybe a mate who works in the mine as a shotfirer. Google probably has something. Some of the old blokes like George would know how to make small blasts. It wouldn't be hard to find out the how-tos.'

Bob didn't look at all sleepy. The adrenalin had hit hard and, like Dave, he was desperate to make some headway.

His mobile phone rang and Bob answered it.

'They've got planes up, scanning the highways,' he told Dave after a moment.

'Good.'

'Aha. I see,' Bob said into the phone. 'Now this is what we've got.' He proceeded to fill Johnny in with their theory. 'Don't suppose the officers who were involved in that accident are at your station?'

Pause.

'Uh-huh. Well, that's enough for you to put out a BOLO for Connie and Tom, isn't it?'

Pause.

'Uh-huh. All we can tell you is they were in a dual cab ute. Maybe check with rego? Yeah. Good. Okay, we'll see you soon.' Bob put the phone down. 'He's confirmed that Mary and Georgia are sisters and that one of the officers from the accident was stationed at Kallygarn, but he was transferred three months ago.'

Dave thumped the steering wheel. 'Yes! There we are. Connection made.'

'Yep, there's the link,' Bob said.

'But Tom . . .' Dave's voice faded. 'Tom is just a loyal friend? Was he mates with Brandan, too?'

The phone rang again, and Bob picked it up. 'Holden,' he said, then he held the phone away from his ear. 'Sorry, you'll have to speak a little softer, I can't understand what you're—'

Dave looked over, frowning, as he heard the tone of the voice on the phone. 'Is that Darryl?'

'Buggered if I know. Sir? Please calm down. I can't help you if—' Bob fell silent and then took in a shuddering breath as the voice dropped and spoke in short, staccato words, loudly enough to be heard through the phone.

'Dead. Drowned. In the dam.'

'Okay, Darryl, have you called an ambulance?'

The answer was muffled.

'Darryl, we want you to take a few deep breaths and drive down to the road so you can meet the ambulance and show them where to go. Dave and I will be with you as quickly as we can. I'll ring the ambulance for you.' He made a hand signal to Dave to turn around.

313

Dave slowed and did a U-turn.

'Yes, we're coming, Darryl. We'll be about two hours.' Bob's voice was gentle. 'The ambulance will be there before us, but they'll know what to do. Hang in there, mate.' He hung up and looked at Dave. 'Jasmine's drowned. In a dam.'

CHAPTER 30

Dave watched the ambulance officers load Jasmine's body into the back of the van. The glare of the stark whiteness from the body bag made Dave's eyes water. Or at least that's what he blamed for the moisture in his eyes.

It didn't seem only four or so hours ago that they were all sitting around the kitchen table. Both Jasmine and Darryl alive.

'Do you know where Darryl is?' Dave asked the ambulance officer. He had a bad feeling about the farmer's absence. 'Have you seen him?'

'He hasn't been here since we arrived,' the younger of the two ambo officers told him. 'There were instructions sticky-taped to the door as to where to find her.'

'We'd better search the farm,' Bob said. 'You all okay here? You'll get her back to the hospital morgue?'

'Yeah, leave her with us.'

They closed the doors and gave Bob and Dave a wave as they started the engine and headed back towards the road.

'What the hell?' Dave exclaimed as they got back into the troopy. 'How did Jasmine get herself to the dam? She could hardly walk five metres when we saw her.'

'My guess is she didn't walk there herself.'

'I was hoping you weren't going to say that. We should have secured the scene. In case he murdered her.'

Bob didn't say a word. He looked weary and worn.

'But we need to find Darryl,' Dave said.

'Shearing shed,' Bob said, his voice heavy. 'You know what we're going to find, don't you? I don't think it will matter about securing anything.'

'Maybe he just couldn't stay while she was in the water.'

'Nice spin, but doubtful. A loving husband, a terminally ill wife. Husband possibly going to gaol. No one to look after the wife, and you really don't think Darryl has committed a murder–suicide? Geez, Dave, you've got a better outlook on humans than I do.'

Dave drove the troopy back to the dirt road and followed it along the fence line to where the country opened up into a compound with a set of sheep yards and a shearing shed. Coming to a halt along the stairs, they both looked at each other before they opened their doors and got out.

Some parts of their job were the pits.

Steeling himself for a body, Dave slid the shed door open and looked straight up at the rafters.

He took a breath.

Nothing.

With his hand on his gun, he walked slowly inside, eyes searching every nook and cranny. He didn't want to be surprised. 'Darryl?' he called. 'Darryl, are you here?'

A flutter of air above him, and a small chirp. A bird brushed the top of his head. Jumping, Dave's hands flew up to protect himself.

A willie wagtail peeped angrily at him and then flew back to her nest.

'Sorry,' he told her.

Bob came to stand alongside him, also on high alert. 'Anything?'

'Not yet,' Dave answered. The pens behind the shearing stands were empty, too. Pushing open the swinging doors, Dave walked around the corner to the engine room.

'Dave?'

He turned at Bob's voice. His partner was now at the back of the shed, where the wool bales were stored.

'Dave, you need to see this.'

Quickly following his previous path, Dave jogged over to Bob.

At his feet, were empty twenty-five-kilo bags, littering the floor and fluttering in the wind. Trails of grey and white granules led out to the door that opened up into an empty space where a truck would have parked to load the wool. It was as if Darryl had wanted to lead them somewhere.

'Fuck,' Dave whispered. 'Where's he gone?'

'More to the point, what's he got the fertiliser in?' Bob said quietly. 'Something big.'

'Where's the number he rang you from?' Dave asked.

'Out in the troopy.'

Dave turned and ran as fast as he could, out the door, down the steps and over to the troopy. He ripped open the door, grabbed the phone and checked the call register.

Before he could hit the last number, the phone rang.

Johnny.

'What's up?' Dave bit out.

The pause made Dave angry.

'What's up, Johnny? I've got a dead body and a missing husband I need to do something with ASAP.'

'Geez! Shit. We've located Tom and Connie's vehicle. About thirty minutes ago. They weren't in it, but we're looking. I'll tell you more when you're free. Who's deceased?'

'Jasmine,' Dave answered and hit the end button.

'Steady, son.' Bob was next to Dave now. 'Take a breath.'

Dave dialled Darryl.

One ring. Two.

Three times.

No dial tone.

It took Dave a couple of seconds to understand that the phone call had connected, but Darryl wasn't talking.

'Hello? Darryl? Are you there?'

Motioning to Bob to hurry up, Dave started the troopy.

'Darryl, mate, is that you? It's Dave here, Detective Dave Burrows.' Adrenalin shot through his body, yet he gathered himself, making his voice calm. Finding first gear as Bob put on his seatbelt, he took off.

'Did they get her?' Darryl asked, his voice thick.

Dave wasn't sure if Darryl was crying or had had a few drinks. Both probably.

'Yeah, mate, the ambos are looking after Jasmine. She's safe.' He paused. 'We're really sorry about Jasmine, Darryl. Whereabouts are you? Can we catch up?' The speedo was climbing quickly.

Darryl laughed. 'I don't think so.'

'Mate, come on. We're keen to make sure you get some help. You've had a pretty tough run.'

'Jasmine was my everything and now she's gone. Not much point in going on, is there?' His voice broke.

Dave spoke gently. 'Can you tell me what happened?'

'She took her pills and went out to the dam. The rest is history. Jasmine's gone. The more important question is, do you know why? That's what you should be asking yourself.'

The ambulance was turning onto the dirt road just in front of them. Dave pushed his foot down harder on the accelerator.

'Do *you* know why?' Dave asked. 'When we visited you Jasmine seemed very calm. Why would Jasmine hurt herself, Darryl?'

'Are you serious? Calm? You saw her break down. You saw her cry. You know exactly why she did this.' His voice kept bouncing as if he was driving down a very rough track.

Frantically, Dave cast around, hoping to see an isolated two-wheel track. Somewhere Darryl could have driven to.

Bob waved his phone in front of Dave and mimed the telephone sign, then mouthed 'Johnny'.

Nodding, Dave understood. Bob would get Johnny on the phone. A direct line to extra back-up, information and anything else they might need.

'How did Jasmine get to the dam, Darryl? I noticed she wasn't walking very well when we were there earlier.'

'It was the court case,' Darryl answered simply, not rising to Dave's veiled insinuation. 'She was terrified of being left alone. And I was petrified of leaving her. What type of government treats their citizens like they don't matter. I've paid my taxes every year, followed the laws and rules of the nation, done everything I was supposed to. Yet they hang me out to dry.' Faltering a little, he continued. 'I couldn't leave her on her own. I could never do that. I loved her too much. Jasmine was so frightened of the future. Ignorance is bliss.'

'What do you mean by ignorance is bliss?'

'Jasmine will never know what happens. She's safe from everything now.'

'Darryl, we'd really like to help you. Where are you?' Dave held the steering wheel steady as the wheel hit corrugations.

'Ha, not likely.'

'Okay, well, if you change your mind, you only need to say the word and Bob and I will come to you.'

Bob was muttering quietly into the phone, telling Johnny what was transpiring.

Dave glanced over, seeing if there were any messages, but Bob didn't look up.

'Bob and I went over to George's farm this morning.'

Darryl laughed. It was a jarring sound, with no mirth. 'Oh yeah?'

'It's strange. The fertiliser he had stored in the shed has gone missing.'

'Has it.' Darryl's voice was flat now.

'Do you know where it could be?'

Darryl didn't answer, yet Dave could hear the road noise.

'Darryl? I've said we're here to help.'

'I've got it.' Low and hard to hear, he finally spoke.

Waving at Bob, he relayed the message by mouthing what Darryl had said.

Bob gave the thumbs up and said as much to Johnny.

What to say, what to say? They had to keep him on the phone. If he hung up, they wouldn't find him until it was too late.

'Okay. We're glad to know where the fertiliser is. Could we come and help you bring it back to George?'

Only road noise again. Taking the phone away from his ear, Dave checked he still had connection and range. Then he heard Darryl start to speak.

'Ever heard the name Brandan Phillips?' The words were loud enough for them both to hear.

Bob's head whipped around and he and Dave locked eyes.

'Fuck,' Bob whispered, the started to tell Johnny the revelation.

Feeling the weight of responsibility, Dave steadily answered him. 'I have. I met his sister and her friend Tom while I was in Stockdale. Was he a mate of yours? Brandan? Or Tom?'

'I knew him—Brandan.'

'What's he got to do with this?'

'Ha! They call you a detective and you can't work out what is right in front of your nose.'

This time it was Dave who said nothing.

'We're attacking the government. The people who make the rules that have shafted both of us. Brandan was killed by the cops. Cops are employed by the government. My life will be fucked by the same institution.

'Um, I've only got half of the fertiliser. It seems only fair to tell you that.' Darryl cleared his throat.

'Tom's got the rest?'

'Yeah. Tom's got it.'

Bob kept relaying the information to Johnny.

'They think they've found Tom and Connie, but they haven't got eyes on them yet.' Bob whispered to Dave.

Dave badly wanted to ask where, but Darryl was still talking.

'Connie doesn't know what Tom's been involved in.' He laughed. 'Ah, well, she might by now. What I do know is that Tom will make sure Connie has revenge on the coppers.'

'Where are they planning to do this?'

Darryl was lost in his own thoughts. His voice dropped and became a monologue. 'I met Connie once. Such a sweet thing, with a broken heart. Like a bird. I felt sorry for her. And her mother, she was so caught up in sadness she couldn't see straight. Just like Jasmine was. It was the kindest thing to do. Make sure she didn't suffer.'

Dave was confused. Who was Darryl talking about? Jasmine? Or Connie?

Shit, was Tom going to hurt Connie, too?

'Tell Johnny that Connie might be in danger,' he whispered to Bob.

Bob repeated the words quickly, his face turning red as he spoke. Dave had time enough to have a second glance at Bob and see how he was, before Darryl spoke.

'It was much easier than I had anticipated. There were pills. Heaps of them. Just ground them up and put them in a cuppa for her. She didn't know anything. Kinder for her, much kinder. Won't be long and we'll be back together.'

Jasmine. He was talking about Jasmine.

'Darryl, I can't wait any more. You have to tell me where you are.' The troopy was bumping through potholes and swinging from side to side. Dave was still unsure of where they were headed. He looked across at Bob for some guidance, but he shrugged.

Dave made the helicopter sign with his finger.

'Tom is so in love with Connie. He only wanted to make her happy. The same way as I fell in love with Jasmine. Connie couldn't see him through her grief and this was the only way for him to make her realise.'

'Do you know where Tom is?' He had to keep his voice even. Although all he wanted to do was scream at Bob to get all the coppers out of every police station in the state. He guessed Tom was on a suicide mission and Connie was oblivious to the danger.

'No idea. Don't want to know.'

'Okay, I've got another question, Darryl, do you mind?'

'You've got about half an hour before I get to where I'm going. I can talk to you until then.'

Dave chose his question carefully, while Bob reported into Johnny.

'Suspect is armed with a bomb,' Bob told Johnny quietly. 'He's about half an hour in front us, destination unknown, but within half an hour radius. We are certain he's aiming for a government department to blow up. Evacuate all government buildings within a five-hundred-kilometre radius of Chapman Hill. Eyes in the sky north of Chapman Hill is requested ASAP.

'Tom and Connie—possible suicide mission. No verification but predict target is one of the police officers involved in the car chase that killed Brandan.'

'Okay, Darryl, why did you and Tom choose Kallygarn as your first target and then again as your second? Why did you blow up the service station?'

'What would be the point in that?' he replied scornfully. 'We're only trying to make everyone see what governing bodies are doing to people is wrong. We're not interested in anything that isn't going to get us attention.'

'You didn't blow up the servo?'

'Nope.'

Bob continued his relay.

'Do you know who did?'

'Nope.'

'Okay, so why Kallygarn?'

'Because it's a helluva long way from here.' He laughed.
'Plus, Tom was aware that one of the coppers involved
in Brandan's death is stationed there.' Darryl gave a low,
rumbling laugh that sent chills up Dave spine. 'It helps to
have someone on site, doesn't it? Local information. The
time cops knock off shift, that type of thing. Makes getting
them easier.'

His sing-song voice made Dave wonder if he'd had some
type of breakdown. Darryl sounded mad.

'Make sure Johnny has got both officers covered, not
just one. And there's a third person,' Dave whispered to
Bob, before turning his attention back to Darryl.

'Sorry? I don't understand,' Dave said.

'Work it out.' Darryl's sigh turned into a sob. 'Anyway,
nothing really matters anymore, does it? Jasmine's gone.
I won't get to go home to the farm. Don't reckon I'd want
to anyway. If she's not there it won't feel right. Why—'
His voice cracked. 'Why did they have to do this to us?'

Bob's voice was loud. He was talking to Comms, rather
than Johnny now: 'Persons of interest are Tom Vincent
and Darryl Wilson. Connie Phillips and Tom Vincent are
together. Unsure if Phillips is aware of what Vincent has
planned. Need to alert other officers involved in Brandan
Phillips' death they are potential targets for Tom Vincent.'
He listened. 'Copy that.'

Bob took the phone away from his ear and started to dial
straight away. 'I'm going to ring George to see if I can get
an idea of what type of vehicle Darryl is driving,' he said.

'Who's there with you?' Darryl asked.

Dave swung the troopy around a corner and headed back towards Chapman Hill.

'My partner, Bob. You met him this morning.'

'Is he trying to rally all the cops together to catch me? Funny, isn't it—Connie loses her brother to the cops because they're hunting him, and I've been helping Tom get revenge on her behalf. Now you're all looking for me. The hunter has become the hunted.'

'Can you tell me what you're driving, Darryl?'

'I'm not that stupid.'

'George? It's Bob Holden.' Bob was holding his mobile phone close to his ear and turned away from Dave, towards the window, his shoulder hunched around him. 'Quick question, can you tell me if Darryl has some kind of a truck that he could mix and transport that fertiliser in?' Bob raised his eyebrows and turned to Dave, concern crossing his face. 'A cement mixer? That's not exactly farm equipment.' He listened. 'Ah, I see. No worries. Okay, thanks. Oh, and George, if you see the vehicle, do not approach Darryl, just ring me ASAP. Make sure you stay the hell away from him.'

'Tell me about Jasmine, Darryl,' Dave asked. 'How did you meet?'

'Why?'

'I thought you might like to talk about her.'

Bob was on the phone again. 'Johnny, do a search on Darryl. He owns and is possibly driving a cement mixer with explosives in the drum. He'll have an electric detonator in his truck. 'How are you going with that plane over

Chapman Hill? We're running blind, but Dave has him on the phone.'

'I could tell you about Jasmine, but what good would that do?'

'I have a wife,' Dave said. 'She's not that happy with me right now, so I know what it's like to have someone you love and to want the best for them. You wanted that for Jasmine, didn't you? The best life she could have.'

Silence.

'Don't lose him,' Bob whispered to Dave. He put the phone back to his ear.

'You wanted a nice house and to be able to buy her lovely things.' Dave gripped the steering wheel, nervously.

'Yeah.' Darryl's voice was low.

'She didn't mind not getting them, though, did she?'

'Nope. I always wanted that, but I never had the money.'

'She loved you and that was enough.'

Again, silence.

Bob leaned towards Dave. 'They got Tom and Connie. At Corrigin. They're contained.'

Allowing himself a moment of relief, Dave closed his eyes and breathed deeply. Then flicked his eyes open as he felt Bob hit his arm.

'There!'

Dave looked out the side window and saw a cement truck parked in a parking bay on the main road. He took his foot off the accelerator and slowed down, not once moving his eyes from the truck.

'You loved her.'

'They fucked it up.'

Bob was talking urgently into the phone. 'We need a roadblock on the Great Eastern Highway, about thirty kilometres west of Chapman Hill. Suspect is stationary in a parking bay. Get the roadblock up now! Clear the area.'

'But legislation and laws are both just that. Rules to be abided by. Did Jasmine want you to clear the land?'

'I didn't talk to her about clearing the bush. It was going to be a surprise for our anniversary. I'd planned to have the pad down by the time she knew.' His sobs were loud. 'I never knew it could get me into so much trouble. You've got to believe me. I never knew.'

'Darryl, I just want you to know, we can see you. Would you like to get out of the truck and come towards us?'

'What?'

They watched as the cement truck lurched forward. 'Stay the fuck away from me. I'll blow this thing sky high, I promise you. I'll get onto the road and drive straight to Perth. I'll—'

'Darryl!' Dave cut through his panic. 'Why don't you come in? I've promised Bob and I will help you. Talk to the courts. See if we can get you a deal.'

'I'll still go to gaol.'

'Your family. Your farm and friends, they all matter.'

He scoffed. 'What family? Jasmine was everything.'

'Come on, mate.' Dave followed the truck at a distance. 'Please don't hurt anyone else. Doing that won't help your cause.'

Bob had the phone raised to his ear now.

'Eyes on the suspect now. Our GPS coordinates are—'
He read them from the screen on the dash. He listened,
then leaned towards Dave. 'Plane isn't close yet. Still about
thirty minutes away.'

'We don't have that long.'

'Do you know what I regret the most?' Darryl asked.

'No, but I'd like to.' Dave replied. 'Could you tell me
face to face?'

'Not telling Jasmine I loved her when I got out of bed
this morning . . .'

'Please don't, Darryl.' Dave's voice was urgent now,
he knew he was losing him. 'Don't hurt anyone else. I'm
repeating myself when I say we want to help you.'

'You can help me by telling those cock-smokers in Perth
that they've got two deaths on their hands. Jasmine's and—'

A mushroom cloud whoomphed into the air, flames
ripping around the truck until it vanished behind the
black smoke. Around the burning vehicle, the air vibrated,
sending shock waves through the atmosphere. Towards
Dave and Bob.

Windows imploded into the troopy, and Dave and Bob
were instantly covered with glass, ash and bits of metal
from the truck.

Scrambling out of the vehicle, Dave, cut and bleeding,
ran towards the cement truck, yelling. 'Darryl! Darryl!'
His voice faded as the heat pushed him back. 'You idiot.'

CHAPTER 31

'Here watch this.' Johnny pressed play on the video and Dave and Bob looked at the computer screen.

A shadowy figure walked in and out of the long shadows of each building on Kallygarn's main street. One jerry can in each hand. Every few steps he had to stop and readjust his grip.

'Now here, look here.' Johnny pointed to the middle of the screen.

The figure unscrewed the cap and sloshed petrol around the fuel bowsers, the edge of the building and then went to the door, where he dripped it underneath, getting fuel inside the shop.

'No wonder it looked like the windows blew outwards instead of inwards. I knew there was some type of accelerant inside. I wasn't sure how got there.

'I tell you what, these cameras are fantastic. I'm going to make sure we've got a lot more around Kallygarn. Talk about making policing easy. We've got everything this bloke's done on video. Shouldn't be any trouble in ensuring the conviction sticks.'

'But who is it?' Bob asked.

'Uh-uh. Wait.'

They watched as the man threw a lit stick of gel near the bowsers and turned, running backwards from the dark shadows. On screen, the image shook and flames illuminated the area.

Johnny jiggled the mouse to change camera views and picked up the man again.

'Look, he's been hurt here.' He jabbed at picture and laughed. 'See him rolling around on the ground.'

'He'll have an obvious injury, even this long afterwards,' Dave said. 'Just gets better and better.'

'Check out what I have here.' From his desk, Johnny picked up a plastic bag and handed it to Bob. 'I'm one hundred per cent sure this is what he was wearing here. You'll notice the synthetic has melted, and when he's peeled it off, there're some hairs here, too, with the roots attached.' Another laugh. 'I'm looking forward to arresting this arse.'

'DNA and everything. God, Johnny, I'm impressed.' Bob grinned.

Dave looked over at his friend. Bob was barely hanging on today. The excitement and emotion from the past few days had worn off. Today, he'd rung Betty and asked her to pick him up. His ride would arrive later today.

Dave still had work to do in Kallygarn with Johnny.

'Want to come with me while I pick him up?' Johnny asked.

'Sure. The final piece of the puzzle. Let's go.' Bob slowly got up off the chair.

Dave waited until he was fully on his feet before he walked behind him as they went to the car.

Johnny folded his large frame in behind the wheel and glanced over at Bob who was arguing with the seatbelt. 'Have you worked out who it is?'

'The way this case has gone, I'm not going to guess,' Bob answered, groaning as he lifted his legs into the footwell. 'I tell you, don't ever get crook,' he said. 'It's got knobs on.'

Neither of the other men answered.

Right then Dave realised that Bob's next round of treatment would take more out of him. He hadn't treated his body kindly while investigating poor old George's stock of fertiliser.

'Right, fellas, get your cameras out, I'm going to enjoy this.' He looked in the rear-view mirror at Dave. 'I'm only joking about the camera.' He winked.

Johnny followed the road around one corner, then another, stopping at a plain house.

Dave assessed it curiously. Edged lawns and a flowering tree of some sort in the garden. No flowers, but the yard was tidy. No bells or whistles about this place.

'Coming?'

'Right behind you,' Bob said, opening his door.

Dave stayed close to Bob, and when they reached the front door, Johnny raised his hand to rap. He didn't get a chance because it swung open, revealing the smiling face of Dan Hinderkin.

Dave sucked in a breath. The shire councillor who had been so self-righteous and opinionated in the pub their first day in Kallygarn.

'Johnny, mate, good to see you. And you've brought some friends. Come in, come in.' Dan opened the door wider to let them through.

'Ah, it's not a social visit, Dan,' Johnny told him, not moving. 'I need to ask you to accompany me to the station to answer some questions about the service station explosion.'

Dan's smile fell away and his eyes turned cold. 'Why would you want to do that?'

'We have reason to believe you were involved.'

'Ah, come on, Johnny.' Friendly again. 'I've already told you where I was. In Perth at a meeting. Can't be in two places at once now, can I?' Charm oozed from Dan.

'Do you recognise these?' Johnny held up the plastic bag with the tracksuit pants in them.

'Never seen them before.' The toothpaste advert smile faltered the smallest amount, but Dave saw it. So did Johnny. He went in for the kill.

'Of course you haven't,' Johnny agreed. Not saying anything, he stared at Dan, who's eyes flicked from one man to the next and the next. Unsure of his next move.

'Dan, we are aware the person who was wearing these will have a burn on their thigh. The synthetic has melted onto their body. In between his thighs as a matter of fact. Would you know anything that could help us?'

'I beg your pardon! What the hell!' Without realising what he was doing, Dan's hand dropped to his jeans as if protecting the burnt area of his leg.

'We are within our rights to ask you to undress, to clarify this injury, but I won't do that in the street. At the station will be fine.'

'That's kind of you,' Dan told him mildly. 'But I won't be coming to the station. I don't know where you've got your theory, but it's just that—a theory. So far I haven't seen any evidence presented against me.'

'Are you sure?' Johnny replied.

'I am very sure.' Dan drew himself as tall as possible, yet found he still had to stare up at Johnny.

'Well, then,' Johnny said, 'Dan Hinderkin, I'm arresting you on the suspicion of bombing the Kallygarn service station.' He continued on, reading Dan his rights while the councillor stood there, open-mouthed.

'What are you doing? This is me, Johnny. Dan. The one who's been keeping this town safe for years.' His tone was bemused. Almost pleading with Johnny not to arrest him.

'Dan, we have DNA on the tracksuit pants, it will only take a test to confirm it's yours. We have you on camera carrying jerry cans. Just put your hands behind your back and make this easy. I won't make a scene if you don't.'

'I don't know what you're talking about. You can't arrest a shire councillor—'

'Yes, I can, and you won't believe how much satisfaction this is going to give me. Turn around.'

Dan turned but he was still shaking his head. 'You're making a mistake.'

'Save it.'

Another police car pulled up and two first-class constables got out.

Johnny clicked the cuffs on Dan and marched him over to the newcomers. 'Take him back and book him. I've read him his rights.'

'Sir.'

'Johnny,' Dan pleaded with the older man, 'you've really got this wrong.'

'If had a dollar for every time a criminal has said that to me, I wouldn't be here in Kallygarn, I'd be in the tropics somewhere. Get him down to the station.' He turned to Dave and Bob. 'We've got one more visit to make before you leave, Bob.'

'Do we?'

'Yup, ready?'

'Why not, since you're being so secretive today.' Bob smiled. 'That was good work, mate,' he said, nodding towards Dan who was being pushed into the police car.

Johnny smiled and clapped Bob on the shoulder. 'You know you were the best partner I ever worked with.'

The smile dropped from Bob's face. 'Now you hold your horses right there. I'm not dead yet. No need to go being nice and shit.'

Johnny laughed. 'Mate, you are going to love what I've got planned. Get in the car.'

Dave raised his eyebrows and Bob shrugged back. Neither had any idea what Johnny had planned.

A couple of streets away, Johnny stopped at a pretty, white weatherboard house, with roses lining each side of the pathway. The front door opened and a slim woman with grey hair came out and waved to Johnny.

Bob looked at his friend. 'What the—'

'Go on, get out and talk to her.'

Bob hesitated. 'Mate, it doesn't matter. It was so long ago.'

'It does matter. To me. Go,' Johnny said.

Dave stayed quiet as Bob got out of the car and walked to the fence. He watched his friend closely, ready to go to his side if he was needed.

'She's going to apologise,' Johnny told Dave, his eyes on his old partner and wife. 'I finally got through to her and she believes me. Only taken god knows how many decades.' Johnny turned in his seat and made eye contact with Dave. 'I'm not proud about what happened that night, and it was nice to have the backing of my partner. I've always regretted not having Bob's back as strongly as he had mine. I was wrong.

'My wife kept saying I didn't have a temper like that. And she would have been correct, you know why?'

Dave shook his head.

'Because, Dave, she'd never seen me lose my rag. But I could and I did. And Bob had to take the flak from her for it. That wasn't fair.

'Now there's a lesson here, young fella.'

'Dare I ask?'

'Georgia and Connie haven't ever seen Mary Fletcher's anger, so they can't believe what she instigated either.' Johnny tried to lean closer to Dave, but the seatbelt cut into his meaty neck. 'I have it on very good authority Mary was with Tom and Darryl the night of the bombing. There's evidence there were three people there. Of course, we can't get Darryl's statement, but Tom has confessed to his part. We still have more questions for him and we believe that he will roll over on Mary.'

'Mary.' Dave shook his head. 'Darryl said before he blew himself to smithereens that there was a third person, but I couldn't get any more information. But Mary? When I questioned her, she was so small and old. Weak even.'

'Weak? Huh! You read the first interview I did with her. She changed the bloody tyre on her four-wheel drive by herself.'

'Yeah, but she's so tiny.'

'Never trust what you see, Dave.'

'Connie is having a bit of trouble, too. Thank god that we found them when we did. Tom had enough fert to blow five stations sky-high. We were very lucky the fellas at Corrigin got their roadblock set up as quickly as they did. Could have ended with more deaths, otherwise.'

'Connie had no idea,' Johnny said. He paused, gathering his thoughts. 'Darryl knew Tom and Brandan through football, and Tom was the one who connected Darryl with Mary. They planned the bombing of the offices. No one was going to suspect an older lady. But here's the thing—Mary used to work on her father's farm and he taught her how to set explosives. They were—'

'—clearing land,' Dave said, remembering Darryl's earlier comments.

'Exactly.' Johnny fell quiet for a few minutes. 'Dave? One more thing—I know you had a theory about the bikies.'

'I did. I can't believe they weren't involved.'

'There's a fair bit of shit that I can't tell you, but the bikies—the Sinners you saw going into Stockdale—they're under surveillance . . . Ah, here he comes. And look at that expression.'

'Tell me,' Dave said, 'Before he gets here.'

'Too late.'

Bob got into the car and looked over at Johnny, a half-smile on his mouth. 'You're a cunning old bugger,' he said and leaned forward to hug his friend.

EPILOGUE

It was three weeks before Dave made it back to Perth.

He'd spent hours with Connie and Georgia, talking about policing and how the job worked. By the time he left, Georgia had ventured out of the house three times and Connie had given him a hug. They were still sad at Brandan's death, of course, but they didn't blame the police anymore.

Dave had slowly and methodically gone over every action of Brandan's fateful day, and when he presented the facts, finally they had agreed that the crash was just a tragic accident.

Connie had been shocked at Tom's actions, and even more at her Aunty Mary's. So devastated, the idea of becoming a lawyer had died. Dave had suggested there was lots of time to work out what she wanted to do.

'Perhaps Connie,' he had said, 'you could still become a lawyer, and help victims of crime.'

Her only answer had been 'Maybe.'

Connie had refused to have anything to do with Mary or Tom since. Her trust had been shattered and she would take a long time to heal. Yesterday, she'd told Dave that she and Georgia were going to pack up and sell their house. Move to Perth to look for work. Stockdale didn't hold anything for them now.

How nice to be able to have a fresh start.

Driving into the stock squad compound, Dave felt like all the weight had lifted from his shoulders. He was home. Back around his team. Back in familiar territory.

Lorri came out of the office and waved as he turned off the car. 'Hey, you're back!'

'So I am. How're things here?'

'Great. Slow. It's nice.' She smiled and held out a letter. 'Here you are. I knew you'd want to see it straight away.'

'I'd forgotten about that,' Dave said, taking it and looking at the envelope. He swallowed hard and stared at the hand-writing until he was sure his face wouldn't give him away.

'Know who it's from?' Lorri asked.

'Yeah.' He cleared his throat. 'Yeah, it's from Mum. She wrote to me a few weeks ago, but I haven't got around to answering her.'

'Oh, that's brilliant! Maybe she's going to invite you back to the farm.' The smile fell away. 'Shit, if she does, you can't go. We need you here.'

'I promise you it won't be anything like that,' Dave said, no emotion in his tone. 'Apparently my brother is missing.'

'Oh good. Well, not good that your brother is missing, but that you won't be going anywhere.'

340

The expression on Dave's face invited no more conversation, so Lorri cleared her throat. 'By the way, there's someone inside waiting to see you.'

Now a smile from Dave. 'He's here?'

'Of course! He knew you were due back today but not what time. He's been waiting for a couple of hours.'

Dave took the steps up into the office in a few long leaps.

Bob sat at his desk, bald as a badger, no eyebrows, but looking happy. Betty was alongside him, her hand on his shoulder. When she saw Dave, she leaned down and kissed Bob's cheek, then touched Dave lightly on the arm as she passed him, leaving the office.

'What's going on?' Dave asked. 'Why's everyone shooting through?'

Bob patted the desk. 'Come and sit down, son. Get everything tidied up at Kallygarn?'

'Yeah, took a bit, but by the time I left, the bulldozers were moving in, flattening both sites and starting to clear out all the rubble. Be ages before the buildings are rebuilt, but at least the sites will look much better by the end of the week.' Dave sat down warily.

'Great work. And thanks for taking me with you on that last run. What an interesting few days that was.'

It wouldn't have taken a detective to know some big news was coming. Whatever Bob had to say, Dave was sure that he wasn't going to like it. The urge to leave was overwhelming. Finally, he asked, 'How about you? How's the treatment?'

'Lost all my hair.' Bob ran his hand over his shiny head. 'I'm told it looks distinguished.'

'Sure does.' There wasn't any humour in his voice.

'Dave . . .' Bob leaned forward, resting his hand on Dave's shoulder.

'Don't,' Dave said.

'Son, I'm retiring.'

There, the words were out. There was no taking them back.

'No.' Dave stood, then sat down again.

'I'm not fit for work and who knows whether I will ever be. I still hope that I'll make a full recovery. If I didn't have hope, I wouldn't have anything.' He took a breath. 'So, my job is up for grabs. You're going to the super's office now. Tell him you want it. You're the only person I'm going to be happy to hand the baton over to.'

'Please, don't,' Dave said. 'Stay.'

Bob shook his head. 'No can do, son.' He let out a heavy sigh. 'I can't kid myself anymore. This is a young—no, a healthy person's game—and I'm neither of those things anymore. I might be back in time, but I'm not going to want the top job again, son. Go on, get your arse over to the super's office. He knows you're coming.'

Bob stood up and clapped Dave on the shoulder. 'It's yours, son.'

ACKNOWLEDGEMENTS

Firstly, a massive thanks to Anna Hill. You're incredible despite what you make me do! #wwammd

Thanks very much to Lindsay for helping me with the bomb-making and setting information. I'm still waiting for the AFP to turn up on my doorstep since both you and I have been reading the same documents. All in the name of research, of course!

I have taken some liberties with the timing of some true events in *Shock Waves*. I hope, dear reader, you'll indulge me, if you work out which ones they are!

To all you readers, thank you. Again, if you didn't read, then I wouldn't write.

To everyone at Allen & Unwin, with special mentions to Robert, Annette, Christa, Matt, Andrew, Shannon.

Gaby—agent, friend and confidante. Thank you for carefully holding and crafting my career over the last fifteen years. Here's to a few more yet!

Booksellers, librarians, you all are an author's biggest asset. Thank you.

Rochelle and Hayden.

DB. Simply the best!

Oh, actually, Cal and Aaron, you're both simply the best, too!

To our fabulous friendship group; it's so wonderful to be among you.

Jack-the-Kelpie. With each passing book you're getting older and I'm not sure any wiser. It's a very good thing I love you, you strange but gorgeous beast.

And please don't forget, #everyoneneedsadave!

With love,
Fleur x